P9-DCW-803

# A Safe Place for Dying

# A Safe Place for Dying

# Jack Fredrickson

THOMAS DUNNE BOOKS

ST. MARTIN'S MINOTAUR 📖 NEW YORK

This is a work of fiction. All of the characters, organizations, and events portrayed in this novel are either products of the author's imagination or are used fictitiously.

THOMAS DUNNE BOOKS.

An imprint of St. Martin's Press.

A SAFE PLACE FOR DYING. Copyright © 2006 by Jack Fredrickson. All rights reserved. Printed in the United States of America. No part of this book may be used or reproduced in any manner whatsoever without written permission except in the case of brief quotations embodied in critical articles or reviews. For information, address St. Martin's Press, 175 Fifth Avenue, New York, N.Y. 10010.

www.thomasdunnebooks.com

www.minotaurbooks.com

Library of Congress Cataloging-in-Publication Data

Fredrickson, Jack.
    A safe pace for dying / Jack Fredrickson.—1st ed.
        p. cm.
    ISBN-13: 978-0-312-35168-7
    ISBN-10: 0-312-35168-2
        1. Private investigators—Illinois—Chicago—Fiction.  2. Chicago (Ill.)—
Fiction.  I. Title

PS3606.R437S24 2006
813'.6—dc22                                                    2006045804

First Edition: November 2006

10   9   8   7   6   5   4   3   2   1

FOR SUSAN

# ACKNOWLEDGMENTS

I have been blessed with the prodding, well-tempered criticism, and encouragement by the finest of individuals. To those who critiqued the whole blooming manuscript, to Mary Anne Bigane, Joe Bigane III, Susan Taylor Chehak, Kelly Fitzpatrick, Lori Fredrickson, Eric Frisch, Missy Lyda, and Beth Smith, I say again . . . and again: Thanks.

To Patrick Riley, who also waded through the words, and then sweated the marketing and applied the Taser at critical junctures, I can say only that you're the best of pals.

To my new friends at Thomas Dunne, to Marcia Markland and Diana Szu, and to India Cooper, who did the copyediting, you made what I did much better.

And to my daughter, Lori, my son, Jack, and to my wife, Susan . . . you make what I am much better.

# Prologue

It was a spectacle even on the four-inch screen of my fifty-nine-dollar television.

Edna Rectenberry, the white-curled fusspot of Chicago P.B.S.'s *Our Prairie, Our Heritage*, was on her knees outside the wall of the gated community, Crystal Waters, barking questions at six preschoolers about the purple wildflowers they'd planted there. She'd just poked her microphone at one fidgeting towhead, in short pants and a better necktie than I'd ever own, when the roof of one of the mansions behind the wall rumbled up like a flaming orange spaceship and vaporized into black smoke. The explosion pounded the ground as glowing cinders of charred wood and shattered roof tile began raining down like hell's own charcoal.

Her cameraman stumbled back from the searing heat, into the suddenly blaring horns and squealing brakes of the cars on the highway, but he kept his videocam rolling as the screaming children and poor, arthritic Edna, her knees bleeding, her white hair clumped with black ash, staggered through the hailstorm of flaming debris into the street.

Nobody died. The people who lived in the mansion were away,

and the wall had protected the children and Edna from all but small burns and minor cuts. And there the story would have expired, as a minor news item on page three of the metro section of the *Chicago Tribune,* along with the worst of the day's other house fires, save for the tape. The videotape of Edna and the screaming kids running from a flaming roof made it perfect Big *T* Television.

All four local news shows hustled coiffures to Crystal Waters, to pose in front of the brick wall and to intone, live at five, six, and ten, that they didn't have much to intone about at all. Voicing over endless replays of the P.B.S. video, they mouthed the obvious: It must have been a gas leak, and there was concern it might happen again.

After enjoying the footage for the sixth time, I blew the sawdust off my gallon of Gallo and poured a celebratory half inch into my coffee mug. I knew Crystal Waters. People from where I'm from drive by it sometimes for a peek at the good life through the iron gates. They call it Gateville.

I call it that, too. But I'd lived there, for the months of my marriage.

And so long as nobody got hurt, I was rooting for another gas leak.

# One

The exploding house disappeared from the news, and already I'd half forgotten it when Stanley Novak called the following week, asking if he could come right over. I hadn't seen Stanley since he'd carted me out of Gateville the previous Halloween, and I knew better than to think it was a social call, especially at 9:00 A.M. I had just enough time to wipe a dry varnishing rag over my two white plastic chairs before the doorbell rang. He must have called from a block away.

I opened the door. It was a cool morning for late June, but Stanley Novak's pale blue uniform shirt was sweat-soaked under the arms like it was high noon in August. Even on his best days, Stanley Novak looked lumpy, like a failed attempt to jam toothpaste back in a tube, but this morning he looked worse than usual. His doughy face was shiny with perspiration, several long black strands of his comb-over had come unglued and dangled limp over his left ear, and he'd missed a couple of spots shaving. He rocked back and forth on his heels, his fingers working nervously at the lip of the tan envelope he was holding.

Stanley was chief of security at Crystal Waters. He was in charge of the guards who manned the gatehouse and patrolled the grounds and was utterly dependable, anxious, and ever at the ready to protect his charges and their micromansions. I'd admired his sense of purpose when I'd lived there. He always seemed sure of what he was doing.

But this morning, Stanley Novak was sweating.

"Stanley Novak, as I live and breathe."

"Mr. Elstrom."

"Call me Dek, Stanley," I said, holding the door open for him. "I no longer dwell among the chosen." I motioned toward the two plastic chairs, the only furniture in what I hoped would one day be a living room I could unload on some urban professional with lots of money and a taste for the unusual.

Stanley stepped inside but ignored the chairs, going instead to the curved stone wall. I was used to that; first-time visitors always need a few minutes to check out the architecture before they want to sit down. The way Stanley was sweating, though, there was more. He was buying time. I sat in one of the chairs and waited.

He moved silently along the wall like he was in a rock museum, reaching out to lightly touch the rough yellow and white limestone blocks. Every few feet he stopped and looked up at the dark, timbered ceiling twelve feet above his head. Dust sparkled in the narrow beams of sunlight filtering through the open slit windows like bits of crystal. Outside, trucks downshifted on Thompson Avenue, lumbering up the railroad overpass.

"I've passed this place a million times, wondering if this was a silo," he said from across the round room. "Then last year I heard it was supposed to be a castle, or something."

"The first turret of one. My grandfather built it in 1929, but he died before he could get much done. It's been vacant since then, except for some mice, a few rats, and a couple dozen pigeons. And me, since last November." I pointed at the two orange buckets of roof patch on the floor next to the table saw. "I'm fixing it up to sell."

He nodded and looked at the curved black wrought-iron stair-case that hugged the far wall. "How many floors?"

"Five. Bathroom and kitchen and maybe an office will be on two, master bedroom on three. I haven't figured yet what four and five will be."

He'd stopped at the small, silver-framed snapshot I'd set on one of the protruding blocks. "Nice picture of you and Ms. Phelps."

I hadn't thought to put it out of sight when he called. "Crown Point, Indiana. Home of the quickie marriage," I said, trying for casual.

He moved along the wall.

"How is she, Stanley?" The words came out too quickly.

"You're not going to drywall this over, are you?" He touched one of the limestone blocks, dodging the question. He didn't like to give things away about the residents of Gateville.

"Everything stays natural."

"This place will really be something when you get it fixed up." He gave the wall a last tap and came to sit in the other plastic chair, the sweat on his forehead gone now in the cool of the turret. He set his envelope on the floor.

"Coffee?" I pointed at the black Mr. Coffee balanced on the cardboard nail box by the table saw, thinking I should have dusted the carafe. It looked furry, like the beginnings of one of those grass-sprouting Chia creatures they sell on television in the middle of the night to people who can't sleep.

"No coffee, thanks." The wide eyes he'd had during his inspection tour were gone; he was all business now. He straightened up on the chair. "Mr. Elstrom, you probably saw it on T.V., last week the house at Sixteen Chanticleer Circle exploded."

"A couple hundred feet from where my ex-wife still lives. Gas leak or something?"

He shook his head. "It was an explosive, most likely set deliberately. D.X.12."

The world had penetrated Gateville. No wonder Stanley was sweating.

"I don't know explosives, Stanley. I'm not that kind of investigator."

"Nobody knows much about D.X.12 anymore," he said. "The Maple Hills police said the Army used it for a time during Vietnam."

"Who uses it now?"

Stanley shrugged. "That's the thing: They think it's long gone. They're checking to see if it's even being manufactured anymore."

"I see," I said, but I didn't. At least not why he was coming to me.

Stanley's eyes took another tour of the room. I waited. Finally he looked back at me. "Mr. Chernek thinks you may be able to assist in the investigation."

Anton Chernek. The Bohemian. I wasn't surprised that he was involved; Gateville was full of his clients, including the one I'd been married to for a time. Anything that would threaten their security would bring the Bohemian. What I didn't get was why he'd send Stanley to me. There were plenty of better private choices, ex-F.B.I., ex-A.T.F., criminal specialists, and none of them the ex-husband of one of his clients.

"Stanley, I'm not the man for this. Even when my business was running and I had a staff, we traced real estate transfers, found current addresses, photographed accident scenes. Document stuff, paper trails, research, for law firms and insurance companies. Explosives are off my turf."

It was true enough, but there was another reason I didn't want to get involved. I wasn't just rebuilding a turret; I was rebuilding my life. And it was going slow. Getting involved with Gateville could knock things back down.

He picked up the tan envelope, reached inside, and pulled out a clear plastic freezer bag containing a white envelope and a sheet of buff-colored paper. "This came two weeks before the explosion." He handed it to me.

I took the freezer bag by its edges. The white envelope inside was ordinary, business-sized, and typewriter- or computer-addressed to the Board of Homeowners of Crystal Waters. The sheet of paper was smaller than letter size, double-lined, and looked to be off the kind of tablet first graders use when learning to write. The words were perfectly hand-printed in block letters, as if drawn by someone using a ruler, and read like a telegram: AVOID PROBLEM. HAVE FIFTY THOUSAND USED TENS AND TWENTIES READY.

I read the note again through the plastic. "I'm surprised the police let you keep this."

"No police. The Board told Mr. Chernek no police."

I looked over at him. His face was impassive. He wasn't joking. I handed back the freezer bag like it was full of anthrax. "Take this to the police immediately. It's key evidence."

He slipped the freezer bag back in the tan envelope and propped it against the leg of his chair. "No police."

"Why the hell not?"

He fidgeted in the chair. "Where in the note does it say a house is going to be blown up? The Board gets crank letters—"

"Crank letter? It says you can avoid problems by paying fifty thousand dollars, and it arrived two weeks before the house was blown up. It's an extortion letter."

"Why blow up the house without first trying to collect?"

"Take it to the cops, Stanley. Let them figure it."

"And look at the amount," he went on. "A piddling fifty thousand. The cheapest house in Crystal Waters is worth three million. Fifty thousand is what the people there pay for a second Mercedes. No, it's got to be from some harmless nut cake."

"If it's harmless, why not give it to the police?"

"The Board knows the police will do what you just did: try to link the note to the explosion at Sixteen Chanticleer. And if that becomes public, it will kill the prices of homes in Crystal Waters.

Mr. Chernek said the houses would lose their borrowing value. The way the stock market's been bouncing around, that could be a disaster for the Members."

Members. I'd forgotten how the residents of Gateville referred to themselves. Members, like in a special club. It was true enough.

"If that note is real, and there's another explosion, they won't be able to give those homes away," I said.

His expression didn't change. And I understood.

"You don't think there will be another note. You think that even if the note is from the bomber, it was targeted only at the—" I stopped. I didn't know their names. For over six months, I'd lived around the curve from the people whose house had blown up, and I never had known their names. Crystal Waters was not a share-the-Tupperware kind of neighborhood.

"The Farradays."

"The Farradays," I said. "The Board believes that if there is a link, it's between the bomber and the Farradays. They were the targets. That's why you're thinking there was never a follow-up letter, because your bomber wasn't really looking for money. You've convinced yourselves the letter was just a ruse."

Stanley shifted in the chair. "You've got to admit the theory makes sense."

"So now that the house has been destroyed, the matter is over?"

"The Farradays aren't going to rebuild," he said. "The Board is purchasing the property. It's already been bulldozed and landscaped with sod and mature pines. You wouldn't know there was a house there last week."

"The police let them obliterate the crime scene so soon?"

Stanley Novak smiled for the first time since he'd arrived. "Actually, the Maple Hills police weren't informed beforehand."

"The Board just went ahead and did it?"

"The village understands how upsetting the ruins were to the

Members. Crystal Waters is very generous in its support of the village."

The speed of big money always astounds me. It defies physics. With big money, the greater the mass, the quicker it moves.

"The Board paid the Farradays to go away, just in case they were the problem?"

He shrugged, but it was a yes.

"Even though this note does not mention the Farradays?"

"Mr. Farraday works at his father's securities trading firm, no other partners. Mrs. Farraday plays tennis and golf and is active in the usual charities. Their kids are popular enough at the Country Day School. The family seemed like typical Members, but you can never know for sure. There are twenty-six other families at Crystal Waters to worry about, and the Board felt that everybody—the Farradays as well as the other Members—would benefit if the matter was put to rest quickly." Stanley spoke like he was reciting scripture, which to him I supposed it was. They were the words of the Board of Homeowners.

"If you think you've got everything under control, then why bring me in?"

"Mr. Chernek would like the note and the envelope analyzed, to be safe."

"You mean to cover the Board's liability for negligence in case another bomb goes off. If you hire me to check out the note, it shows you didn't just sit on your hands." Sometimes I think at the speed glaciers move, especially when I'm being handled, but this one was too obvious.

Stanley didn't answer. He reached into his shirt pocket, came out with a check, and held it out so I could see. It was for three thousand dollars.

I like to think I hesitated. I had big doubts about keeping the note from the police. But as I paused to be righteous, my eyes fixed on the two orange cans of roof patch next to the table saw. It had been a wet spring, my roof dripped like a spaghetti strainer, and I hadn't worked in weeks. Three thousand would buy a roof repair good enough to stem the floods that came for Noah.

"You would report to Mr. Chernek," Stanley said, still holding out the check. "No need to actually go back to Crystal Waters." He was remembering the night he drove me away.

It was just an insurance job, I told myself, the kind I would take any time. An ordinary, five-hundred-dollar paper trace. This one just had an extra twenty-five hundred tacked on for keeping my mouth shut.

"You ought to go to the police," I said again.

But I was reaching for the check.

# *Two*

His name was Anton Chernek, but people like my ex-wife knew him as the Bohemian. Not like from the western part of what used to be Czechoslovakia—that was too broad an origin, home to too many peasants—but from the Bohemia before that, the old Hapsburg kingdom. Mention the Bohemian to people around Chicago with a net worth north of fifty million, chances were certain they'd heard of him. If they were lucky, they had him on retainer.

He was an attorney, a C.P.A., and a certified financial manager, but the degrees were wall shingling. He was really an overseer, not just of financial portfolios, but of whole lives. Big money can have special problems, and for many of the wealthiest families in Chicago, he was their arranger, their go-to guy, their fixer of problems too thorny or too embarrassing to entrust to ordinary retainers.

I'd met him once, the previous October, in a mahogany conference room at the top of the fourth tallest building in Chicago. He was my height, six-four, but twenty years older, around sixty, and built solid, like a bronze horse. He had a country club tan, wore his silver hair combed straight back, his beard closely trimmed, and had teeth whiter than the perfectly starched collar of his two-hundred-dollar Turnbull and Asser shirt. He'd come to sit in with the three lawyers representing Amanda, her father, and her various trusts during the dissolution of our marital assets.

My lawyer couldn't attend. He'd had a zoning hearing for another client who wanted to put up a miniature golf course behind a gas station. I'd told my lawyer no problem; I didn't want anything of Amanda's. Besides, I'd sold just about everything I'd owned and had nothing left except five hundred dollars in passbook savings, the three cut-glass jelly jars I'd gotten for opening the account, and a rusting red Jeep that had been my second car. Since I'd already eaten the jelly, and the Jeep was the small model, with stick shift, no air, and a hundred thousand on its odometer, I didn't anticipate the meeting would last long.

It didn't. I was out of there before they could get embarrassed about not offering me coffee. In return for signing a document promising I would make no claim against Amanda's assets, I got to keep the savings account and the Jeep. Custody of the jelly jars never came up.

During the meeting, the Bohemian sat alert but silent at the polished table, his fat black fountain pen lying capped next to his closed leather folio, never once checking a note. That's what large money buys: preparation. If my lawyer had been there, he would have spent the first few minutes fanning the reused, dog-eared folders jammed in his briefcase for one with my name on it, struggling to remember why he was there.

The meeting lasted twenty-one minutes. I wasn't sure of much those days, but if I'd thought about it as I left that room full of good-smelling lawyers, I would have been positive I'd never see the Bohemian again.

The telephone receptionist at Chernek and Associates sounded delighted to hear my voice, but she had the kind of trained, unhurried diction that would have come across pleased if I'd announced I was calling with great deals on burial insurance. My name must have been on the put-through list, because she rang me right in.

"Vlodek Elstrom." The Bohemian rolled each syllable slowly and distinctly, with just a trace of Eastern Europe softening the vowels. "Vlodek, such a good Bohemian name. What is the Elstrom—Swedish?"

"Norwegian."

"Of course," he said.

I skipped the smooth and tossed him the same question Stanley Novak hadn't answered: "Why me and not the police?"

"Discretion, Vlodek. Plus, you know the community."

I knew Gateville about the way the whitewash guy knows the White House, but I let it pass. "Stanley Novak said you think the letter either is from a crank or was a ruse to disguise that this was a hit on the Farradays and not aimed at all of Crystal Waters."

"Those are the likeliest scenarios. The Board gets threats occasionally—feeble, harmless attempts at shakedowns. It might have been coincidence that this letter was received two weeks before the explosion."

"And the Farradays?"

"There has been speculation that some of Mr. Farraday's brokerage clients suffered unusually heavy losses in one of the recent stock market downturns. Perhaps one of them became unhinged."

"Blow up your stockbroker's family because he gave you bad advice?"

"Never underestimate the rage of people who lose significant sums of money, Vlodek. Murders are usually about money."

"All the more reason to go to the police."

"I showed Mr. Farraday the letter and offered to forward it to the police. He seemed quite sure he was not the target. He's content to leave the matter alone."

"Given that you probably paid him a substantial premium for

his property, contingent upon him keeping quiet, he must have been very content."

"Vlodek—"

"What about the third scenario, the one you're avoiding?"

"That it's a real extortion letter?"

"That's the one."

"The bomb already went off, Vlodek. What kind of extortionist threatens to do something unless he's paid, then carries it out without first trying to collect?"

"Let the police figure it."

"It's best to keep the matter quiet."

"Because of the potential loss in property values."

"Without breaking any confidences, I can tell you that some of the Members are quite leveraged—"

I cut him off in mid-drone. "Your Members borrowed to buy stock, then pledged those shares as collateral to buy even more stock. Such greedy little piggies they were. Still, it was an OK strategy so long as stock prices went up, but your piggies guessed wrong; the stocks tanked. The value of the shares slid below what they owed for them, forcing them to pledge their houses against the loans, to cover the loss in stock value and keep their snouts above the manure. Now, incredibly, a bomber has shown up. If word of that gets out, those homes they pledged to cover the loans will become worthless—you can't sell mansions in a minefield—and the brokerages will demand more collateral, which your people don't have because they're all tapped out. Your Members will disappear into their own manure."

"Inelegantly put, perhaps, but that's it exactly." His voice softened. "Vlodek, we're not being irresponsible. The police are already involved. They're telling us the D.X.12 was most likely left behind by a landscaper, blasting tree stumps long ago, and that somehow it got triggered."

"Knowing you received that letter just before the house blew up might change their minds."

"Yes, though incorrectly, and at great expense to the Members, as you've pointed out. All I'm asking you to do is check for finger-prints, find out about the printing and the typing, perhaps learn where the paper and the envelope might have been purchased, and from where it was mailed."

"You're using me to cover yourselves with your insurers."

"Of course, but where's the harm? If we think it's a real threat, we'll bring the matter to the police, after we've conducted our own investigation, discreetly."

"You know I'll have to hire a document examiner. You could do that yourself, skip the middleman."

"We trust you, Vlodek."

He meant he could control me. He knew I'd keep a lid on it be-cause Amanda owned one of the houses in Gateville.

I looked down at the check lying on the card table I use as a desk. "One more thing. If there's another bomb, and this becomes public, using me to show your insurers you took action could backfire. I'm tainted goods."

He made a laugh. "Stop trying to talk yourself out of a job. You were exonerated. Life goes on. Find out what you can."

We hung up. I'd told him to go to the cops. I'd pressed it enough to almost convince myself I was a stand-up guy, not some schlump on the make for a roof. He said enough to convince me he wasn't telling me everything. I picked up the check from the table, folded it, and put it in my shirt pocket. One thing was sure: It was going to rain again.

I called Amanda's home phone, said hello to her voice mail, and left a message. We hadn't talked in months. Then I called Leo Brumsky and told him I'd buy him a hot dog.

Leo reclined in the driver's seat of his black Porsche roadster, his pale, bald head angled at the sun, his eyes hidden behind enor-

mous sunglasses, tapping his fingers as Astrud Gilberto sang about
the girl from Ipanema. It was one thirty, and the gravel lot in front
of Kutz's Wienie Wagon was empty of construction workers and
truckers. I stopped next to him, revved the tinny Jeep engine like a
greaseball going home alone after a no-score Saturday night, and
killed the ignition.

He didn't open his eyes. "You're late," he said above Astrud's se-
ductive voice.

"I'm worth the wait."

He nodded, shut off the C.D. player, and eased his five feet, six
inches out of the Porsche. He wore pilled gray polyester slacks and
a drooping, shiny blue Hawaiian shirt with red parrots on it that I
hadn't seen before.

"How much did you pay for the shirt, Leo?" I asked as I got
down from the Jeep.

"Four bucks, on closeout, at the Discount Den. They only had
double XLs," he added, as if I hadn't noticed the way the shoulder
seams hung down to his elbows.

"Could be handy," I said as we started across the lot, our shoes
crunching the gravel. "You can invite people inside your shirt if it
starts to rain."

He nodded, all chin-up cool behind the sunglasses, and veered
off to scope out the ancient picnic tables around back. Kutz lets the
squirrels and the pigeons do his cleanup, but sometimes they get
bloated from the peppers and the onions and start ejecting more
than they pick up. Then it can take a while to find a dry table.
While Leo searched, I walked up to the trailer window and ordered.

Kutz's—first the old man, and now Young Kutz—has been sell-
ing hot dogs out of the peeling white wood trailer under the
Thompson Avenue overpass since the days when the trucks rumbling above were delivering hootch to the speakeasies in Rivertown. Oldtimers say nothing about the place has changed much

since then, except perhaps for some of the water Young Kutz uses to boil the hot dogs.

Young Kutz, who's pushing eighty and is mad about it, piled the five hot dogs, the double-large cheese fries, a huge root beer, and a small diet cola on the flimsy red tray and pushed it through the window. I could feel his eyes hot on my hands as I picked up the tray by its underside, palms up, fingers splayed. I paused to look through the window at him, *mano a mano.* He gave me the nod, a gesture of respect from one warrior to another. Young Kutz uses thin, cheap trays that flex in the middle and are easy to drop. It's how he builds repeat orders. But not with me; I haven't dropped a tray since high school.

I went around back. Leo sat at a brown plank picnic table near the dented, galvanized trash cans. He'd chosen well; there were very few white clumps on the table. I took one hot dog and the small diet off the tray and pushed the rest across the wood.

Leo Brumsky was already balding the summer we graduated from Rivertown High School. That was when Ronald Reagan was in the White House, and much had been said about him being the oldest man ever elected president. Maybe so, I remember thinking that summer, but Reagan, with his impossibly brown hair and rouged cheeks, still looked younger than Leo Brumsky did the day he graduated high school.

"How's Ma, Leo?"

He was already through half of his first hot dog. He kept chewing until the swelling in his cheeks went down, then set the half-eaten dog on the tray next to the others he'd lined up like torpedoes.

"The usual." He picked up a French fry oozing with the yellow stuff Young Kutz tells everybody is cheese. "Ailments."

Leo lived with his mother in Rivertown in the house where he'd grown up. He was a provenance specialist, authenticating and dat-

ing items for the big auction houses in New York, Chicago, and
L.A. When he wasn't traveling, he worked out of the basement of
her brick bungalow and made upwards of four hundred thousand
dollars a year. His Porsche cost double what his mother's house was
worth, but the pilled, too-loose clothes hanging on the one-
hundred-forty-pound frame and his worried, thin, pale face made
him look like he slept under cardboard and foraged for dinner in
alley barrels.

"And Endora?"

"Mercifully, also the same." He smiled around the French fry.
Endora was Leo's twenty-five-year-old girlfriend. She was thin,
quirky, dark-haired, and gorgeous and had an upper-register I.Q.
to match Leo's. She was a researcher at the Newberry Library and
dressed for it, in shades of charcoal and black that kept everything
tight and controlled. But in the summers, after work, on the beach
or on the sidewalk, she wrapped things lighter. Then even the birds
stopped to witness. I will go to my grave wondering what incredible good deeds Leo did in a previous life to merit Endora.

He picked up the half-eaten hot dog and took another big bite,
replenishing his cheeks. "How's the turret coming?"

I told him I was going to buy a new roof. He nodded, chewing.
Sometimes we joked that thirty years from now, he'd still be living
with Ma, and I'd still be working on the turret.

"I've got this document job, Leo."

He tapped his bulging cheek. "I figured there was a reason for
the big spending," he said through the food.

"It's about that explosion last week at Gateville."

Leo's eyebrows, thick and black, moved up his pale forehead, almost touching, like caterpillars about to mate.

I'd brought Stanley Novak's tan envelope. I pulled out the
freezer bag and set it on a clean spot on the table, out of range of
his cheese fries. "This arrived a couple of weeks before the house
blew up."

Leo leaned over to read through the plastic.

"They think it's either a coincidental scam attempt or a ruse, disguising the real objective of killing the people who lived in the house. My fear is it's neither, that the letter is a threat aimed at all of Gateville, with more explosions to come. Whatever it is, there's been no follow-up to collect the money demanded."

He looked up from the freezer bag. "They gave you the originals?"

"They haven't gone to the cops."

"Jeez." He started to shake his head, then stopped when the obvious hit him. "Why hire you?"

"To show their insurance company they acted responsibly in case the threat proves to be legit. Plus, they think they can control me because of Amanda."

"Ah, Amanda." His eyebrows kissed at the top of his forehead.

"It's a job, Leo. I need a roof."

"You betcha." He glanced down at the hot dog wrappers and sodden French fry tray that now held only a tiny, coagulating puddle of the cheese-colored substance. "How much are they paying you?"

"Three grand."

"And my cut?" He smiled, because we both knew he wouldn't take a dime.

"You just ate it." I put the freezer bag back in the tan envelope.

"Not quite," he grinned. "I'd like another root beer."

After lunch, I went to the bank drive-up, pleased that I remembered the way. It had been two months since my last deposit. I put the Gateville check in the scratched plastic canister, punched the button, and watched the vacuum suck it up like a Kansas tornado. The gray-haired lady behind the bulletproof glass gave me a wink and a grape lollipop with my receipt, and I motored out of there, sucking on my lollipop, knowing exactly what it was like to be Bill Gates.

All I could do was wait for Leo's examination, so I drove to the Rivertown Health Center. I fight to keep my weight at the plumpness of an overinjected Thanksgiving turkey, but it's a battle I lose. Still, I go to the health center to keep the dream alive. And to take hot showers. A water heater is on my list for the turret, but it's halfway down.

The parking lot was nearly empty, except for the usual dozen abandoned cars rusting on their axles. I crept along the rutted, weed-spotted asphalt to my regular space next to the doorless '73 Buick by the entrance. I got out, checked my doors twice to make sure they were unlocked, and went in. My Jeep has a vinyl top and plastic side windows, and I don't need anyone slitting them to verify I don't have anything worth stealing.

The Rivertown Health Center had once been a showplace Y.M.C.A., with a big exercise room, an indoor pool, and five floors of temporary rooms for good Christians new to town. That was in the 1950s, when there'd been manufacturing jobs in Rivertown. Now the sheet metal on the roof streaked tiger stripes of brown rust down the yellow bricks, the last of the paint had flaked off the gray, sun-rotted wood windows, and the good Christians had fled, leaving the upstairs rooms to trembling winos hanging on for the salvation of fresh pints at the first of the month, when the disability and public aid checks arrived.

Downstairs, the pipes leaked, the running track was a greasy, crumbling obstacle course of silver-taped rips, and the locker doors had all been beaten in by punks hunting for watches and wallets. But it was cheap, the water was hot, and so long as I got out of there before the punks came to hang out in the late afternoon, it was safe enough for a workout and a shower.

I changed into my blue Cubs T-shirt and red shorts and went upstairs. Barney, Dusty, Nick, and the rest were there, roosting on the rusted fitness machines like crows on fence posts. Old men, retired from the tool cribs and stamping rooms of the factories that used to be in Rivertown, they came early every afternoon to reassure themselves that they were all still alive. Nick told me a joke, the same joke he told every Tuesday. I laughed. He smiled, proud of his wit. It was ritual.

I left them to their talk and ran laps and did maybes. Maybe the Bohemian was too practiced at telling his clients money could make their problems go away, maybe the threat in the letter was real, maybe there would be another bomb, maybe somebody would get killed. Maybe I should not let myself be used, insist instead that the Bohemian take the note to the cops. Maybe I shouldn't worry about Amanda's house. After six laps I staggered off to hug the wall, sucking air. There was no maybe about me carrying too much weight.

I hit the showers and thought about the only thing that wasn't a maybe.

The Bohemian was holding something back.

# Three

Leo called at 9:00 A.M., two days later.

"Can you come over?"

I could hear something tapping, his heel maybe, or a pencil.

"You don't want to extort another gourmet meal?"

"I don't want to waste any time."

I told him I'd be right over.

Leo's mother's place was seven blocks away, a narrow dark brown brick bungalow in the middle of a block crowded with narrow dark brown brick bungalows. They had been built in the late 1920s, when Rivertown had Florida bungalow fever. And hope.

Blue television light flickered behind the lace curtains as I went up the cement stairs to the porch and rang the bell.

Leo opened the door almost instantly, as if he'd been waiting with his hand on the knob. Ma didn't look up as I stepped into the living room. On the big-screen television, a woman was interviewing a man sitting on a couch next to a chimpanzee. The chimp looked life-sized on the forty-five inch screen. "So nice Leo has friends," Ma murmured, her eyes fixed on the television. "Yes, ma'am," I said. The chimpanzee smiled. Leo and I walked through to the kitchen.

I followed Leo down the stairs and through the basement, past the broken Exercycle, the train set on plywood I'd helped him put together in seventh grade, and the decorated three-foot artificial Christmas tree they shook off and put on the T.V. every December. We went into the space Leo had walled off under the living room for an office.

There was no door, and he'd never gotten around to priming the drywall or putting tile or carpet on the bare concrete floor. Equipment—magnifiers, three tall gray file cabinets, a light table—took up every available inch. Nothing was out of place. It was all pure Leo: functional and without a nod to aesthetics. Just like his shiny Hawaiian shirts.

He went behind the scarred, beat-up wood desk he'd found in the alley, sat backward on the listing chair, and wrapped his thin arms around its slatted back like he was hugging it for warmth. I dropped into the sprung green overstuffed chair that must have felt fine under Leo's bony one hundred and forty pounds but always made me feel like I was bungee jumping.

On the wall above the light table, shiny photographic enlargements of the Gateville envelope and letter were clipped to a metal holder next to an old poster of a wet but excited Bo Derek.

"Sorry about taking two days, but I wanted a friend of mine at the I.R.S. forensic lab downtown to take a look." Leo's heels started beating a light riff on the cement floor. When Leo is on to something, his feet tap, and his fingers stretch and curl, probing for anything they can pick up. Today he twirled a yellow wood pencil between his fingers.

He pointed the eraser end at the blowup of the white envelope. "There's nothing remarkable about that; millions like it are sold in stationery stores and discount places. It's got a self-adhesive flap, so

I doubt there's potential for saliva D.N.A. It's postmarked at the main Chicago post office, and so it has plenty of fingerprints, none of which will help us. It was addressed recently with an ink-jet printer, probably a Canon, the kind that's in every public library."

"No typewriter with a raised, cracked *e*?" I said, doing my growl of Humphrey Bogart doing his growl of Philip Marlowe.

Leo's eyebrows crawled up into a tired black arch. "Must I suffer your mimicry?"

"Forgive me, schweetheart. What about the note?"

"Much more interesting. Pencil lettering, done with a ruler to disguise the writer's hand as you suspected. And of course, the paper is from a kid's tablet, old stock."

"Old stock?"

"The manufacturer discontinued this particular paper twenty years ago."

"You're saying the note was written a long time ago?"

"That I can't tell." He opened a desk drawer, rummaged inside, and pulled out a spiral-bound notepad with a school crest. He fanned the pages to a blank sheet in back. "This paper is old, too. I've had it since college. Means nothing; lots of people have old paper lying around. As for the lettering . . ." He shook his head. "I can't tell its age. Pencil lead doesn't change much with time."

I pointed at the enlargement of the note on the wall. "Fingerprints?"

"None."

"So nothing can be learned."

"Not so fast, Holmes." His wide lips split into a grin. "To begin with, the lettering is precise, but also the color is consistent on every character. A ruler can help that, but the pencil pressure still had to be controlled throughout." He stood up, went to the blowup, and used the pencil eraser to draw an imaginary line under the words. "See the evenness of color? Nice and consistent. No urgency, no anxiety. If this had been written by some nut as a quick scam, one might expect evidence of agitation: uneven color, a trailing line, a missed connection between two lines, or any of a number of other things that would suggest haste. But this is precise and controlled. Your letter writer is serious."

"Or he's a shakedown artist on Valium. What else?"

Leo came back to sit behind the desk. The smile was gone. "Why hand-print the letter at all? Why not type it on the library computer, or wherever, when he did the envelope? Why fool with a pencil and ruler to write the words and risk finger or palm prints?"

I thought for a minute, came up with nothing.

"It's a huge clue," Leo went on, tapping again with the yellow pencil, "but we're not smart enough to figure it. This needs to go to the police."

"The Bohemian thinks the problem's over. If the letter's not from a nut, it was a ruse to keep the focus off the Farradays, and they're gone."

"How fortunate for the Farradays," Leo said, his voice heavy with sarcasm.

"No, I don't think the Bohemian hung them out to dry. He said he showed Farraday the note, let him decide whether it should go to the cops. He said Farraday declined."

Leo shook his head. "Somebody's got to take this to the cops."

"The Bohemian won't allow it unless he's convinced the threat still exists. There are twenty-six homes still at Gateville. Figuring conservatively at three million each, that's seventy-eight million worth of real estate that could become close to worthless overnight."

"Including Amanda's." Leo watched my face.

"I need a roof, Leo." I pushed myself out of the folds of the green chair and picked up Stanley Novak's tan envelope off the desk. "As for Amanda, sure, I want her house to keep its value. Nobody takes a three-million-dollar whack easily."

"You betcha," he said, standing up.

We went up the stairs. On television, Ma was watching a deeply tanned woman wearing a white towel say something to a deeply tanned man wearing a white towel. It's always nice when people with similar interests find each other.

Leo opened the front door. "Will the Bohemian listen to you?" he asked as I stepped out.

"I don't know."

"He'd better. He's got to call the police," he said through the screen.

I checked my phone for messages as I pulled away from Leo's. Amanda had returned my call a half hour earlier and had left an international phone number. I swung back to the curb, shut off the engine, and called. She answered right away. It was a lousy connection, but there was no missing the wariness in her voice. It was the third time we'd spoken since our divorce. The two earlier times had been the previous October. I'd been drunk.

"I'm not pickled this time, but I'm going to sound just as foolish."

In the background, I could hear cars and trucks, and people shouting in another language.

"Amanda, where are you?"

"Paris, in a little café across the Seine from the Louvre, drinking American coffee from a yellow cup on an orange saucer."

The tight spot in my neck relaxed. She was nowhere near Gateville.

"What time is it there?" It was all I could think of to say.

"Just past five in the afternoon. Dek, are you all right?"

"Are you going to be over there long?" I asked, counting on the background noise to make my question sound casual.

"Through the fall. I'm doing an art history book for middle schoolers. Are you sure you're all right?"

"Absolutely."

"Is your business coming back?"

"Slowly. You know lawyers, cautious as mice. I sent them all copies of the exoneration story in the *Trib*. It was two paragraphs long. You're sure you'll be away for a while?"

"Yes." She paused, waiting. She was tensed, afraid I'd suggest I come to Paris.

When I asked a couple of quick questions about her book project instead, the relief in her voice was louder than our words. We filled another minute talking about the crowds of summer tourists, and then she asked, "What were you going to say?"

"What?"

"You said you were going to say something that would sound foolish."

"I did? That was foolish. I just called to hear how you are. Paris for the summer sounds great. I've got to run." I clicked off. There was no need to fumble with an explanation of why she should stay away from Gateville; she was going to be safe in Paris. Still, I wouldn't have minded talking some more. There were plenty of other foolish things I wanted to say.

It's the little stuff that haunts. The sound of her laughter, as it made something I'd said sound wittier that it was, or the way the burgundy highlights in her dark hair caught the fire of the sun. Little stuff, that comes at me in the middle of the night.

I first saw her on an unseasonably balmy February evening the year before. Chicago weather does sometimes, tosses out a lily of a springlike day in the middle of winter to lull everybody before burying them in a ton of snow in April. That night, the false spring made the walls of my tiny condo so tight they almost touched. I'd gone outside and walked west, restless, to Michigan Avenue.

She was standing just inside one of the small art galleries, a beige trench coat draped over her arm, frowning at an oil painting on the wall. She was about my age but wore it better. She had short, dark hair, a pale complexion, and lips that looked like they could offer salvation.

She must have felt my eyes. She turned, smiled, pointed at the oil on the wall, and surprised me by motioning me to come in. I did, not pausing to wonder why she'd beckoned. Opportunity of that sort rarely knocked on my dusty door.

"What do you think?" she asked, pointing again at the painting she'd been staring at. Her voice was soft, lilting.

"My taste in art runs to blues festival posters."

"Does that prevent you from forming an opinion of other art?" Her brown eyes sparkled mockingly.

I pretended to study the painting. It was abstract, I supposed; a mess of indeterminate shapes, mostly green.

"There's a lot of green," I offered finally.

She laughed. "Anything else?"

I bent closer to the frame. The little card said it was being offered for one hundred and twenty-five thousand dollars. "It's obviously very good green."

"Actually, it's not very."

"Very what?"

"Good green. It's just very expensive."

"Do you want to have a drink?"

She surprised me again. She said yes.

We drank beer in a dark booth in an empty ersatz Cockney pub on the ground floor of one of the shopping towers. She told me she wrote art history books that were too expensive to sell anywhere but to libraries. That was good enough for her, because of the potential that some kid might pick up a copy and get a switch turned on that would lead to a lifelong interest in art.

I told her I ran an information service, chased down records and photographs for lawyers and insurance companies. That was good enough for me, because it got me out of Rivertown where most of the art was spray-painted in four-letter words, on the walls of abandoned factories.

We talked until the Cockneys threw us out at midnight. By then, I'd been enchanted, captivated, bottom-line crazy-in-love for three hours.

We met the next four times by the bronze lions in front of the Art Institute. She was teaching a class there that semester. We'd walk to one of the small places for dinner and we'd talk. We didn't do the theater, or the movies, or the clubs. There wasn't time; we were both in too much of a hurry chasing something we'd each thought had passed us by. And we had too much to say about not much of anything, before we ended up at my condo closet on the lake, where we wouldn't talk at all.

I proposed on our fifth date, at a little trattoria three blocks west of Michigan Avenue.

"I want you to have dinner at my place before I give you my answer," she said.

Things froze in my mind then. It had been too fast, too wonderful. She read it on my face.

She smiled and reached across the red-checked tablecloth to squeeze my hand. "Just have dinner at my house, Saturday night." And then she told me she lived at Crystal Waters.

I hadn't put it together that she came from huge rich. She dressed simply, wore little jewelry, and drove an old Toyota. She'd told me once that she lived west of Chicago, and that had been enough. We were in a hurry, and there were other things to talk about. Or not.

That Saturday evening, I got off the Eisenhower Expressway at Rivertown. I drove past the houses where I'd lived growing up, past the graffiti-blighted high school, past the abandoned, ruined turret that had been my grandfather's dream and folly. Rivertown was less than fifteen miles west of my lakeshore condominium, but I hadn't been back in twenty years.

I didn't linger. I took Thompson Avenue out of Rivertown and followed it to where it widened to four lanes and the shallow, cookie-cutter colonials began. Red brick facades, skinny white pillars, little green ribbons of side yards. "Fronts," people in Rivertown call them, but they say it with envy.

The money real estate begins a mile farther west. That's where the houses get big and different from one another, each one set back from the road, framed in its own setting of full, rich trees. Gateville is three miles west of there, six total from Rivertown. But that's as the birds fly. Measured by money, it's as far away as the moon.

A half mile east of Gateville, I drove up the hill that always seemed like it had been put there to give pause before the beauty of the good life down below was revealed. I'd looked at Gateville plenty of times but had never known anyone who lived inside.

The guard at the gate checked my name on a list, gave me a half salute, and waved me through. As I pulled past the guardhouse, I saw him pick up the phone.

Amanda was waiting outside her front door. "I'm not here much," she said as I got out of the car. It sounded like she was apologizing.

"Quite a house to not live in very much," I said as we went through the huge walnut double doors. And it was. Beige brick, gray tile roof, three-car garage, and lots of tinted windows around what I later counted to be ten rooms.

She led me through an unfurnished foyer to the center hall. She bypassed the arched entry to the living room and started the tour in the dining room. It was a bare room, empty of anything except a lone oil portrait of a man's face hanging on an interior wall, where it couldn't be seen from the hall. It was a stern face and looked vaguely familiar.

"This used to be my father's house," she said, her voice echoing in the empty room. "He took all his furniture except for the stuff in the living room when he moved to the North Shore."

"That was recently?"

She laughed and led me out to the hall. "No."

We walked through to the kitchen. White tile countertops, stainless steel refrigerator, big restaurant-sized stove—and, strangely, a junk-store porcelain-top table and two white-painted chairs. The table had been set with white plastic plates.

We continued through an unfurnished family room and a cherry study whose built-in bookshelves were crammed with art books but which also had no furniture. We came back to the foyer, climbed the stairs to the second floor, and walked down the hall past four empty bedrooms. At the rear of the house she stopped. "My bedroom, growing up." It was the smallest of the bedrooms, and the only one that was furnished, with a twin bed, a dresser, a nightstand, and a student desk with a computer. It looked like a room in a college dorm. She cocked her head up at me and smiled. "Any questions at this point in the tour, Dek?"

I had about a hundred but narrowed them to one. "Why live here?"

"The answer is downstairs." We went down to the arched entry off the first-floor hall. Unlike the rest of the rooms on the first floor, the living room was nicely furnished. "Mostly Louis XIV reproductions," she said of the cream-colored chairs, the tables, and the two settees. "My father left them. He was going for a different look in his new place."

She paused in front of a small oil painting hanging above a Chinese lamp on a little table. The oil was of a woman in a long white gown, reading a book. "Pierre-Auguste Renoir," she said. She turned and pointed to several other small oils, naming artists I'd never heard of. The two-foot bronze of a cowboy, though, I knew was by Remington.

"You asked why I live in Crystal Waters?" She moved to stand in front of a larger painting, perhaps two feet by three, of water lilies on a placid pond. It hung above the fireplace, in a gilt frame with hexagonal corners. She looked at it for a minute without speaking, as if she were seeing it for the first time. "Claude Monet. It has never been shown publicly." After another minute, she smiled at me. "If there were ever a fire, I would get the Monet out of the house before I'd call the fire department."

She led me to one of the antique white sofas. "These were my grandfather's favorite pieces. Collectively worth nine point eight million dollars, at last appraisal."

I'd been worrying she had money. I hadn't let myself fear she had that kind of money.

"Was that your grandfather's portrait hanging in the dining room?"

"No. That's my father. He left it behind when he moved. He said it would remind me he was keeping an eye on me."

Then I had it. I'd seen that face in the newspapers. He headed Chicago's largest electric utility, along with being a big time fundraiser in Democratic circles.

"Your father is Wendell Phelps?"

She nodded. "We don't get along."

Over dinner of bakery baguettes, marinara heated in the jar in the microwave, and undercooked pasta, she filled in the blanks. She was one of eight grandchildren of an enormously wealthy steel magnate. "My share of my grandfather's estate was just over twelve million. I didn't want his money; I wanted his art."

"So you gave up your share for the pieces in the living room?"

"And used the rest to buy this house from my father," she smiled. "Strange?"

"Not the art part. But I don't understand why you live here in this big empty house."

"Security. Constant surveillance, monitored neighborhood, the gatehouse. It costs every dime of what I make to live here, but it's the safest place for the art."

"Does all this mean you won't marry me?"

"It means I wanted you to see how I must live before you ask."

"We're so different, Amanda."

"Precisely."

"Will you marry me?"

"Of course."

She hadn't bought dessert. We didn't notice.

That was in March of last year. Every day, when I think of that evening, it cuts like it happened yesterday.

Back at the turret, I called the Bohemian before I got out of the Jeep.

"You've got an enemy," I said. "I just met with the document examiner. The envelope is common, available everywhere, and was computer-addressed with the kind of printer that can be found in every public library. There are no fingerprints on the note, the paper is old, and the lettering looks controlled, not the work of a quick scam artist firing off a false threat."

"Thank you, Vlodek," he said too quickly.

"Not so fast. A handwritten note makes no sense when your man obviously had access to a computer. It would have been much safer for him to type the letter on the computer as well, not chance leaving fingerprints or other clues. You need the police to puzzle through his motivation for using a handwritten letter."

"I'll take that under advisement," he said, in a flat tone that meant he would do no such thing. "Send me a report."

"You should take the police a list of anyone who might wish to harm Crystal Waters."

He sighed. "I can think of no one, and everyone."

"Let's start with everyone."

"People who wish harm to Crystal Waters?"

"Yes."

"Pull out the phone book, Vlodek. List everyone who has lost a job, add those who are just barely getting by, along with those who resent wealthy people because they think they never lift a finger.

Add in anyone else who feels envy, and for good measure, stir in those people with mental problems and those who hear voices from outer space. Are you understanding this?"

"Sure, we're still with every name in the phone book. Let's narrow it down to people who are familiar with Crystal Waters and who need money."

He paused and then said softly, "Like you?"

It stopped me because he was right. We were looking for people like me.

"People other than me," I said. "Like caretakers, contractors, service workers, landscapers, anyone who had access to Crystal Waters recently, anybody who could have gotten close enough to the Farraday house to plant a bomb."

"I wouldn't know how to begin such a list," he said.

"My point exactly. That's why you need the police."

"It's premature."

"What about the guards? Are any of them recent hires?"

"I'll check with Stanley."

"What about the Members? How many of them need money?"

"I would imagine all of them, given the recent fluctuations in the financial markets. But fifty thousand? Somebody who will risk planting a bomb to extort fifty thousand dollars? I think those Members who are in dire need of cash require a hell of a lot more than fifty thousand. I think you can eliminate the Members from your list, Vlodek."

Maybe he didn't mean it to, but it came across arrogant. "Fifty thousand is a lot of money to most people."

"Of course it is, but don't let us forget that our letter writer never followed up to collect."

"All the more reason to look for an amateur, someone who got cold feet and couldn't follow through with another letter."

"It's not a Member, Vlodek."

"Then you're back to the phone book, and for that you need the police."

"The letter either was written by someone harmless or was meant to confuse the Farraday investigation."

"So you'll do nothing?"

"I will be very deliberate regarding the next step, Vlodek. Please, send me a report."

I gave it up because there was nothing else to say. I hung up and went into the crumbling tube I call home, past the table saw, the plastic chairs, and the buckets of roof patch that so far hadn't done much to keep out the rain. I went up the flaking, rusted metal stairs to the second floor, sat at the ancient card table, and turned on the six-year-old computer that was all that was left of my business. I supposed the Bohemian was right about everything being a matter of perspective. Fifty thousand was chump change to the Members of Gateville, but it would be enough to transform a lot of what was wrong in my life.

I typed a full-page summary of Leo's findings about the envelope and the letter and ended it with my recommendation, in capital letters, that the Bohemian take the note to the police immediately, so that they could begin compiling a list of suspects from everyone who had recent contact with Gateville. I printed my report, called a same-day messenger service, and told the girl who answered that I wanted something delivered and signed for that morning. I started to yell when she told me they might not get to it until that afternoon, but then apologized. She sounded nice, like someone to whom fifty thousand dollars would have mattered.

I shut off my computer and stared at the dark glass screen. It was a document job, I told my reflection. I'd done what I was supposed to do.

# Four

I live in a limestone turret because my grandfather was a bootlegger. There are other reasons—a courtroom scandal, a tanked business, a vaporized marriage—but it remains that, were it not for my grandfather, dead decades before I was born, I might still be tiptoeing around the fragrant puddles on the upper floors of the Rivertown Health Center.

My grandfather would have insisted he be called a brewmeister, because that's how he apprenticed in Bohemia, but there were no brewmeisters in America in the twenties. Prohibition had made them all outlaws. Bootleggers.

As bootleggers went in those days, he was small time. He worked out of a dozen garages in Rivertown, brewing pilsner the right way for the Czechs and the other Slavs who lived on Chicago's west side. Family lore had it that some weeks he made money, other weeks he lost. It depended on how often his operations got trashed by the police or his bigger competitors. He had more bad weeks than good, though, and died broke, of a heart attack, in 1930. But not without marking me. I would get his first name, Vlodek, and I would get the beginnings of his castle.

In the spring of 1929, six months before the stock market crashed, the illicit, big vat brewers and whiskey runners in Chicago started killing each other in a vicious series of gang wars. The police weren't particularly distressed, viewing the wars as a kind of weeding, but they had to make a show of trying to stop it. For months, with the outfits and the cops so occupied, no one had time to raid my grandfather, and he enjoyed a season of unrivaled prosperity. He must have thought it was going to rain money forever. Because, flush for the first time, he did what anyone with too much money and a lunatic sense of grandeur would do: He began building a castle on the bank of the Willahock River in Rivertown. He had grand plans and bought a pile of limestone big enough for twenty rooms, four-foot-thick walls, and a five-story turret at each corner.

But within weeks of the delivery of his small mountain of limestone, the gangs reached an accommodation, and they and the cops slipped back into their old, comfortable routines of preying on tiny rivals like my grandfather instead of each other. And the money quit raining. My grandfather got only one turret and a small wood storage shed built before he died, broke, a year later.

My grandmother tried to sell the turret, the shed behind it, and the pile of limestone, but the Great Depression was in full fire by then, and the demand for limestone, let alone single turrets and medieval dreams, was nonexistent. The turret and the heap of blocks sat neglected until the end of World War II, when the city fathers of Rivertown, as slimy a bunch of lizards as had ever scuttled down a dark alley, raised up their heads and sniffed the coming of postwar prosperity. They would need a proper city hall from which to dispense building permits and accept donations and appreciations. And so it went. They condemned my grandmother's pile of stone and the two acres on which it sat and built a four-story limestone city hall of magnificent executive offices and tiny public rooms, all set on terraced stonework leading down to the Willahock River.

They hadn't wanted the rat-infested turret a hundred yards away, with its skinny windows, nor its rickety storage shed, and they sat empty for another six decades as ownership passed from my grandmother to my uncle and then to his widow, my aunt. Each tried to sell it, but always, the fees for clearing an old title clouded with murky, vague city liens were more than the property was worth. My aunt, in a last act of maternal protection, left the property not to her own four children but to me, her least favorite nephew.

In my right mind, I would have viewed the inheritance the way the owner of white carpeting sees the arrival of a St. Bernard suffering intestinal distress. But I was broke, exiting a ruined business and a failed marriage, and I needed a place to live. Of such is born delusion. I figured I could fix up the turret, clear the title, and sell it for a tidy profit, to get a grubstake for a new life.

I was full of new optimism, that day after Halloween, as I walked across the grass from the turret to city hall to get an occupancy permit. It had been less than a month since I'd met with Amanda's lawyers and the Bohemian to dissolve my marriage, but it was a new day, a sunny day, bright and warm.

"How long you been gone?" the building commissioner asked. His name was Elvis, and I remembered him from high school. He'd been the mayor's nephew. He'd slathered lots of Vaseline on his hair back then, and I used to wonder if a fly landing on his head could free itself before it dissolved. Now, it appeared he enjoyed hair spray, scented sweet, like coconuts. His hairline was in full retreat, but what was left, halfway back on his head, was sprayed straight up, like a little wall meant to hide the patch of shiny skin behind.

"Since high school, Elvis. I lived in the city while I went to college, stayed there when I got a job."

"Heard about your job." He smirked with his mouth open so I could admire his bad teeth.

"I was cleared."

"Put your ass out of business, I heard. Got you throwed out of Gateville, too."

A month earlier, I would have gotten in his face. Now, though, I was showering at the Rivertown Health Center while standing in what I hoped was just water. I needed the occupancy permit.

"Damned right," I smiled. "I prayed I could be returned to my own kind."

The top of his head glowed crimson all the way back to the hair wall, quicker than he could think. Instinct must have told him there'd been an insult, but the words had come too fast to process. He bent over the counter, head still glowing, and began filling out a form. When he was done, he hit it with a rubber stamp and pushed the permit across the counter.

I looked down. He'd stamped "Historic" in red ink at the bottom. "What's this?"

"Your property is a historical. No changes." He laid a dirty fingernail on a tiny drawing in the upper right corner of the permit.

It was a rendering of the turret. The City of Rivertown was using my turret as its symbol.

"What do you mean, no changes?"

"Check with us before you do anything, so's you don't spoil the integrity of the structure and we make you rip out what you done."

"I want to make it into a residence."

He shook his head. "No can do, even if it wasn't a historical. It's zoned municipal."

"What's that mean?"

"Mean's the property's only approved for city buildings."

"I know what municipal zoning is. I meant, how can private property be zoned only for public buildings?"

"Your aunt approved it after she took sick." The corners of his mouth twitched; something funny had penetrated his consciousness.

"Why the hell would she do that?"

"Might have been because of us waiving sixty years' worth of unpaid taxes and penalties. Municipal property don't pay tax, so there'd be no liens against her estate." He showed me his bad teeth again, in the kind of feral grin hyenas give to fresh meat. "You been away a long time."

"Does this mean I can't live there?" I was struggling to maintain an even tone.

"It's a municipal. Still, I suppose I could give you a temporary exception, so's you can repair the place and all." He batted his eyelashes like a virgin bride, dropped his head, and started making a notation on the permit. He wrote slowly, giving me time to fish in my pocket for a fifty to express my gratitude.

I didn't have the fifty. Nor the gratitude.

He finished writing. I scooped up the permit before he noticed I wasn't flashing any green and started for the door.

"Hey!"

I stopped and turned.

Elvis had his index finger in the air. "Just you can live there, and only to fix up the place on the inside. No wives," he snickered, "no girlfriends. I catch wind of anybody else living there, you're gone."

I went out quickly, before I got stupid. Like the movie cop said, a man's got to know his limitations, and mine were screaming to be let loose, all over Elvis's oily head.

The next afternoon, I saw a zoning lawyer who told me, for a billable hour, that I'd been away a long time. Rivertown was under new management, he said. Grandson and granddaughter lizards had taken over, and the new lizards were college educated, not to be satisfied with small-change pimp and pinball money. They wanted Mercedeses, not Cadillacs, and for that they needed condominium developers with big, greasy wads of building application and zoning variance cash. But to get those developers, they first had to shake off the old Rivertown tank-city image of wet-floor bars, gambling houses, and strip joints. So they hired consultants

who came up with a marketing campaign. Rivertown Renaissance, they called it. To kick it off, they chose the turret—my turret—as the symbol of the rebirth of the town. They put it on the town's stationery, police cars, fire trucks, and municipal Dumpsters. They even put it on the portable toilets in the town's one park.

I could fight, the attorney said, but that would take money I didn't have. Since I'd already moved in, he recommended I rehab cautiously on the inside and, when I could afford his three hundred an hour, take the City of Rivertown to court to change the turret's zoning into something I could sell. Until then, he suggested I keep a low profile. Don't provoke.

My hour expired. I left the lawyer's office mumbling to myself. The dominoes of my life were still tipping over.

In the beginning, it wasn't difficult to follow the lawyer's advice. As November changed into winter, I had more pressing things than a zoning conversion to worry about. Like heat. I got a small personal loan at the bank, bought pipes, electrical conduit, and wiring—and three space heaters—and spent the winter clearing out seventy years' worth of pigeon droppings and squirrel carcasses and repairing the rudimentary plumbing and wiring my grandfather had installed. With a used microwave oven and plastic washtub sink, the turret, with its bad roof, had all the comforts of camping out in an abandoned house, but as I reminded myself on an almost hourly basis, at least I was not at the health center. The zoning lawyer would have been pleased; through that winter and spring and into the summer, my profile was lower than a garden snake's.

Late one afternoon, I was on top of the turret, leaning against the stone wall that rose five feet above the roof, arguing with Elvis. A long week had passed since I'd messengered my report to the Bohemian, and I'd stayed busy by calling every roofer in the yellow pages and trying to convince myself that the Bohemian was right in not going to the cops.

Elvis had seen the roofers' trucks coming by all week, and each time one pulled away, he came blustering over to make sure I wasn't violating any of his rules.

"A membrane roof is a big rubber sheet," I said for the fourth or fifth time. I kicked at the loose stone pebbles on my roof. "It won't leak like this tar and gravel. Besides, this wall hides it. I could put a pink roof on, and you'd never know."

"I'd know." Elvis touched a large dark red pimple on the tip of his nose. "I'd know."

"You saw the buckets downstairs. This place leaks."

"I'd know."

The loving way he was fondling the zit was mesmerizing.

"I'd know," he said again.

"What?" Engrossed by the way he was caressing his apple red nose, I'd lost the thread of what he was saying.

"If you were putting a pink roof on this place," he said.

I'd paused, searching for the right one-syllable words, when my cell phone rang. A crisp British voice introduced herself as the Bohemian's secretary and said, "Mr. Chernek requests that you go to Crystal Waters immediately. Mr. Novak will be outside the front gate."

My heart started banging like an old pump. "What's this about?" I shouted into the phone.

"Please go there, Mr. Elstrom. Immediately." She hung up.

Elvis's lips were working under his inflamed nose, but I couldn't hear his words. Guilt had shut down my sound as my mind raced. Thirty pieces of silver, three grand; I'd been Judas. I'd sold out, hadn't forced the Bohemian and Stanley Novak to go to the cops. For money, for a roof. Jesus. Now there'd been another bomb, and maybe somebody had died.

I hustled the startled Elvis down the five flights, mumbling something about a family emergency, jumped in the Jeep, and aimed it west.

I couldn't risk getting stuck in the trucks clogging Thompson Avenue; I ran the stop signs on the side streets, past the bungalows and the dark shells of the abandoned factories, and shot back onto Thompson Avenue by the Fronts at the outskirts of Riverton, where the highway widens to four lanes. I raced along the highway, swerving around the slow-moving trucks, dodging the occasional car pulling out of one of the long driveways. Cars horns blared; drivers fumbled to lower their windows to scream at my recklessness. I didn't care. I was Judas, and now people had died.

I got to the hill just east of Gateville and sped up toward the crest with my head out the side window, scanning the sky for black smoke. But the sky was clear and blue, and there were no sirens above the sounds of the traffic. I got to the top of the hill and looked down.

The white marble gateposts of Crystal Waters stood like Corinthian soldiers at rest, calm against the dark green yews by the entrance. No smoke, no flames, no flashing lights. Just three men standing next to a pale blue pickup truck parked on the grass outside the brick wall, right next to the entrance. I rode the brake down the hill, taking deeper breaths.

I got close enough to recognize Stanley Novak, talking to two workmen in pale blue coveralls. All three were staring into a hole in the ground like they were discussing planting a tree. They looked relaxed. I tapped my horn and waved to Stanley, swung around, and parked fifty feet down along the grass shoulder. He hurried up to the Jeep before I could get out.

"Chernek's office told me to get right over here," I said through the open side window. "What's the rumpus?"

Stanley leaned closer to be heard above the traffic going past. "Something blew that lamppost out of the ground, but I don't think it's related to our problem."

He opened my door before I could stop him. I got out.

"Those workers don't know about the note," he said, closing the door.

"Mum's the word."

We started toward the two workers.

The hole was rough-edged, three feet in diameter and three feet deep. Next to it, a black metal lamppost, jagged at the base where it had been ripped from its cement footing, lay on the grass like an uprooted tree.

The taller workman was down on his knees, sniffing inside the hole. "I still don't smell anything," he said, getting up. He looked at Stanley. "Best we call the gas company." Next to him, the other worker nodded.

I bent down. The inside of the hole was strewn with chunks of broken cement. I couldn't smell anything except the sweetness of freshly cut grass.

"Get your shovels and poke down in there first," Stanley said quickly. "See if you can locate the pipe."

Both workers looked at him, surprised. I did, too. "The shovels might give a spark," the taller one said.

"Use the wood handles, then. Let's make sure there's a gas pipe down there before we call the gas company."

Neither of the workmen moved.

"Look," Stanley said to the tall workman, "after the explosion at Sixteen Chanticleer, any reporter getting hold of this will see it as the same kind of explosion, and then it will hit television or the papers. Let's be sure it's gas, is all I'm saying."

The tall workman looked back at Stanley. "What else could it be?"

"Kids, with a coffee can full of cherry bombs." Stanley turned and touched my elbow, ending the discussion. We started walking back to the Jeep.

I waited until we were out of earshot. "You really think that big iron lamppost was toppled by kids with fireworks?"

"Fourth of July was last week. Kids here, their parents buy them cherry bombs, M-80s, skyrockets. Put enough of that stuff together, you can blow up anything."

We leaned against the hood of the Jeep and watched the workmen pull blue-handled shovels from their pickup truck. It occurred to me then that everything matched in Gateville: the truck, the workers' coveralls, Stanley's uniform shirt, even the shovel handles. It was all pale blue, the color of a clear sky, as if serenity could be painted on.

"Tell me what happened."

Stanley looked at his watch. "Four hours ago, at two thirteen, I was making my rounds."

I remembered the way he cruised Chanticleer Circle in his blue station wagon, lap after lap, scanning the empty lawns and the shut-tight houses for movement that didn't belong. I used to wonder how he stood the monotony, because hardly anything ever moved in Gateville. The residents were never out. The women didn't talk across hedges, their kids didn't toss footballs on the lawns, their toddlers didn't wobble big-wheeled tricycles down the sidewalk. The hedges had been grown tall, to seclude, not to talk over. There were no sidewalks. And the kids were shadows, invisible, gone after school to supervised activities and then later whisked down to basements, to numb themselves with home theaters and video games. What movement there was in Gateville came from landscapers pushing lawnmowers, house painters carrying cans from trucks, maids or nannies exiting beat-up cars left respectfully out on the street. Caretakers, silently serving unseen masters, like workers in ghost towns.

"I heard a loud noise out by the road," Stanley was saying. "I looked up and saw dirt and dust in the air outside of the wall. I figured a car accident—a car rolled, kicked up dirt. I drove out the gate, met one of my guys running from the guardhouse. We saw that." He pointed ahead at the lamppost lying beside the hole.

I looked at him. "No note?"

He shook his head. "I checked the Board's mailbox right after the explosion. Nothing."

In front of us, the two workmen, holding their shovels by the blade, poked gingerly into the hole.

We watched for another minute, and then Stanley asked, "Anything new at your end?"

It surprised me, because I thought he would have talked with the Bohemian. "I haven't done anything since my report to Chernek. I told him the threat could be real, that you should take the letter to the police."

"I was wondering if you are investigating other things."

"I just did the letter and the envelope, Stanley."

We went back to watching the workmen. They probed into the hole slowly with their shovel handles, as if at pythons coiled in a pit.

Traffic had picked up on the highway alongside of us. It was approaching six thirty, white-collar rush hour. Every few minutes, a Mercedes, B.M.W., or Jaguar, every third one of them painted black, slowed to turn into Gateville, their drivers oblivious to the workmen outside the wall. When I lived there, I used to wonder what it was with all that black. It wasn't just the men with their luxury sedans. It was their pert, frosted blond wives, too, driving the most enormous of S.U.V.'s. Most of those were black, too, each looking big enough to haul four caskets, stacked properly. Amanda drove a white Toyota. Reason enough to love her, I'd told her once.

The tall workman set down his shovel, bent down, and began lifting chunks of cement out of the hole. Then he got down on his knees and started scooping out dirt with cupped hands. After a minute, he stood up and gave us a wave. We walked back to the hole.

"I don't understand it, Mr. Novak," the worker said, brushing off his hands on the sides of his overalls. "No gas pipe, just the wiring for the light post."

I bent down to look into the hole. Electrical wires of every color, reds, blues, greens, yellows, and more, severed by the blast, spilled out of a ripped metal utility pipe and lay on the black dirt like multicolored baby serpents. There was no gas pipe.

I kept my face calm, trying to ignore the vein pulsing in my forehead, as I thought about how much force must have been needed to pulverize the concrete. Stanley cocked his head slightly, warning me with his eyes to say nothing. He turned to the workmen. "Loose-fill the hole so no one can fall in."

I started back to the Jeep. He caught up with me.

"No way that was done with cherry bombs," I said. I jerked open the door to the Jeep before Stanley could pull at it like a doorman, got in, and looked back out. His forehead sparkled with beads of sweat.

"Call the cops, Stanley, or I will." I twisted the ignition key, fed the engine too much gas, and cut ruts into his precious green parkway as I lurched onto the highway.

# Five

My cell phone rang at seven thirty the next morning, one minute after I'd switched it on. It was the Bohemian, and he didn't take time to schmooze.

"You can't go to the police."

"Your bomber is sending you another message."

"By blowing up a lamppost?"

"By showing you he can do it anyplace."

"We must wait for his letter."

"What if he doesn't send one? He never did send a follow-up to collect money the last time."

"We must wait."

"Go to the police, or I will."

"You think the Maple Hills police can solve this?" His voice rose.

"No, but they'll pass it off to the F.B.I. or the A.T.F. They'll check the soil around the lamppost for D.X.12 and start a professional investigation."

There was a pause. "It was D.X.12," he said.

"You know this already?"

"I had Stanley take a soil sample to a lab last night."

"That kills your theory that the first bomb was aimed at the Farradays. Your bomber is targeting all of Crystal Waters."

The Bohemian said nothing.

"The Feds might be able to trace the D.X.12," I said.

"The police tried after the Farraday bomb. D.X.12 hasn't been manufactured since the sixties. There are no sources to trace."

"Then somebody's got an old cache," I said, "and that's a clue you, Stanley, or I don't know how to handle. The Feds might."

"People will be ruined."

"People will be dead."

He gave an exasperated sigh. "Vlodek, ask yourself: Does he want to kill, or does he want money? He blew up a house when nobody was home. Now he's blown up a lamppost safely outside the walls. He's an extortionist, not a killer. He wants money. The lamppost increases the pressure, perfects his position. He's priming us. He'll send another note, we'll pay him, and he'll go away."

"How can you be sure? He hasn't contacted you for payment. He might just keep setting off bombs."

"He will communicate. He's a businessman. He wants money."

The Bohemian sounded so cocksure: a bomber as businessman, rational, perfecting his position. It made it all the more chilling.

He went on, each word calm and well reasoned. "Our bomber knows publicity would ruin house values. That's his lever against us. But it cuts both ways. He fears publicity, too. If this gets out, we'll have no choice but to bring in the police, and that will end his chances for money. That's why he won't kill. This is a kind of blackmail, Vlodek. We must handle it ourselves."

"We just wait?"

"He'll contact us for the money."

"And once paid, he will stop?"

"He knows our resources are not infinite. If he gets too greedy, he knows we'll have no choice but to involve the authorities."

"Is everything in your world always so logical, or are you just practiced at making it sound that way?" I struggled to keep my voice as sure as his, to not let him hear I was furious with his calm logic—and furious with myself, because he was manipulating me, and I didn't know how to stop it.

"The lamppost was a heads-up, a little notification. Obviously it will be followed by a money demand, with instructions."

"What if you're wrong? The police can give you security that Stanley Novak and his band of gatekeepers can't."

"Do you recall the two groundsmen digging in the hole yesterday?"

"Yes."

"A tall man and a shorter one?"

"Yes."

"Describe the shorter one."

I thought for a minute and realized I couldn't, at least not well. The tall man had drawn my attention; he'd done the talking.

"The shorter groundsman is from a private security firm," the Bohemian said. "You didn't see it, but he had a gun. There are others as well, acting as landscapers or contractors."

"None of them did any good yesterday."

*"It was outside the gate."*

"The police need to see the note, and they need to know about yesterday."

"Let me handle this, Vlodek." He clicked off so smoothly it took a few seconds to realize I was listening to dead air. He'd flicked me off like lint.

I went over to the Mr. Coffee, thought better of it, and balanced my cup on the pile in the sink instead. I was already breathing like I was running uphill. I went outside to sit on the city bench facing the river.

The only thing worse than being a paper tiger is being the last one to realize it. I could growl in the air all I wanted, but the Bohemian had me pegged. He knew I wouldn't call the cops.

Point One: I wasn't a licensed investigator, or an attorney, but the Bohemian would have checked around, learned I always respected the confidentiality of my clients. Point Two: If I ever did go to the cops against the wishes of a client, I'd be ruined in the business I was trying to rebuild, and afterward, the best I could hope for would be a greeter's job in a discount store. Point Three: Amanda's three-million-dollar house was involved. She didn't have much cash, just that big-buck residence and a fortune in art. Losing the house would jeopardize her ability to keep the artworks, and the Bohemian knew I'd go to any length to protect her.

Points One, Two, and Three were why the Bohemian hired me in the first place; he was sure of the control he'd have over me before he sent Stanley flashing a check. I could protest and threaten all I wanted, but the Bohemian knew I wouldn't go to the cops.

But there was a Point Four: The sand was running out of the hourglass. The Gateville bombs couldn't be kept quiet forever. A Board member would tell his wife to get the kids out of town; she'd tell someone, and someone else—a cleaning woman, a gardener working under an open window—would hear and sell it as a news tip to a radio station for twenty-five bucks. Word was going to get out, unless the bomber sent a note soon, he got paid, and he went away. Quickly—and for good.

Point Four was where my brain dead-ended: Why did the Bohemian think he could get the whole thing resolved before it became public, and why was he so certain that, once paid, the bomber would go away forever?

What did the Bohemian know?

I watched the river, but the river offered up nothing but empty eddies.

I got up. Maybe the answer was simply that the Bohemian understood money motives better than I. He was managing multimillion-dollar portfolios while I sniffed varnish, trying to cobble up enough for a roof and a hot water heater. I went into the turret for my gym bag.

Except for the trucks lumbering through town along Thompson Avenue, the streets were empty. It was nine thirty in the morning, too early for the commerce of Rivertown, too early for the pawnshops, video arcades, bars, and working girls. That would change when the lizards got the condo builders to start stacking young urban professionals along the Willahock. Then the latte emporiums, trendy clothiers, and organic-broccoli peddlers would come, daytime places for daytime people with daytime needs. Until then, Rivertown would stay a nighttime town.

And that was fine, at least until I could finish the rehab, get my zoning changed, and unload the turret. Because when the developers did come, the first thing they'd push over was the health center, to chase out the drunks. Yups won't pay a half million for a condo if they're going to be greeted mornings by some grizzled fellow in urine-stained pants, savoring an eye-opening splash of muscatel against their bricks because he couldn't find his way back to his room.

I needed that health center, too, except I needed it for the hot water and for the times when the inside of the turret got too tight.

I pulled into the lot and crept around the potholes to the husk of the doorless Buick. The locker room was empty except for the guy asleep on a towel bag. He had a room upstairs but slept down by the lockers in the summer because it was cooler. I put on my workout duds, went up, and walked more laps than I ran, so my gasping wouldn't drown out my voice of reason, should it decide to speak up. It didn't. After forty-five minutes, I went down to the showers, no closer to understanding why the Bohemian thought he could buy off the bomber for good.

I spent the rest of July like a man waiting for bad news from a doctor, trying not to jump at the first ring of the phone or tap at the door, for word that another note—or worse, another bomb—had come to Gateville.

I sent out letters to former clients, newsy little bundles of lies about how busy my firm was, yadda, yadda, yadda.

I called the roofers, had them come out again, peppered them with too many questions about how each would fix my roof. And then waited by the door for Elvis to come huffing over, so we could yell at each other while he inspected my roof and I inspected his complexion.

I hung dark oak trim on the first floor of the turret, CD player blasting Brownie McGhee and Sonny Terry, Son House, Lightnin' Hopkins. Blues men from blue times.

I went to the health center every day and laughed at Nick's jokes and did circles around the track like I was doing in life.

And I went nuts a little, because all I'd really been doing was waiting for another bomb to go off. So, on the tenth long day after I'd messengered my report to the Bohemian, I launched a minor war against city hall.

I'd spent the morning and all afternoon on a long ladder, caulking the gaps around the slit windows on the second and third floors, and being subjected to the whining voice of some adolescent outside city hall, counting to three, over and over, sound-checking a P.A. system. Across the lawn, workers were setting up green-and-white-striped umbrella tables along the terrace, and they'd hung a huge RIVERTOWN RENAISSANCE IS READY banner across the front of city hall. The lizards were holding their first evening soiree for contractors and developers.

The reception started at five o'clock, and from my ladder, it looked to be high style for city hall: candles on the tables on the broad limestone terrace overlooking the Willahock, strings of brightly colored Christmas lights woven into the bushes, an out-of tune, two-sax-with-drums trio, and, judging by the volume of shrill laughter as the soiree got under way, plenty of booze. No doubt there were also cocktail wienies on toothpicks, but I can't verify that because none of the lizards thought to acknowledge me, up on my ladder, by sending over a sampling on a paper plate.

I quit working about eight o'clock. The sun was going down, and I had a pounding headache from the off-key music and the liquor laughter from next door. I had just slid the ladder into the shed when the combo stopped abruptly, as if somebody had mercifully pulled the plug of the P.A. The sudden absence of missed chords calmed the night like painkillers on a toothache, and I stopped outside the shed to breathe in the quiet.

The silence didn't last. A minute later, the two saxophones attacked the first notes of the theme from *2001: A Space Odyssey*. The drummer fought to keep in time. And some fool flipped a switch.

Four spotlights hit the turret with enough mega-wattage to light a microsurgery. The combo screeched louder; people clapped. I froze, caught in the glare, staring into the white light coming from the city hall they'd built with my grandfather's limestone, on the land they'd stolen from my grandmother. It was supposed to be high drama, the stark illuminating of the symbol of Rivertown's renaissance. But to me it was assault.

The bastards didn't bother to turn off the spotlights after the last of the developers had tipsied away. The slit windows of the turret are narrow, too skinny to admit much sunlight, but that night the interior of the turret was as bright as a bus station waiting room. I couldn't sleep at all, from the glare and the anger, and spent the night on the roof, in a small patch of shadow cast by the top of the stone wall, staring at the floodlit water of the Willahock. If not now, then soon, the turret would be floodlit all night, every night.

And sometime, just before dawn, a switch of my own got flipped.

The next morning I pulled into the parking lot of Mabel's Mature Fashions. I'd found it in the yellow pages.

"What are the largest-sized ladies' undergarments you carry?" I asked the pink-wigged woman in the orange tunic behind the counter. She looked to be sporting the very sizes I was interested in.

She raised one caked eyebrow.

"Not for me," I added quickly. My skin felt hot, and I wanted to giggle. It was probably from the lack of sleep.

"Fifty-quadruple-D in bras, 6X in panties." She looked me up and down. "Might be a little large."

I ignored it. "Do they come in colors?"

The other caked eyebrow went up. "White only in those sizes, sir, but they're all cotton. You could dye them to suit yourself."

I turned away to clear my eyes as I fumbled in my wallet for my credit card. This was not funny; this was war. I bought six sets.

After Mabel's, I went to a hardware store for clothesline, clothespins, and Rit Dye. Back at the turret, I boiled water on my hotplate, mixed the dye, and became Michelangelo. As a kid, I'd tie-dyed all my T-shirts once, in a quest to become a ten-year-old hippie. That had been decades before, but I hadn't lost my touch. I transformed the panties and bras, big enough for prizewinning pumpkins, into bright, psychedelic works of what could be called art. I spread them out on my table saw and over the plastic chairs, and when they were dry, I set them on top of my new coil of clothesline.

They would be the battle flags of my war against city hall.

The second reception was the same as the first: umbrella tables, colored lights, eighty-proof chatter, and the same two saxophones, sounding like they'd wasted not one minute on practice. As the last of the sun disappeared from the sky, the combo went silent, just as it had during the first reception. Only this time, I was behind the turret, tensed for the first shrieking notes of *2001*.

A minute passed, then another, and then both saxophones bleated into the night air, fighting to approximate the same note.

The four spotlights hit the turret with white light.

I started feeding my flags onto the clothesline I'd strung on the property line facing city hall.

I played them out slowly, letting the bright colors unfurl with their own drama. By the time the second pair of tie-dyed 6X panties—these scarlet, gold, and Kelly green—hit the white light and started flapping in the night breeze, the cocktail chatter next door had dissolved into shrieks of raucous laughter. The band stopped, confused, as the people roared, louder and louder. I fed two bras, the first one magenta and yellow, the second neon green, onto the line. The people clapped and cheered.

And that brought Elvis.

He stormed across the lawn, chasing his own shadow made long by the spotlights behind him. He wore a greasy powder blue dinner jacket that had the look of something discarded after a prom.

"You got a woman living here, Elstrom," he screamed, his face contorted, his hair wall glistening in the glow of the floodlights. A hundred yards behind him, the well-lubricated contractors and developers shrieked, drunk enough to think this was a skit, done for their amusement.

"This is not underwear, Elvis," I announced. "It's art." I clipped a bright purple and orange bra that I was particularly proud of onto the line. In the shadows of city hall, the developers hooted and clapped, a hundred happy hands.

That infuriated him further. "It's underwear, damn it." Bits of spittle bubbled at the corners of his mouth. "Get her out here so I can throw both of you out."

"There's no woman, Elvis." I smiled and bent down to my laundry basket for something pink and yellow.

"When I catch her, you're gone."

At that point, someone must have cued the combo, because they took off into their approximation of "Fly Me to the Moon," each saxophone flying in a different key. It made further discussion impossible. I closed my mouth and beamed at Elvis, mellow as a panda on Percodan.

Across the lawn the people kept clapping, and the drummer began singing about Jupiter and Mars.

Elvis wasn't done. He leaned to within an inch of my nose. "What the hell do you want, Elstrom?" he screamed, spraying spittle into my face.

"Change my zoning to residential or commercial. I'll sell and leave," I yelled back, waving at the still-clapping crowd behind the glare of the floodlights.

"No can do," he shouted. His lips gave a final twitch, and he stalked off. Someone at last thought to kill the floods, and the developers gave a final burst of applause.

My stunt was stupid and childish. That night, I slept better than I had since I'd moved into the turret.

The lizards held two more receptions. They didn't risk the floodlights again, but the ambient glow from the colored Christmas bulbs was enough to light up my undies, and the effect was mostly the same. Each time I'd start stringing my flags, the crowd would roar, and Elvis would march over, his oily face shining red above the pale blue of his prom jacket.

"Change my damn zoning, and I'll leave," I'd yell.

"No can do," he'd scream back.

And the drummer would sing about Jupiter and Mars.

That was how July died. Every evening I ran up my flags, to remind the lizards that I was twitching for a fight. But after the fourth reception, no more were scheduled, and that was just as well. My little battles were just diversions, things to keep my mind from circling around what I was really doing, which was holding my breath, waiting for Gateville.

So I felt a sick kind of relief when, at the steaming beginning of August, I answered the door just after lunch and found Stanley

Novak standing outside, clutching another tan envelope. He didn't say anything. He didn't have to. The sweat on his face said it all.

I'd been varnishing, and Stanley didn't look like he could survive the fumes, so I led him down to sit on the bench by the river. I took the new freezer bag out of the envelope and read the note on the child's paper through the plastic: NEXT TIME SOMEBODY DIES. FIVE HUNDRED THOUSAND SUNDAY NIGHT SAME PLACE. The perfect pencil lettering, the computer printing on the envelope, and the Chicago postmark were the same as the first letter's.

I looked at Stanley.

"It came this morning. Mr. Chernek wants it analyzed to make sure it's the same guy before he pays."

"It's the same, Stanley; you can tell just by looking at it. What I want to know is—"

He stood up. "Please, Mr. Elstrom, have it analyzed. Then we'll talk."

I didn't waste the words. He was a blind pawn on the chessboard, like me. I walked him up to his station wagon and told him I'd have it checked right away.

I drove to Leo's. Up on the porch, television sounds came through the window screens. I knocked, waited, knocked again. After five minutes, Ma opened the front door against the chain, her head still aimed at the T.V. in the living room. People were grunting. Leo was in L.A., she said, but would be home that evening. I passed the envelope in, and as I did, Mr. Jack Daniel himself came wafting out through the crack in the door. Cocktails had started early. I made a polite grab to retrieve the envelope, but she was already shutting the door. The grunting inside had reached a fevered pitch. I let it go. I could only hope she'd drop the envelope on the hall table as she teetered back to her chair.

Leo had told me she only drank when he was out of town. As long as he kept his trips to one-nighters, he'd said, he didn't worry. He even brought her back the disposable plastic hotel cups she buried at the bottom of the kitchen garbage so she could think she'd left no visible evidence of her drinking.

I called Leo's cell phone before starting the Jeep and told his voice mail I'd left another note with Ma but that she'd been vaguely disengaged. He'd understand. Hurry home, Leo.

It was two o'clock. The turret would feel like a cage until Leo looked at the letter and I could press for a meeting with the Bohemian.

I drove west, meandering, wrestling with the last words on the note: SAME PLACE. Words that meant the Bohemian or the Board already knew where to drop the money, words that meant there had been other communications, letters, maybe even phone calls they hadn't told me about. Fair enough. I was the document guy, hired to be a cog, not the whole wheel. I didn't need to know.

But need and want are two different things.

I swung over to Thompson Avenue and headed west to Gateville. If I showed up unexpectedly, I might be able to open up Stanley Novak about what had happened in the past.

From the crest of the hill, Gateville once again looked like paradise: green lawns, big houses, shading oaks, all nestled inside a protecting wall in its own little valley. I drove down the hill.

A stake truck loaded with plastic flats of flowers was stopped diagonally in front of the wrought-iron gate, blocking the entrance. Its engine was off, but its driver was still behind the wheel. I pulled onto the shoulder across the street and shut off the Jeep's motor.

Two masons in white overalls were tuck-pointing the outside wall, troweling small amounts of mortar from wood pallets into the brick joints. It looked to be slow, painstaking work, pushing in the little amounts of mortar and then smoothing the joints with a jointer. One tuck-pointer sang to himself, his lips moving softly.

Two pale-blue-uniformed guards came out from between the white pillars, waited for a break in the traffic, and crossed the street toward the Jeep. Each wore a gun belt, something the Gateville guards had never done when I'd lived there. The retaining straps of their holsters were unsnapped.

It was good. The landscaping truck blocking the entrance and the slow-moving tuckpointers were security. The one tuckpointer hadn't been singing; he'd been speaking into a microphone to alert the guardhouse that a Jeep had stopped across the street.

I put both hands on top of the steering wheel where they were easily visible. One guard came up to my side window as the other moved to the front of the Jeep.

"Dek Elstrom, working with Stanley Novak. Would you like to see a driver's license?"

The guard nodded.

I kept my right hand on the wheel and extracted my wallet with my left. I thumbed it open, slid out the license, and passed it out. The guard bent down to compare my face with the photo, then backed away from the Jeep to use his cell phone. After a minute he came back and handed me my license.

"Mr. Novak said if you need to speak with him, to call him at home."

"I just saw him a couple of hours ago. Is he ill?"

"Not him. His wife."

"Nothing serious?"

The guard shrugged. "Call him at home if you need him."

He motioned to his partner, and the two guards walked back across the street. I watched them disappear between the white pillars and thought about another time.

Nine months before, in the black of the night of Halloween, Stanley Novak had escorted me out from between those same pillars, at the direction of my ex-wife.

# *Six*

It hadn't been an acrimonious split. We'd only been married for a few months, not long enough to build up a big list of hatreds. Instead, our divorce had been a last, loving gesture of Amanda's, a veering away, before my unraveling of my life caused us to despise each other.

Driving her to O'Hare on that gray drizzling October day, Amanda told me in a soft voice to take whatever time I needed to move out. She wouldn't be back from Europe for six weeks. I told her I was going to get my life back together so we could try again. She kissed me good-bye at the international terminal like she believed me.

I drove back to Gateville, packed what clothes I hadn't given away in two black plastic garbage bags, and piled them inside the front door. But the next step, the one that had me turning the doorknob, throwing the bags in the Jeep, and driving away, was too big. I mixed a weak whiskey and walked slowly through the empty rooms of her enormous house. I didn't want to stay; I didn't want to go. An hour went by, then the afternoon, then the next day. And then the rest of that October passed, as I shuffled from empty room to empty room, pausing only to mix watery whiskeys just strong enough to keep a veil over my thoughts. I microwaved things on occasion, and slept, sometimes on the bed, sometimes on the carpet. But mostly I paced from room to room, a ghost of something I'd been, looking at nothing at all.

I came to life, sort of, on Halloween. In the middle of the afternoon, I put ice in the sterling silver bucket that was a wedding gift from the mayor of Chicago, filled Amanda's grandfather's Baccarat punch bowl with fun-sized Snickers, and set out a fun-sized quart of Jack Daniel's for myself. I settled in one of Amanda's antique white Louis XIV reproduction chairs to wait for princesses, goblins, and Harry Potter.

But nobody came. Not a gremlin, not a goblin, not a Spider-Man or a Superman. At dusk, I levered myself out of the chair, pulled back the brocade drapes, and looked outside. In the glow of the landscaping lights, the smooth emerald lawns were empty, save for a few errant leaves that had had the nerve to fall since the twice-a-week lawn crews had last been by.

There were no trick-or-treaters, not in Gateville. They must have been hurried inside when I wasn't looking, home from some organized function where they'd been supervised by nannies, au pairs, and specialists at conducting controlled Halloween parties.

It was wrong.

What the hell was Halloween without trick-or-treaters?

I aimed myself back to the chair, had more whiskey and fun-sized Snickers, and reflected on that. And, at about nine o'clock, I had an inspiration. None of the kids in Gateville knew how to trick-or-treat because they'd been raised too stuck-up-the-ass rich to go out to grub for candy.

I'd show them. I'd be the Pied Piper of tricks and treats.

Fueled by the whiskey and, by then, half a cut-glass punch bowl of fun-sized Snickers, I got up and started hunting around the house for a mask. Of course there was no mask, but it did take some time, many overturned drawers, and four torn-apart closets to conclude that. And every time I stepped through the center hall—carefully, one foot in front of the other so as not to spill a drop—Wendell Phelps, who I didn't suppose would like me one damn, mocked me, unseen but not unfelt, from his place on the other side of the wall.

After the fourth or fifth such pass, I went into the dining room to confront Wendell Phelps, key Democrat, C.E.O. of Chicago's largest electric utility, and advisor to senators, congressmen, and other people like himself. I stared at the portrait. It was life-sized, but just of his head. Amanda had said it was a good likeness. Wendell Phelps was all head.

The liquor and the sugar had not drained me of all my resources. After staring at the portrait for several moments, I had a second inspiration. I would go trick-or-treating as the great man himself, Wendell Phelps, C.E.O., counselor, knower of everything worth knowing.

The canvas of his portrait, despite being stiffened by layers of crusted oil paint, was surprisingly flexible. Wielding a sharp razor knife with great care so all could be put back as it was, I excised his face from the portrait, cut out his eyes so I could use my own, poked holes at his ears, and tied on a rubber band—which took some doing, being that deep into the Jack. But, after a time, I had my mask. I filled my glass to the brim, as a soldier does his canteen before a long march, and went out trick-or-treating.

Stanley's guys got me before I could pound on the door of the second house. They did not believe I was Wendell Phelps. They took me to the guardhouse and called Stanley at home. He told them to call Amanda, which took a while because she was in Portugal. When they did get through, she was in no position but to approve my eviction, what with nine point eight million dollars' worth of colored oil hanging on her living room walls and me with a razor knife and the potential for more inspiration. By that time,

Stanley had gotten there and eased me into his station wagon, and out I went, flushed gently through the big white pillars of Gateville, with a fading buzz and my clothes in garbage bags following behind in the back of my Jeep, driven by one of the guards.

I managed to tell him to take me to Rivertown, because it was where I was from, and it was what I was. I slept at the health center the rest of that night, in a Lysol-drenched room that had just been vacated by somebody who had died in his own vomit. The next morning, with a banging head, eyes recoiling from the white of a too-bright November sun, and the certainty that I had, at last, sunk to the bottom of the pond, I moved into the turret.

Nine months ago, I'd finally come full circle. I was back in Rivertown.

I was asleep in the shiny blue vinyl La-Z-Boy, twelve bucks truly used at the Salvation Army store, when Leo called at ten o'clock at night. He'd just gotten in and told me to come over. Ma answered the door, said with minty breath that Leo was in the basement, and sat carefully back in her chair. Naked people were getting acquainted on the television. I went through to the kitchen and down the stairs.

Leo, still in his gray business suit and wearing white cotton gloves, was hunched over his light table, peering through a Luxo magnifier at the second note. His face was ghoulish in the green underglow. Astrud Gilberto sang about Corcovado from the cheap boom box on top of a file cabinet, but too softly to drown out the lustful things the man and woman were saying on the television upstairs. I knocked on the raw wood of his office doorjamb.

"Same sender?"

"Same old, same old," he murmured, continuing to peer at the note. I leaned against the jamb and tried to shut out the drama going on above my head. The man and woman had stopped talking and were communicating now with squeaking bedsprings, as Astrud sang softly of love, oblivious to the lust going on just above her head. Mercifully, Leo finished his examination, switched off the magnifying light, and turned around.

"When did this arrive?"

"This morning."

He slipped the note and the envelope back into the freezer bag, brought it to his desk, and pulled off his cotton gloves like a doctor after surgery. He sat down and I dropped into the overstuffed chair.

He held up the freezer bag by its top edge, pointed to the last two printed words on the note, and arched his eyebrows.

"Same place," I recited.

The bag and his eyebrows stayed up.

"They've dealt with him before," I added.

He waited, his face coaxing. I hadn't yet said the magic words.

"I've got a no-win choice: the cops or my career?"

"Ah," he said, as his face relaxed. But there was no humor in his eyes.

I didn't sleep.

Leo and I had kicked around my options until the middle of the night, looking for good ones, but they kept boiling down to one of two bad alternatives: Tip the cops to what was happening, watch the news ruin the people at Gateville, and find another line of work. Or keep my mouth shut, like a good employee, and wait for people to die.

I got home at three in the morning, no closer to knowing what I should do. I didn't bother with my cot. I went straight to the blue vinyl of the La-Z-Boy, shifted into full recline, and watched the insides of my eyelids for a couple of hours. I nodded off a few times around four o'clock, but it was only to dream, in bursts, of big houses disintegrating into fireballs. And, strangely, of snakes—red, lavender, green, black, and white snakes—writhing on their tails, twisting together in the orange light of the burning houses. Over and over I dreamed of those snakes until, exhausted, I gave it up at five thirty. I made a pot of coffee, filled my double-sized travel cup, and took it and my cell phone up to the roof. I keep a folding lawn chair up there for nights when old times come to haunt and I go up to wait for the sun.

I sipped coffee and thought about the snakes in my dreams. Endora, Leo's girlfriend, says everyone knows dreams are the mind's way of resolving the unresolved. Leo laughs and tells her that's got to be true with me, because my daytime mind is too weak to power both motor and cognitive functions. Leo jokes that I should concentrate only on eating and walking when I'm awake and save my thinking for my dreams.

Screw Leo. But he's more right than I'll tell him. During the weeks when my reputation was being trashed, my business was collapsing, and my marriage was destructing, I learned to trust my dreams to work through what I couldn't make sense of during the days. Or didn't dare.

Up on the roof, though, I couldn't figure the snakes.

I drank coffee and listened to the night. A mile away, long-haul trucks on their way to Indiana and Wisconsin rumbled over the corrugated rub strips on the toll road. Closer, the bells at the railroad signal started clanging. Long-haul trucks and railroad trains made sense to me. Dreams of snakes did not.

I picked up the cell phone and then set it down. It was only six o'clock, too early to call the Bohemian.

To the east, the sky was getting lighter over Chicago. It seemed impossible that, just a couple of years before, when I lived downtown on Lake Shore Drive and was full of enthusiasm for such things, I'd get up early to watch the sun rise over Lake Michigan. August dawns were the best, because the moisture rising off the lake would sometimes combine with the early heat to create incredible colors.

But now, drinking coffee on the roof of my grandfather's aborted dream, the day's first reds, oranges, and yellows licking at the blue-black of the night sky reminded me only of the snakes that had twisted and contorted through my dreams.

At seven o'clock I called the Bohemian's office number. He picked up the main line himself.

"Vlodek. I was just going to call you," he schmoozed. "The note is from the same sender?"

"Surprise, surprise. How about I drop it at the cops—"

"—Vlodek—"

"—on my way to your office. We need to meet. You, Stanley, and I."

"About what?"

"The first payoff. The one you haven't told me about."

The oil went out of his voice. He told me he'd have Stanley Novak in his office at nine.

I got in line inbound on the Eisenhower Expressway behind a gray-primered Chevy Caprice with a wired-up back bumper. At eight in the morning, the traffic crawling east into Chicago is thick with rattling old cars. More and more, the good stuff—the high-end imports, the sixty-grand S.U.V.'s—is across the elevated tracks, going the other way, aimed at suburban offices from the rehabbed Chicago lofts, renovated row houses, and brand-new city communities of red brick, black wrought iron, and green sod that have popped up, like God's own blooms, over what used to be hardscrabble urban blight, glinting of ancient cinder and broken glass.

The Bohemian's office was just west of downtown, in one of the first rehab districts. His were the only offices listed for the top floor of a ten-story, yellow-brick former factory that towered over everything around it. I punched the button and was admiring my khakis, blue Oxford cloth shirt, and navy summer-weight blazer in the elevator mirror when I noticed the splotch of dried ketchup on the coat sleeve. I was still scratching at it when the elevator chimed at the top.

The door opened right into the reception area of Chernek and Associates. The room was dark and discreet, lit softly by green glass-shaded lamps. The six high-back chairs and two Chesterfield sofas were upholstered in dark green leather that was lightly creased, like old money. I crossed the burgundy oriental rug to the black walnut desk. The receptionist was young and blond and upholstered in red silk. The only crease I could see on her was one perfect inch of tanned cleavage.

"Dek Elstrom to see Anton Chernek."

"Of course." She smiled and touched a button on her telephone console.

A dark-haired older woman with a helmet haircut appeared almost instantly at a side door. She wore a blue suit with a white blouse buttoned to the neck and had the pinched-face demeanor of someone wearing tight underwear. Certainly her cleavage had never seen the sun. I recognized the British accent when she told me to follow her. She was the Bohemian's secretary.

We went through the door and down a row of cubicles, two of which had empty cartons set on their worktops. She stopped outside a small conference room with a single window, more dark green leather chairs, and a round walnut table. She told me Mr. Chernek would be with me shortly. I went in and sat down.

A large oil painting of an English hunting scene hung on the beige-papered wall. I studied the dozen red-coated riders, tensed astride their burnished black horses, their faces all purpose and concentration as they followed the pack of hounds. I tried to fit myself into the scene. The Bohemian would be the lead horseman, of course, his whip raised, his face confident and sure. Just as the rider immediately behind him, dutifully sounding the hunt with a curved brass horn, would have to be Stanley Novak. But I couldn't fit myself in with the rest of the riders; they looked too well born, too comfortable in their riding clothes, too obviously suited to the hunt. They could only be the Board members of Crystal Waters. I stared at the painting until I finally decided I was the only dog straggling behind the riders, his head canted to the side, distracted by something in the underbrush. Yellow, green, and red snakes, maybe.

The Bohemian opened the conference room door and came in. For a big man, he moved softly, like a panther. He wore a charcoal chalk-striped suit, a soft blue shirt, and a muted burgundy tie. He had the same tanned skin and bright teeth I remembered from my divorce meeting. I got up, and we shook hands. His hand was big, the hand of a man who had done manual labor long ago. We sat down, and he folded his big hands on the table and waited for me to speak.

"Stanley Novak will not be joining us?"

"He's been delayed but will be here shortly." The Bohemian glanced at the table and then shifted to look at the floor by my chair. "You've not brought the envelope and the letter back?"

"I thought it would be safer back at my place."

His face remained calm. "You've not given it to the police." It was a statement, not a question.

"Not yet."

He leaned back in the chair and studied my face. "Vlodek, so little trust."

"Why go through the charade of bringing the second note to me?"

"We have to make sure we're paying the right man."

"You mean the same man—"

The quick tap at the door cut me off, and Stanley came in. He didn't look well. His uniform was neatly pressed and his comb-over was intact, but he had dark smudges under his eyes and his lips were shiny. He sat down like he'd been carrying cement.

"How is your wife, Stanley?" the Bohemian asked.

"She'll be fine." Stanley pulled out a handkerchief to wipe his mouth. "What have I missed?"

"Vlodek spotted the reference in the second letter."

Stanley nodded. "As you expected," he said, looking at the Bohemian.

The Bohemian turned to me. "In April of 1970, just a few weeks before the first Members were scheduled to move in, the developers received a note demanding ten thousand dollars. It did not make a specific threat and said nothing about where to drop the money. We took it to be a prank because it was so vague—some Maple Hills resident, perhaps, upset about the development."

"What did the letter look like?"

The Bohemian glanced at Stanley. "From what I remember, exactly like the two we've received this summer: double-lined child's paper, block printing, capital letters in pencil."

Stanley nodded in agreement.

"And the envelope? Was it white like the ones you received this summer?"

"Yes . . ." The Bohemiam hesitated, looked to Stanley.

"Except it was addressed in pencil, block lettered like the note. Obviously not ink-jet computer printed, not back then," Stanley said.

The Bohemian went on. "A week later, there was an explosion at the back of the guardhouse. It wasn't a big explosion, nothing like the Farraday house, but it did enough damage to require rebuilding the rear wall. We assumed it to have been set off by the person sending the letter."

"Why didn't you go to the police?"

"We did, Vlodek."

"Mr. Chernek came to me," Stanley said. "I was a patrol officer on the Maple Hills force, moonlighting at night as security on the construction site, but my hat was in the ring for the security chief's job at Crystal Waters. After the guard shack blew, Mr. Chernek called me in and showed me the note they received."

"And you did what?"

"I told him hundreds of construction workers had access to the development, as did truckers delivering materials, utility company people, even Maple Hills cops, for that matter. Cops are like everybody else. Some of them get resentful at all the money in a place like Crystal Waters."

"So there were lots of potentials. What did you recommend?"

"That he contact the sheriff's police."

I looked at the Bohemian. "You didn't do that."

The Bohemian met my gaze, said nothing.

"Let me guess," I said. "If word got out, nobody would move in, and the developers would be out millions."

"Tens of millions," the Bohemian said.

"So you did nothing until the bomber sent you another letter, telling you where to leave the ten thousand."

Stanley took out his handkerchief and wiped his mouth again. "The second letter said, 'Put the money in a plastic garbage bag. Drop it in the Dumpster behind Ann Sather's restaurant after dark on Sunday night.'"

"Where was that?"

"On Belmont, in Chicago."

"Same pencil printing, same double-lined kid's paper, same postmark as the first?"

Stanley nodded. "Like the two we've received this summer."

"You delivered the ten thousand?"

"That next Sunday night."

"And you never heard from him again?"

The Bohemian spoke. "That ended it."

"Until now," I said.

The Bohemian tapped his forehead with his forefinger in a vague salute. "Until now."

"So you think that by paying him, you'll get him to leave you alone for another few decades?"

The Bohemian stood up and went to the window. The sun was getting higher, wiping away the morning shadows on the surrounding rooftops. "The objective was then, and is now, money, not murder," he said, looking out. "Our bomber is a professional. He does his research. He knows when the houses will be empty. He knows the places outside the wall where no one will be standing. And, being a professional, he knows our resources are not limitless. He knows we can raise five hundred thousand; it's less than twenty thousand dollars per house. He also must know he can't keep coming back, that if he presses for more, we will be forced to consult the authorities. I think he'll leave us alone when he gets his money."

"You speak of him respectfully," I said to the Bohemian's back. "You might be giving him credit he doesn't deserve. The mailman and the paperboy could have known when the Farradays would be gone, too."

The Bohemian turned from the window, the trace of a smile on his face. "You've forgotten. No paperboys, no mailmen. Everything gets left at the guardhouse. I'll say it again: This man is a businessman."

"Like most of the men who live in Crystal Waters," I said.

The half-smile on the Bohemian's face didn't flicker.

I went on. "As I told you before, this could be an inside operation."

"I can't see how any Member would benefit as much as he would lose. The current demand is for a half million. That's one-sixth of what the typical house in Crystal Waters is worth."

"Another insider, then: a contractor, a landscaper, a housepainter." I looked at Stanley. "A guard."

"Vlodek, please—"

"I don't understand either of you." I said to the Bohemian. "Why go through the charade of having me look at the second note? Obviously, it's the same as the earlier one this summer."

Stanley answered. "We needed to be double sure it's the same person. We knew you'd pick up on the reference to our 1970 payment, but we also knew we could trust you to keep this matter private. We have to be sure it's the same man."

"The man who, if given what he wants, can be relied upon to stay away for years and years?"

"Exactly, Mr. Elstrom." Stanley looked at the Bohemian. "We will proceed with payment, Mr. Chernek?"

The Bohemian turned to me. "Will you allow us to continue without the authorities, Vlodek?"

I didn't need much convincing, which was the shame of it. Playing it out, seeing if the half million would be enough to make the guy go away again, got me off my little moral hook. I wouldn't have to choose between what was left of my career and going to the cops, at least for a while.

"Fair enough." I stood up. Suddenly, I was anxious to get out of there, away from both of them. I wanted to think. I told them I'd call Monday morning to find out how the drop went and left.

On the way back to Rivertown, I kept hearing the admiring tone in the Bohemian's voice when he talked about the man targeting Gateville. Professional, he'd called him. A businessman. A careful man, who does his research.

It sounded like he was describing himself.

# Seven

Saturday morning, early, I drove to Ann Sather's restaurant on the north side of Chicago. I wanted to check out the place where Stanley Novak was going to leave half a million dollars on Sunday night.

Ann Sather's neighborhood was in the first grunts of going upscale. At nine o'clock in the morning, the parking places along Belmont were already taken, the sidewalks already teeming with pairs of slim young men and clusters of black-haired teenaged girls wearing resale-shop clothes. They are the forward guard, the anointers who can declare an area worthy. They have no money; they come for weak tea and candles and used compact discs. But from their terra-cotta perches downtown, the big-money urban developers watch them, and when the anointers come in sufficient numbers, the developers strike with the sureness of hawks—optioning, demolishing, rehabbing, and sending the prices of real estate to the moon. The grungy, curtained incense shops and tiny, linoleum-floored groceries get pushed out by rents gone exponential, to make way for upscale boutiques and bakeries. And then the commodities traders, lawyer couples, and professional urban trendies come to smile and pirouette on the sidewalks, and there are lattes and grandes and little square dessert items for everyone.

I turned off of Belmont into the narrow side alley next to Ann Sather's. It led back to a parking lot. All the spaces were taken, and several cars filled with spaghetti-string tops, purple makeup, and hormones were circling, so I threaded past them and out the main alley that ran parallel behind the restaurant. I had to drive a mile west before I found a spot in front of a used furniture store. The proprietor, no fool he, had put a hand-lettered sign on an aluminum lawn chair in the window: AND ANTIQUES. I walked back east into the crowds tightening along the sidewalks.

Ann Sather's Swedish Diner looked like any of the blue-plate restaurants that dot Chicago's older neighborhoods, the kind of place that always has good meat loaf. It had a pale brick front with full windows facing the sidewalk, offering views of people in booths miming various levels of table etiquette.

I went in. Thirty people, waiting for tables, pressed around a glass case filled with cinnamon buns and loaves of fresh-baked bread, talking loudly to be heard above the clatter of plates and metal silverware. Every few seconds, the window-aisle waitress, who looked like she ate there for free, cut through the throng like Moses parting the waters, balancing plates of omelets and thick-cut potatoes.

I made my way into the long dining room. The back exit wasn't visible, which meant it was normally accessible only to employees. That, and the window card saying the restaurant was closed Sunday night, ruled out the possibility that the extortionist, posing as a patron, was planning to snatch the money from the Dumpster and come back through the diner to escape out the front.

I went back to the foyer and looked in the glass case. For camouflage, I bought a dozen cinnamon buns in a blue and yellow box, the colors of the Swedish flag. It was necessary that I look like a day shopper, and the expense might be tax deductible. Compelling reasons like those don't come along every day. I tucked the receipt in my wallet and took the buns outside.

I walked around back, taking out a cinnamon bun to activate my disguise. The bun was moist, fresh, nothing like the varnished, petrified, pseudo-cinnamon horrors sold at shopping malls and toll road plazas. I ate the bun slowly, a guy killing time, eating a lard pill, waiting for his wife. My favorite cover.

The small blue Dumpster where Stanley would drop the money the next night was just outside the back door of the restaurant. It looked like it would hold ten garbage bags. I took another bite of the cinnamon bun and let the last bit fall from my hand. I bent to pick it up, opened the hinged Dumpster lid, and tossed it in. There was one white plastic bag of garbage inside the Dumpster.

To maintain my cover, I ate another cinnamon bun as I scanned the backs of the buildings lining the main alley. All were classic Chicago four-flats, yellow-brown brick, with latticeworks of gray-painted wood stairs hung on their backs like external vertebrae. Any of those buildings would offer a safe, hidden view of the Dumpster the next night.

I walked down the long back alley, turned the corner, and went around to the parallel street behind Belmont, the one fronting the four-flats. I was looking for an apartment for rent, a place I could put down a deposit to get a key, but there were no signs in the windows. At the end of the block I turned left and came back up the alley from the other end, almost full circle. And got saved.

An old woman in a faded beige housedress was hanging clothes on a line in one of the tiny backyards. I stopped at her chain-link gate.

"Do you know of any apartments for rent around here?"

She had four wood clothespins in her mouth. She shook her head.

"How about garages?"

The wet blue towel she was raising to the line went still. The clothespins came out of her mouth.

"Yah," she said in a heavy Polish accent. "Mine."

She dropped the towel into her basket and motioned me to come through the gate. She met me at the service door to the garage, pushed it open, and stepped aside.

I went in.

There was just enough light coming from the dirty side window to see. The cement slab was cracked into a dozen pieces, and the wood smelled damp from mildew and rot. I felt the wall along the side door for a light switch.

"No electric," she said from outside.

I walked across the broken slab to the side window, took a quick casual look, and went on to the overhead door. The big door was swelled shut, probably from the rot I smelled. I jiggled it loose enough to muscle it up, as if I cared that it worked. I'd already seen what I wanted. The side window had an unobstructed view of the Dumpster behind Ann Sather's.

"How much?"

"Tree hunnert." Her dentures clicked.

When a neighborhood is in play, when the developers come and start bidding everything up, garage rents are among the first to rise. Forget the faded housedress and fractured English; this babushka had her ear to the ground.

"I just want one stall."

"Tree hunnert, cash."

"I'll give you one seventy-five."

She shook her head. "Tree hunnert."

"Two hundred cash." It was all I was packing.

"Two fifty, plus two fifty security. Five hunnert, up front."

I pulled down the overhead door and walked across the cracked concrete. The hinges of the service door wiggled in the spongy door jam as I started to close it. "Two hundred cash, no security," I said as I stepped out.

She nodded, put the clothespins back in her mouth, and extended her hand, palm up.

I gave her four fifties. It was all transacted Chicago style: no lease, no signed receipt. The money disappeared into the pocket of her faded housedress. We were done.

From the Jeep, I called Endora, Leo's girlfriend, at the Newberry Library. She usually worked Saturdays.

"You still driving that little purple '94 Grand Am?"

"My lilac-mobile."

"Can I borrow it tomorrow night?"

"Got a date you want to impress, Dek? Some new lovely you don't want to bounce around in your Jeep?"

Endora had many interests. Resurrecting my love life was in the middle of her list.

"No. I need your car for surveillance."

"No problem. Listen, there's a new lady who's been coming here, doing research for her dissertation. I think she'd be perfect—"

"Can I just borrow the car?"

"Leo will switch with you tomorrow."

Leo was a lucky man.

"A stakeout? Isn't that over your head?" Leo shot the basketball. It arched over the backboard, bounced off the top of a rusty metal upright, and rolled across the crumbled asphalt into the corner of the rusty chain-link fence.

"I should go to the Feds instead?" I called as I ran to get the ball.

"No," he said as I came huffing back. "You rat out your clients, you're done working for lawyers."

"Then what do I do?"

He shook his head. "I don't know. It's just that if you need a car your own clients won't recognize, you've got a problem."

I'd called Leo after I talked to Endora, to arrange to swap cars and to ask him to make a few phone calls. He suggested a workout late Sunday morning at the outdoor basketball court behind Rivertown High School. We'd been shooting bull and hoops there since freshman year, though neither of us had ever learned to drop a basket. A game of horse could run three hours and end scoreless. The workout came from fetching the ball.

I turned around for my over-the-head backward shot. Leo snickered, but I could hear the fear in it. I rarely dropped such a shot, but when I did, it was a marvel to behold. I leaned back and sighted upside down at the backboard behind me. Some poet had spray-painted EAT SHIT in neon green letters on the gray, flaking plywood. I aimed at the space just to the right of EAT, held my breath, and let the ball fly. It hit the underside of the backboard, banged against the fence, and skittered along a rut toward the far end of the blacktop.

"Haven't lost your touch," Leo yelled, but it was in relief. He ran to stop the ball before it rolled into a puddle.

"People could die," I said when he came back.

"And you staking out the drop site will prevent that?" He put the basketball into the small of his back and used it to lean against the rusty fence. A cut from that fence needed a tetanus shot. "Look, I checked around as you asked. Chernek's lost some clients, and a couple of his analysts have quit, but those things happen when the market takes a tumble. Financial guys get blamed, they lose clients, and the junior associates take off for other pastures."

"The Bohemian is hurting for money."

Leo wiped his forehead with his T-shirt sleeve. "Like almost everybody, including thousands of brokers. But they're not going around setting off bombs. Besides, you've got a direct link with the bomb that went off in 1970. Same paper for the note, same kind of explosive. Why not concentrate on that?"

"I don't like the way the Bohemian's so willing to fork over half a million dollars to whoever it is. Maybe he doesn't mind because he's giving the money to himself."

"He's doing what he's told. He's taking his orders from the board of rich people, like you are taking orders from him."

"What if the bomber is one of them?"

"One of who?"

"One of the Members. I told the Bohemian the bomber could be an insider, a Member."

"I'll bet he loved that."

"He brushed it off."

"Of course he did."

"I don't like it, Leo. The Bohemian should be looking at everybody as a potential suspect."

"He's doing the obvious, paying off the guy like last time, hoping he'll go away for another few decades." Leo shook his head and pushed himself off the fence. "What are you going to do tonight when it's collection time? Jump out of your garage and yell, 'Stop, bomber'?"

"I'm going to take a few pictures. Get the license plate number, maybe follow the car."

"What if he spots you? What if he's got a gun?"

"I'll stay well back. The important thing is not the tail, it's the license plate and the description of the man."

Leo stepped in front of the basket and prepared to shoot. "Dek, half the things I see are forgeries. I do my analysis, make my report to the people who hired me, and that's it. What they do with the information is up to them. Sometimes, a bad piece I've examined pops up later at a different house, with a fake attribution. I don't second-guess my clients, I don't rat them out, don't announce they've passed off a forgery. I just do what I'm hired to do."

"No one dies because of that."

Leo aimed the ball and fired. It hit the backboard and dropped onto the metal rim, where it teetered for a full five seconds before, incredibly, wobbling and falling through the hoop.

"Yes," Leo shouted, waving his skinny white arms like a scarecrow on speed. "Game called on account of victory." He snatched the ball before I could grab it, tucked it tight against his stomach like a wide receiver hugging a miracle catch, and started running for the opening in the fence. I hustled to catch up with him.

"Didn't you tell me Chernek has increased security at Gateville?" he asked as we slowed across the hard dirt and tufts of crabgrass.

"Yes."

"Isn't that doing the right thing?"

"Of course."

"Isn't paying off the bomber the most reasonable thing they can do? Especially since the last time they paid off, the guy stayed away for close to forty years?"

There was nothing to say because he was right. We got to Endora's purple Grand Am.

Leo's worried eyes scanned my face. "You're sure it's wise to watch the drop behind their backs? What if you scare the guy away, and that causes him to blow up another house?"

"What's my alternative?"

"Let it alone. You've done what you were hired to do, which was to have the letters examined."

I held out the keys to the Jeep. He shrugged, shook his head, and gave me the keys to Endora's Grand Am.

I got to the parking lot behind Ann Sather's at five thirty. Though the temperature was still in the upper eighties, I wore my blue Cubs cap, dark Ray-Ban sunglasses, and a tan jacket with the collar turned up. I looked like a pervert.

I pushed up the overhead door, drove the car in, got out, and pulled the door down. The mold cultures in the garage were fetid from steaming in the sun all day. I took off my jacket, cracked open the service door for some air, and tried not to breathe. Stanley had said he would make the drop right at dark. I had three hours to kill.

I'd done a couple of dozen surveillances. Most of them were for insurance companies, on people who'd filed false injury claims, but two were for runaway kids, and one was on a guy suspected by one wife of having another wife. All were agonizing, hours and hours of looking at nothing. I like surveillance like I like warts.

I pulled out a small, old wood kitchen chair from Endora's trunk and sat in the shadows of the side window with my beat-up college copy of Thoreau's *Walden*. I need to read Thoreau every few weeks because he chucked it all and went to a rustic cabin in the woods to think. For him, life got understandable when he realized that rich people were herd animals. I wondered what he would have thought of people lumbering along in mammoth S.U.V.'s, chatting on cell phones about luncheon plans or tennis games with other people lumbering along in their own big S.U.V.'s. Thoreau was a pacifist, an environmentalist, and a nonviolent person, but I like to think that he would have been mightily tempted to drive the whole herd, still chattering, into Walden Pond.

I read Thoreau until eight thirty, when it got too dark to see the words. I put the book back in the car, took out my ancient Canon F.T.Q.L. with the long lens, set it on the folding tripod I'd brought, and checked the focus. It was just about dark. I pulled the chair closer to the window to wait.

At nine, a big, square light went on behind Ann Sather's, likely from a timer. It flooded the area around the Dumpster with bright light, and I wondered if the bomber had thought to check out the back of the restaurant at night before he sent the note. When he came for the money, he was going to be lit up like Wrigley Field during a night game. It was dumb, and he hadn't made dumb moves before.

At nine twenty, two kids came out of the shadows of the side alley, bouncing a basketball. It echoed loudly off the brick walls of the buildings. The kids moved diagonally across the empty parking lot, passing the ball back and forth in one-bounce shots, and disappeared down the main alley.

At five minutes to ten, a blue full-sized Chevy van fitted with a wheelchair side lift pulled into the east edge of the lot. It cruised slowly behind the buildings until it nosed to a stop next to Ann Sather's Dumpster, right under the light. The driver's door opened, and Stanley Novak, wearing red plaid shorts, an untucked dark knit shirt, and a yellow baseball cap, got out. He reached back into the van and pulled out a filled black garbage bag. He carried the bag slowly around the van to the Dumpster, lifted the lid, and set the bag inside. The bag didn't go all the way down. He bent into the Dumpster and moved things around until the bag disappeared. He closed the Dumpster lid, got back in the van, and drove out of the lot.

All of his actions had been slow and easily visible in the bright light. Stanley had made sure that the bomber, wherever he was hiding, had gotten a good look at him leaving the money.

I peered through the lens to check the camera focus once more and sat back to wait.

At eleven fifteen, an old green Ford sedan with a faded cardboard temporary license taped inside the rear window pulled into the lot and rolled to a stop in the shadows a hundred feet from the Dumpster. I swung the telephoto lens on the car, but it was too dark to read the numbers on the temporary license. I turned the lens back to the Dumpster sitting isolated in the white light, double-checked the focus, and lifted my head to watch the Ford.

No one got out. Ten minutes passed, then twenty. I left the camera aimed at the Dumpster but kept my eyes moving back and forth between it and the green Ford. Another thirty minutes passed. Then, suddenly, a woman's voice yelled out angrily in Spanish. A Hispanic girl, nineteen or twenty, clambered out of the Ford, furiously tugging at her skirt. She spun back to the open door, screamed something else, and stomped off, hips swinging, across the lot. I watched the Dumpster through the telephoto lens, my index finger resting lightly on the shutter button. Nothing moved. A couple of minutes later, the engine of the old Ford started up. I spun the camera on the tripod and tried to change the focus to the car, but the Ford had disappeared into the dark at the end of the alley before I could snap a picture.

Nothing happened for the next three hours. Everywhere else, people made love, argued, slept, worked night shifts, as the planet turned. But in my little part of the universe, a rotting garage across a parking lot from a Dumpster, time stood still. Nothing moved. I'm sure of it.

At least until sometime past two in the morning, when I got the nods.

No honest person who does surveillance will say it doesn't happen. It does, and often. Surveillance is grinding monotony. For someone like me, who doesn't sleep well at night anyway, it's impossible to stay awake for extended hours.

That night, in that molding garage, I fought it. I sat tilted on the back legs of the chair I'd brought, my best old trick, knowing that when I nodded off, the chair would start to move and that would wake me.

I remember I looked at my watch at two fifteen. At two eighteen, I checked the view of the Dumpster through the telephoto lens. I checked it again at two thirty. Then I leaned back on the rear legs of the chair, steadying myself with the back of my head against the garage wall. It wasn't comfortable, but I didn't want it comfortable.

The big diesel engine boomed off the brick walls of the entry alley, jolting me awake. My chair crashed down on its front legs as the headlights swept the parking lot. The garbage truck turned and rumbled to a stop next to the Dumpster. I pushed out of the chair, my neck throbbing from being jammed against the wall, and hobbled on stiff legs into a contorted run across the broken garage floor. I ran out the service door, pulled at the chain-link gate, then sprinted across the empty parking lot, my legs loose now, shouting at the man in coveralls standing by the open lid of the Dumpster.

He stopped, surprised.

"I put something in the garbage by mistake," I yelled out, slowing to a walk.

The driver must have heard the commotion, because he had shut off the engine and was coming around the side of the truck. I pulled out a twenty and handed it to the tailgate man standing by the Dumpster.

"It'll only take me a minute."

The driver and the tailgate man looked at each other and shrugged. The tailgate man stuffed the twenty into his overalls and pulled out a pack of cigarettes. The driver climbed back in the truck cab.

I looked in the Dumpster. And lost the air in my lungs.

Three white bags, lumpy with food garbage, lay at the top. I pulled them out, threw them on the ground. But the bags underneath were white, too.

The black bag of money was gone.

I ripped open the top bag in the Dumpster. Pork chop bones, dinner rolls, half heads of rotting lettuce embedded in strands of blood red spaghetti, glistening and exposed in the glare of the back-door light like the viscera of a corpse. I tore at the second bag. More garbage, just as wet. Frantic, my heart banging, I bent in and tore at the rest of the bags in the Dumpster. Every one was filled with decomposing food. I dropped to the asphalt and pulled at the tops of the bags I'd thrown on the ground, ripping at them like a crazy man. It was no use. There was nothing there but food waste.

I rocked back on my heels. Something bright glinted high, to my right, above the rooftop. The sun. I stared up at it, uncomprehending. Until, disbelieving, I thought to look at my watch. It was five fifty-eight in the morning. I'd been asleep for over three hours.

And the five hundred thousand dollars was gone.

# Eight

I drove out of Ann Sather's alley fast, and angry, with the windows down. I needed the fresh air to force away the stench of damp-rot garage, spoiled food, and failure. I'd slept right through the one opportunity to stop the bombings at Gateville.

I got to the health center at seven, put a quarter for a towel on the counter next to the greasy head of the sleeping attendant, and headed for the showers. I wanted a long soak to draw the disaster out of my pores. I turned the water on hot and reran the night.

A couple of kids bouncing a basketball, Stanley Novak, an angry Hispanic girl, two men in a garbage truck—and a Dumpster bathed in white light the whole time. Everything had been in plain sight, and that's what nagged. He had to know someone would be watching. Sure, he could have come at the Dumpster from the back of the restaurant, moving low to stay hidden from anyone at the fringes of the parking lot, the garages, or the four-flats beyond, but why take the risk at all? It had been a lousy place to pick up extortion money, too well lit for someone who'd been as cautious as a church mouse with his delays and his careful, ruler-printed letters.

I toweled off and got dressed. None of that mattered anyway. I'd fallen asleep. I still stank of failure.

At the turret, I made a cup of weak coffee and called the Bohemian because he would have been suspicious if I hadn't.

"How did Stanley do with the drop?"

The Bohemian sounded ebullient. "He called me from his van about ten thirty last night. Everything went smoothly."

"Now what?"

"Now we pray the matter is over."

"It might take more than prayer."

"Vlodek, Vlodek." He paused. "You don't sound like your usual chipper self. Been getting enough sleep?"

If it was a veiled inference that he knew I'd been watching the Dumpster, it was either daring or astute. I let it go because I was too tired to think. I mumbled something about staying in touch and clicked off before he could pick up on anything else.

I went upstairs to the cot and dreamed of nothing at all.

Loud banging woke me at one thirty. I threw on a T-shirt, paint-splattered Levi's, and Nikes, and clanged down the metal stairs to open the door. Leo stood outside in the bright sunshine, wearing an enormous purple shirt and khaki shorts. In the glare of the midday sun, the purple made his white skin look translucent, like he'd been bled out in a medical experiment gone wrong. He hurt my eyes—but he had hot dogs from Kutz's. I grabbed sunglasses, and we walked down to the bench by the river.

"I brought back your Jeep to save you the trip," he said as we sat down. "But I really came to find out how the surveillance went." He handed me a hot dog and pointed at the smaller of the two soft drinks on the bench.

"I think I slept through the pickup."

He set down the hot dog he was unwrapping and stared at me. "Jeez, you must feel stupid."

"Thank you, Leo, for the salt for my wounds. I was worried I might not have enough of my own." I took a bite of hot dog. Stupid people need to eat, too.

"What happened?"

I chewed for a minute before I spoke. There was no good way to put it. "I don't know. Stanley showed up behind the restaurant a little before ten and put a black garbage bag full of money into the Dumpster. He did everything nice and slow under the light. Then he drove away."

"And then you fell asleep?"

"No." I told him about the couple in the beater Ford. "My guess is the guy dipped a little too deep, the girl took off on foot, and the car pulled away a few minutes later."

Leo chewed through two more hot dogs, looking at the river. "You're thinking the girl was a diversion, to draw your attention while somebody else made a move on the Dumpster?"

"Could have been, but the car was close enough to the Dumpster to keep both in sight. Even so, I didn't take the chance. I kept my telephoto lens on the Dumpster, ready to take a picture. But nothing approached it. I suppose a pickup man could have come from behind the restaurant then, low, but with all that light from the back door, he took a big risk getting spotted."

"Did you get the license number of the Ford?"

"No plate, just a sun-bleached temporary tag in the back window. I turned the telephoto lens on it as the car pulled away but couldn't get it focused in time to snap a picture."

"Jeez, Dek, if you're going to do this kind of work, you need to get a rig with an automatic lens."

"Too expensive right now."

"It's cheaper than guilt. Why won't you let me loan you money?" I said nothing to that.

"When did you start falling asleep?" he asked after a minute.

"Sometime after two thirty." I shifted on the bench to look at him. "I'd planned for it, Leo. I brought a chair, sat tilted on the back legs so I would wake up instantly if I dozed and the chair started to move." I paused, going over it again in my mind.

"And?"

I shrugged. "The night passed. I got the nods, but plenty of times the chair wobbled and woke me. The problem is that I don't remember checking my watch until after a garbage truck showed up just before six. Since I'd seen nobody approach the Dumpster, I broke my cover and hoofed it across the parking lot to grab the money before they could haul it away as garbage. But when I opened the Dumpster, all I saw was white bags. The black bag wasn't there. I slipped the back-end man a twenty to let me go through the bags anyway. I ripped every one of them apart. The money was gone."

Leo looked across the water. "Did you tell Chernek?"

I looked at the water, too.

He turned on the bench. "You've got to tell him, Dek."

"I don't like him keeping out the cops and the Feds."

"You don't like him having money problems, either, but none of that puts him behind the bombs."

"I don't like that he's using someone like me instead of a pro."

Leo waited for a minute, then spoke softly. "You've considered, of course, that you were spotted before the money was picked up?"

"Sure, but that doesn't explain how he got away with it. My eyes were on that Dumpster all night."

"Except for lapses."

I turned to look at him, ever Leo, ever my friend, trying to spin my screwup.

"Is that what I can call falling asleep for three-plus hours? A lapse?"

He shrugged.

"It gets worse, Leo."

"Worse?"

"It could have been the garbage guys, inadvertently. They might have already tossed the top bag from the Dumpster into the truck as I was charging out of the garage. I didn't think of it at the time."

"Jeez."

"Exactly. That money might be landfill now."

Leo spoke slowly. "Chernek is your client, Dek. He needs to know all this, regardless of your concerns about him. Unless . . ."

The word dangled. Leo took a slurp of his Coke and picked up another hot dog, but it seemed like a forced move. He didn't look hungry anymore.

I looked over at him. "Unless what, Leo? Unless I'm worrying about more than the Bohemian? Like about the *Tribune?*"

Leo didn't answer. He was too good a friend.

There's a Guy Clark tune that compares life to taking candy from a gorilla. Grabbing the candy's not tough when the gorilla's not around—but get used to the easy grabbing, start taking easy pickings for granted, that's when the monkey shows up.

I'd gone to a city college in Chicago, majoring in getting out of Rivertown. I hustled for nickels and dimes, busing tables, washing city trucks, cleaning classrooms. And I started a gopher service, mostly for lawyers, picking up take-out dinners, or going for pizzas. They worked late; I worked cheap. It was a perfect marriage, and soon I was getting enough daytime work, running documents between law offices and courthouses, photographing accident scenes, and looking up information in the newspaper morgues, to quit my other part-time jobs.

At graduation, the best my marketing degree got me was an offer to sell toilet components for half of what I'd been making as an undergrad, so I rented a third-floor walk-up office four blocks beyond the fringe of what was respectable real estate in downtown Chicago, got some raised-ink letterhead, and expanded my list of services to include document traces, missing persons location, and a bunch of other things I hoped I could do. It was an odd-job little research business, not all that far removed from the pizza pickups I'd begun with, but by the time I met Amanda, I had three employees, a heavily mortgaged condo overlooking Lake Michigan, a five-year-old Mercedes ragtop I'd bought used, a stainless Rolex, and comfortably diminishing memories of Rivertown. It might not have been much by rich-folk standards, but from my Rivertown-fed point of view, the candy grabbing had been good enough.

But then, two months after Amanda and I married, the monkey showed up.

She came named Evangeline Wilts. She was the mayor of a small suburb just outside of Chicago, and she was on trial for taking kickbacks for steering city funds into a mob-controlled insurance company. Her lawyer hired me to trace canceled checks that he said would prove his client's innocence. The checks showed the proper endorsements. I testified to that in court, and based on my findings, Mayor Wilts was acquitted.

But I'd been set up. The checks I'd traced were dummies, processed by a bought-off bank vice president with a fancy set of rubber endorsement stamps he'd used to mask the path of the real checks.

A *Tribune* reporter discovered the scam. There were rearrests and more charges, and a new trial was scheduled, this time sure to convict Ms. Wilts. Because of the egg I'd left dripping on the prosecutor's face in the first trial, I was charged briefly, as an accomplice. Nobody believed I was involved in the deception, but it was a way for the prosecutor, a Republican appointee, to vent anger—and get a lot of press. For I was, as was pointed out on the front page, the son-in-law of that Democrat powerhouse Wendell Phelps.

I hired a lawyer, who hired experts. The prosecutor dragged out the pretrial period, milking the publicity until the press got weary of it, at which point he dropped the charges against me. I was guilty, though—of being a fool. It didn't matter that the setup had been professional, virtually undetectable. I was in the accuracy business; all I had to sell was accuracy. Without that, I wasn't in business.

After the *Tribune* stories, none of my lawyer clients would risk using me, and my little company blew away like a twig hut in a tornado. The Lake Shore Drive condo, the Benz, the Rolex, and anything else I could sell went for to pay the legal bills and the remaining months of the lease for an office where the phones no longer rang.

So, too, went my ability to function. The sudden loss of my business and my money, my public humiliation, and maybe most of all the shame I'd brought on my new wife left me a zombie, prowling the empty rooms of my bride's house. Amanda tried as hard as she could, offering to fund a restart of my business, but we'd been a whirlwind thing created by two people from vastly different cultures. She was inherited rich. I was stained Rivertown, with all the resentments that could bring to a suddenly untethered mind. I started drinking and did stupid things like giving away my books and most of my good clothes. I needed to shed everything I used to value, like I was no longer worthy of anything. And, with the perfect clarity of a newly practicing drunk, I started rearranging facts. In a matter of days, I had my downfall blamed on the fact that I'd married a big Democrat's daughter.

In my disorientation, I needed to shed her, too.

Amanda tried. She hugged me and screamed at me and hugged me some more. When that didn't work, she invented a reason to go to Europe, hoping I'd snap out of it if left alone. But she came back to a house littered with empty whiskey bottles, discarded pizza boxes, and a husband, beached and numb, alternately yelling and staring at the walls.

She got me sobered up enough to talk. She told me she loved me enough to throw me out while I could still leave on my feet. I loved her enough to know she was right. She went back to Europe. I packed what I hadn't sold in garbage bags. Then I sat, until I went trick-or-treating on Halloween.

Leo pulled me out, spoon-feeding me charity assignments he could have skipped altogether. At first, he had to work like a man tugging a mule from a tar pit, coaxing and pleading, and when I began to stagger on my own, he put the arm on a few lawyers who needed him more than he needed them, and I started photographing accident scenes and running down addresses again. It was a beginning.

But if the good, gray, Republican *Tribune* ever got wind that Wendell Phelps's ex-son-in-law was somehow involved in a bombing extortion at Gateville and had slept away the stakeout of the money drop, the news would get sprayed on the front page, and everything would start spinning again. No lawyer would ever dare think about hiring me again.

And I could never tell Amanda again that I loved her.

"I staked out the money drop last night."

The Bohemian inhaled sharply at the other end of the connection.

"I hid in a garage and watched Stanley drop off the money, and then I watched the Dumpster for the rest of the night."

"*What did you see?*" His words were terse, clipped. If he was acting, he was good.

"I fell asleep."

"*What do you mean, you fell asleep?*"

"I didn't see anybody pick up the money."

"*Damn it, you don't think the garbagemen—?*"

"I don't know. They showed just before six. I broke my cover, went through all the bags. The money was gone."

"So it was picked up." His breathing came easier.

"That's what I think, but I'm worried the bag got tossed into the garbage truck before I got to the Dumpster."

"For God's sake, Vlodek. What are we to believe?"

"That the bomber got to it sometime between two thirty and six, when it was still dark."

"When you were asleep."

"Yes."

"What were you doing there, Vlodek?"

"Trying to get a photo of the bomber, or a license plate number."

"Did Stanley authorize this?"

"No."

"You took the initiative to jeopardize Crystal Waters by yourself?"

"No extra charge." I sounded hollow. And stupid.

"Yet you saw nothing?"

"Nothing."

He stopped talking. If he was involved in the extortion, he was relieved that no one had seen the money get picked up. If he was innocent, he was furious—and might spread the word through the legal community that I was unreliable and should not be hired. Even if I were sitting across from him, watching his face, instead of waiting at the other end of a phone, I doubted that I'd be able to tell what was running through his mind.

I was right. He surprised me.

"What is your billing rate?"

"One hundred twenty-five an hour for research; one fifty for field work, plus expenses."

He had enough style to not laugh. Even when I had a full-fledged office, I rarely got my clients, insurance companies and lawyers, to pop for more than sixty-five an hour.

"Start your meter now, Vlodek. You will report to me on everything pertaining to this case. You will also keep me apprised, beforehand, of your steps."

"What about the Board?"

"Your contract with them was completed. They hired you to analyze the notes."

"What are you really hiring me to do?"

"Follow your nose, as I said. But don't risk Crystal Waters again."

I told him I'd think about it. He was shrewd, and maybe a

bluffer of the highest order. He wanted to know what I was thinking, up front, before I made a move. He wanted me in a bag, tied tight by the double knot of forewarning and client confidentiality.

The question was whether that was important—and why.

# Nine

The sky had turned overcast while I was on the phone with the Bohemian. After I hung up, I set out my buckets, pans, and wastebaskets on the top floor, guessing at the drip points. Then I called Stanley Novak and told him I was driving out to Gateville. I was guessing at that, too, figuring ace investigators substituted movement for thought when they didn't know what to do next.

The sky to the west was black when I got to Gateville. A heavy, studded steel beam hinged to a thick iron post had been installed in front of the decorative wrought-iron gates. The tuckpointers were gone, but there was a man up on a ladder, cleaning the glass globe of one of the lampposts. I would have bet there was a Glock in his plastic tray, next to the Windex. I pulled off the road and parked next to the entrance.

Stanley and another guard hurried out of the guardhouse as I shut off the engine. Stanley recognized the Jeep, motioned for the guard to go back, and came over. He wasn't wearing his usual smile.

"Mr. Chernek called after he spoke to you. He said you staked me out."

"Not you. The bomber."

"You took a big risk."

"We're all taking a big risk, Stanley."

"Mr. Chernek said you didn't see the pickup."

There was nothing to say to that.

"So what are you going to do now, Mr. Elstrom?"

"Chernek told me to follow my nose, but to do it with my mouth closed."

Stanley smiled, a little. Things were thawing.

I opened the door and got out. "I thought I'd start with 1970."

Thunder clapped far in the west.

"The guardhouse explosion?"

"Or before."

Stanley shook his head. "We never found any link to anything, back then. There was the first note, then the guardhouse bomb, then the second note with the payment instructions."

"Then the ten-thousand-dollar payment, and the bomber went away."

"That's it, Mr. Elstrom."

A few drops of rain fell. Fifty feet away, the guy on the ladder continued polishing the lamp glass. In the rain. Clever, that disguise.

The lights on the entrance pillars and the row of lampposts came on, bright as surgical lamps. I turned away from the glare.

"Have you upped the wattage on those bulbs?"

"No." Stanley gestured at the guy on the ladder. "But as you can see, we're keeping the glass really clean."

"I don't remember these lights being so bright."

"You only saw them from your car, Mr. Elstrom, coming or going at night. They're brighter when you stand next to them."

Ten feet away, the lamppost that had been blown out of the ground sat on a new metal base, on new concrete, surrounded by fresh sod. I walked over to it.

"Our man could have pulled off the highway, faking a flat tire,"

I said. "He could have dug down with a little collapsible shovel or a garden trowel while he was hunched down by the tire, twisted a dial or pressed a button and dropped the device into the hole, then scooped the dirt back in and taken off. What would you guess that would take? Two or three minutes if he'd practiced, from the time he pulled off to the time he got back on the highway?"

He nodded.

The raindrops started falling heavier. Stanley looked up at the darkening sky.

"But none of your guys saw anything like that?"

"No. I had to be careful how I asked, because they don't know about the letters or the D.X.12, but they didn't see anything. Remember, we weren't watching outside the walls back then," he said, his gaze shifting to the man on the ladder. He held his palm up to catch a few drops. "It's raining, Mr. Elstrom."

"Here's my question, Stanley: There are five of these iron lampposts strung out along the wall on each side of the gate. Why blow up the one closest to the entrance?"

He wiped a raindrop that had fallen on his nose. I couldn't tell whether he was thinking about my question or worrying about the approaching storm.

I touched the repaired lamppost. "At night, this one's not only illuminated by its own bulb but also by the lights from the entrance. Why risk burying a bomb under the best-lighted lamppost? Why not plant the bomb in the shadows at the end of the wall"—I pointed down the road—"where it's darker and less visible?"

Thunder boomed closer in the west. Big raindrops started falling, dotting Stanley's pale blue uniform shirt. We started toward the entrance.

"Is that important, why he chose one particular lamppost?" he asked over his shoulder as I opened the door of the Jeep.

"Beats me."

The rain came down then, hard. Stanley ran for the guard shack. I shut the door of the Jeep, started it, and pulled away.

I drove a half mile west, took a right, and went north through the woods, past the sculpted yews of the golf club that stretched down to the road. It cost a hundred grand to drive through those yews, and that was just for openers. The rain was falling in sheets now; the golfers were inside, deepening their sun flushes with gins, tonics, and limes. I doubted that any of them had set out pickle buckets before coming to the club.

The Maple Hills Municipal Building is a single-story, redbrick confection with stubby white pillars and black shutters, meant to look like it's been there two hundred years longer than it has. It holds both the library and the village hall. I parked and ran through the rain to the arch that opened into the library. Two old men in pastel shorts, *National Geographic*s spread open on their laps, dozed in big nubby chairs across from the reception desk.

I asked the sturdy woman behind the counter for old issues of local papers. She led me to the microfilms of the *Maple Hills Assembler*. I remembered the *Assembler*; I'd leafed through a couple of issues Amanda hadn't gotten around to throwing out. It was a ten-page local shopping and good news rag, just right for the bottom of a hamster cage, so long as the hamster wasn't looking for much beyond wedding announcements, real estate ads, and recipes for dishes that blue-haired old ladies could eat with little spoons. I threaded the spool for the 1960s and forwarded it to 1968.

The first mention of Crystal Waters came in September. The *Assembler* reporter—a woman with the same last name as the publisher, and whose own recipe for corn soufflé took up half of page three—gushed with the news that Maple Hills, population 868, had been selected as the site for a new, high-security residential development. Coming so soon after the "unfortunate events of Martin Luther King, Robert Kennedy, and those riots," she wrote, "it is welcome news that occurrences such as those will not be taken lying down. Crystal Waters is going to be the state of the art, a virtual Tomorrowland of personal security."

The rest of the article read as though it had been lifted intact from a sales brochure. Twenty-seven homes, each in excess of five thousand square feet, each with a library, a three-car garage, multiple alarm systems, and access to a bomb shelter, among other amenities too numerous to mention, were to be designed by name architects and constructed on one-acre lots. The exteriors would be of brick, with cement tile roofs, to make them impervious to fire, and had been carefully designed to blend with one another to create a "harmonious whole." An unnamed representative of Safe Haven Properties, the developers, said the homes would have features that would make them virtually impregnable, details of which, of course, could not be released. Surrounding the development would be a high brick wall with a guard structure at the only entrance. The *Assembler* article ended with the news that potential purchasers had already been invited to submit applications to the new development, and construction was expected to begin the following spring.

Safe, snobbish, and selective. No wonder the corn soufflé lady had gushed.

I slow-forwarded through the next issues. The year 1968 may have been a rough one for America—assassinations and "those riots," as the reporter had put it—but in Maple Hills, all the news was good. A vegetable market opened, a flower show was well attended, and the developers of Crystal Waters donated a new fire truck to the village. Even the recipes I read, in case I ever graduated past Lean Cuisines and microwaved macaroni and cheese, sounded positively delightful.

The next mention of Crystal Waters came two months later, just before Thanksgiving. The corn soufflé lady reported that over four hundred applications for the twenty-seven homes had been received, some from as far away as Europe. All, she noted, had been accompanied by the requisite one-hundred-thousand-dollar deposits. I wondered how the reporter came up with such a tidbit. Good, hard journalistic investigation, I supposed, or perhaps she'd bribed one of the Safe Haven developers with a soufflé.

The vetting process must have been extensive, because it wasn't until March of 1969 that the *Assembler* reported that twenty-seven families had completed their final interviews with the developers and had been notified that their one-hundred-thousand-dollar deposits would be retained. It must have been a grand day for all.

Ground was broken the next month, and the *Assembler* carried periodic updates and photographs throughout 1969 and early into 1970, all of them on the front page. In May of 1970—the month students protesting the Vietnam War at Kent State had been shot by nervous National Guardsmen, an event that went unreported by the *Assembler*—the paper ran a photo of a group of deliriously happy Mexicans laying the last bits of sod outside the wall at Gateville. There had been no report of the guardhouse explosion, as I'd expected.

I advanced the film through June, the month the Members moved in, and then through July and August. The next mention of Crystal Waters came on the Wednesday after Labor Day, in a photograph on the front page. It was a grainy close-up of a dozen children waiting for a school bus in front of a brick shelter outside the wall of Crystal Waters. I stared at the photo, only dimly aware that my heart had started pounding like an oil derrick.

I leaned closer to the microfilm screen. To the left of the shelter stood a lamppost, and immediately to the left of that, in the upper corner of the photograph, appeared a fragment of an ornate shape. I stared at that shape in the corner of the photo for a full minute, then fed a dime into the printer and ran a copy of the picture. I rewound the spool and went out into the hall connecting the library with the village offices, trying to tell myself that odd little ornate shape might mean nothing.

I followed the signs on the wall, every one of my footfalls echoing loudly down the green tile stairs. I turned the knob on the frosted glass door marked BUILDING DEPARTMENT. Only one of the six gray metal desks inside was occupied. A three-hundred-pound man in a plaid shirt, with a plastic shirt-pocket protector full of different-colored felt tips—an assortment I would have killed for in third grade—looked up from the newspaper spread out on his desk. By the hard set of his jowls, he didn't appear delighted by the interruption.

"What do you need?"

*The security of a city job,* I almost snapped at him, but that would have been the knots in my gut talking. "I'd like to look at the site drawings for Crystal Waters," I said instead.

His oak swivel chair creaked as he shifted his attitude to look at the wall clock. It was ten to five. "Can't do."

"Can't do or won't do?"

"Can't do, won't do, whatever. We don't have them."

"I thought site plans had to be submitted to get building permits."

He took another look at the clock. Only nine minutes to quitting time now. He was probably thinking he still had to throw away his newspaper.

"You a resident of Crystal Waters?"

"I used to live there. I want to check an easement."

He leaned his bulk back. The chair groaned. Oak is strong, big grained, but if it's stressed too much, it'll give up. Just like people.

He picked up his newspaper and started folding it. "Crystal Waters is like a separate country. They convinced the mayor their security would be breached if we had their prints." He snorted, shaking his head. "You people. Always special needs."

"I told you, I don't live there now."

"Whatever." He dropped the newspaper into his wastebasket and shifted his girth. He was preparing to stand up.

The clock ticked loudly, echoing off the gray metal of the desks. A site plan would have been good, but only to double-check what my fear already knew, and I did have the microfilm photo. I went out, letting the door slam, and up the stairs.

It had stopped raining, but the air was hot and thick and gray, as if it were holding the drops suspended, ready to unleash them in one sudden torrent of fury. To the west, lighting crackled in the dark sky, signaling the next storm front that was about to come through. I unzipped the driver's-side plastic window and drove back to Gateville, parking across the road from the entrance. I got out and waved at the guard who had moved out from between the pillars. He was the same one who had come out with Stanley earlier. He waved back in recognition but remained by the gate, watching me.

I held up the photocopy of the *Assembler* photo and studied the brick wall across the street. There was no bus shelter there now, nor had there been when I'd lived at Gateville with Amanda. But I wasn't looking for that, I was looking for the fragment of the ornate shape in the upper left corner of the picture.

I found it right away, as I knew I would back at the library. It was the finial atop the marble column to the right of the entrance to Gateville. I moved a few paces until I was looking at the exact perspective the photographer had used.

Thunder crackled then, and the sky let go, pelting me with hard, cold rain.

I stood unmoving, letting the rain hit. There was no doubt. Across the road, immediately to the right of the entrance column, the repaired lamppost stood gray and indistinct, ghostlike in the downpour.

Right where those kids had stood in the newspaper photo.

# *Ten*

Monday night rush hour traffic jammed the four inbound lanes on the Eisenhower, every driver frantic to beat the next wave of the storm slinging in from the west. The radio said it was still ninety-four degrees at six o'clock. I was soaked from standing in the rain at Gateville, the inside of the Jeep was dripping like an Indian sweat lodge, and the closest I was to air conditioning was the 7 Series B.M.W. in the next lane, driven by a suit talking on a cell phone. I wanted to kill him but supposed it was because I was angry about other things.

I'd called the Bohemian's office as I raced away from Gateville. The British-voiced secretary said he was on another call and was already late for a dinner engagement—a dinner with important people, she added. I told her to stuff a candy bar in his face and tell him to wait, then hung up before I got even more personable. Finding out I'd been handled had not made for a mellowing afternoon.

I got to his building at seven o'clock. In the elevator mirror, my damp hair, soaked T-shirt, and paint-splattered Levi's made me look like a guy who didn't have any money. Or one who had too much.

The reception area was empty, but the Bohemian's secretary, whose name I didn't know but decided must be Griselda, materialized at the side door before I could drip much on the oriental carpet. She must have heard the elevator chime. She led me back to the conference room, left, and returned with a roll of paper towels, all without uttering one articulated word. No doubt she was smoked by my tone on the phone, though it could have been she was afraid I'd cause the furniture to mold. I dried off my hair and blotted at my T-shirt with the paper towels.

The Bohemian came in five minutes later, resplendent in formal black trousers with a silk stripe down the side, a pleated white shirt with a high collar, and a black bow tie with enough irregularity to it to show it had been hand-tied. Guys in his crowd don't wear clip-ons. He looked every bit the man off to an important dinner, as Griselda had said. If I'd worn that outfit, people would assume I was a waiter in a French restaurant.

"Vlodek." He said it as a necessary pronouncement of fact, without enthusiasm, like something he'd discovered stuck to his shoe. He sat down without offering to shake hands.

I pushed the damp picture of the kids at the bus shelter across the table. It left a wet streak. "That was target number two."

He barely glanced at it. "The children don't take the bus anymore. A van picks them up at their homes. That shelter was torn down in 1982."

"You knew the significance of that site. It wasn't just some damned lamppost, outside the wall."

He shrugged. "I checked the old Crystal Waters blueprints. As I said, the shelter was torn down in 1982."

"Your bomber was telling you he can blow up kids."

He leaned forward abruptly, both meaty forearms on the table, and glared. "I know no such thing. You can't assume that's the message he was sending."

"Let the police decide."

"He's been paid, Vlodek."

"We *think* he's been paid."

"That's right. Thanks to you, we cannot be sure. However, I continue to believe the matter is over."

"Like 1970?"

He leaned back. "Exactly." His wide, Slavic eyes didn't blink.

"You said you checked the blueprints for Crystal Waters. I went to the Maple Hills Building Department today. They don't have site plans for Crystal Waters."

"For security, I have the only set." He folded his big hands. "Why were you looking for them?"

"To verify the location of that." I pointed at the picture of the bus shelter. "I want to see those prints."

"For what?"

"For the next strategic target."

The skin around his eyes tightened. "Strategic target?"

"That lamppost was not a randomly chosen little reminder. It was a strategic target, as you well knew, blown up to send a very specific, and frightening, threat: He'll kill children."

"We've done what the man demanded, Vlodek. We've paid."

"An installment. If getting five hundred thousand is that easy, he'll be back for more."

He looked out the window at the rain beating against the glass. "When do you want to look at the prints?"

"Now."

He pulled an antique gold pocket watch out of his trousers pocket and flipped open the lid. "You may look, but you must leave them here," he said, closing the lid with a soft click. "I have to leave. I'm expected at a fund-raiser for our junior senator." He stood up and looked down at me. "Wendell Phelps, your former father-in-law, will be there."

"Tell Wendell I send my love."

"Indeed." He moved to the door but paused, and the corners of his mouth twitched. "Trick or treat," he said as he went out.

Griselda brought me the big roll of plans, then went out again and returned with a thermal pitcher of coffee, a pale blue Wedgewood cup and saucer, a little china basket of cream containers, and a bowl of white crystals that could have been sugar or could have turned me into a toad. I gave her a winning smile and told her I didn't use sweetener. She frowned and left. I poured the coffee and unrolled the blueprints.

The top sheet showed the site plan for the whole development: the footprints of the residences, road, streetlamps, guardhouse, and school bus shelter.

Crystal Waters had been built around one elongated oval street, Chanticleer Circle. Ten homes were inside the oval, on wedge-shaped lots that sloped gradually down to a center pond. The remaining seventeen houses were strung around the outside, backed by the brick perimeter wall. The whole plan resembled a doughnut, squeezed at the sides.

The Farraday house had been the first residence on the outer circle to the right of the guardhouse, driving in. On the blueprint, the inside of the Farraday house outline was slightly lighter than the bluish tint of the rest of the sheet. I bent down closer to the drawing. Someone had penciled, and then almost completely erased, a light *X* on the Farraday house.

The small rectangle of the school bus shelter, outside the wall, across from the Farraday house, had also had an *X* drawn on it and then erased. I studied the two little rectangles for a minute but could see no relationship between the two other than proximity.

I flipped slowly through the rest of the blueprints. They contained the detailed construction specifications—the material lists, cross-sections, and dimensions that had been needed to build Gateville. There were nine sheets for the road alone, a dozen just for the landscaping. Electrical, plumbing, concrete, sewerage, they all looked normal enough.

I went back to the site plan on top, and this time I noticed a little triangle of torn paper hanging from the binding. A previous sheet, perhaps a cover, more likely a contents index, had been torn off.

I went through the prints again. This time I counted pages. It didn't take long, because the sheets were numbered. Blueprint numbers fourteen, nineteen, twenty-seven, forty-one, and fifty-eight were missing.

I checked the little list by the conference room phone and called the Bohemian's extension. Griselda answered on the first ring. She told me he had left. Her hurried tone suggested she'd left her broom idling by the outside door and was anxious to leave, too. Outside, rain was coming down heavy, obscuring the lights from the surrounding buildings. I checked my Timex. It was past nine o'clock. I told her I was finished.

She was there in a minute and walked me out to the foyer. Once she had me safely blocked inside the elevator, she handed me a thick cream-colored business card, almost the same shade as some of the paint splats on my jeans. ANTON CHERNEK, the card read, in raised dark green letters, along with his office telephone number. There was no address. Another phone number had been handwritten in green fountain-pen ink below the printed number.

"Mr. Chernek requested you call him when you finished. That's his private cellular number." She made no move to step aside to let me back in to use the reception phone.

I ran through the rain to the Jeep. I tried the Bohemian's cell phone before starting off, but it forwarded me to voice mail. I left a message saying that I would try back in a few minutes.

I started the Jeep and put it on the Eisenhower, not wanting to use the cell phone again until I was sure traffic would keep moving. Steering and shifting a Jeep in traffic, especially in the rain, is, at minimum, a two-handed sport, but three hands are needed if a cell phone is being used, and four if it's all to be done in the proper Chicago style, with one arm waving an upraised finger at the other oblivious morons talking on their own cell phones.

It's bumper cars, played with obscene gestures, but I have hope for the future. Evolution ultimately corrects physical limitations, and I have no doubt that in a thousand years, humans will have sprouted cellular antennae and the necessary two extra hands.

Two miles west of the Bohemian's office, traffic opened up enough to call. This time he answered right away. In the background, I could hear the clink of heavy glasses and the loud laughter of scotch drinkers.

"Do you have more blueprints?"

The clinking and the laughter got softer. He'd moved away from the noise so he could talk. "You have everything I have. What are you looking for?"

"Some pages are missing." I didn't say anything about seeing the X's drawn on the two bomb targets.

For a minute the only thing that came through the phone was people talking in the background, and then he said, "Can you tell which pages?"

"No, just the page numbers. Was there an index page, a cover sheet?"

"I don't recall," he said. "I just keep them in safe storage."

"Who has had access to them?"

"Over the years?" He paused. "All kinds of people. Contractors hired by the Members come over to reference them all the time."

"Do they take them with?"

"Absolutely not."

"So those prints have never left your offices?"

For a minute, the only sounds coming through the phone were background voices at his party. "Except for the Board," he said finally.

"Board members have taken them out?"

"Why is this important, Vlodek?"

"I don't know." I went on. "Does anyone think the D.X.12 was buried outside the house, or could it have been inside?"

"Nobody has established that."

"Nor will they, given that you bulldozed the site. Our best shot now is the lamppost. Because of the depth of the hole, I'm thinking the bomb must have been buried two or three feet down, under the base."

"You told Stanley it could have been left by a guy faking a flat tire. Would he have had time to dig that deep without being noticed?"

"I don't see him taking the risk, but it's still my best guess. You're sure there are no other sets of blueprints?"

"They don't exist, not anymore. The developers numbered each set and then made sure those drawings were seen only by the contractors who really needed them. When the project was done, I got them all back. I destroyed them myself, except for my own set."

"You covered every base, didn't you?"

"Good security comes from absolute attention to detail. Electrical, plumbing, and sewer pipes are all ways into Crystal Waters, even if some of the pipes are less than a half inch thick. We tried to think of everything."

"The Farraday bomb might have been planted by someone posing as a landscaper, squatting behind a bush," I said, "but the lamppost, lit up, out in the open, bothers me. Someone planting a bomb there, even with the car jacked up and a spare tire on the ground, took a big risk of being seen digging, and that doesn't fit with the caution our man has been using."

"Unless the explosive was pushed through a pipe or something, from inside Crystal Waters?"

"It's a speculation," I said.

"Surely not that electrical conduit pipe beneath the lamppost? It was too small to push anything through."

"As I said, it's just a speculation."

"Jesus, Mary, and Joseph."

In the rain, in the traffic, I couldn't make out the inflection in the Bohemian's voice.

"Jesus, Mary, and Joseph, exactly," I said.

The snakes came again that night. All colors of them, backlit by the orange flames of the burning houses, writhing and contorting as first one house, then another and another, blew up like monstrous firecrackers on a long string, sending sparks and flaming roof rafters high into the night sky. Until, at last, all the houses were gone, and the ground was flat, scorched black, and nobody was left alive.

# Eleven

I shifted so I could see Leo's reaction to what I was going to say. It was eight thirty Tuesday morning. We were drinking coffee from Ma's scratched porcelain mugs, sitting on his front steps. The rain had stopped in the middle of the night. After emptying the buckets and wastebaskets out the windows on the fifth floor, I'd spent the rest of the night on top of the turret, riding my lawn chair, spinning fancies, and I wanted Leo to tell me I was crazy.

"We've got old explosives and old paper. The first explosion occurred in 1970."

"Right." He sipped his coffee.

"The note they received last June, just before the Farraday explosion, demanded fifty thousand dollars. Small change by today's standards."

"But big dough in 1970?"

"I'm getting there."

He motioned for me to continue and took another sip of coffee.

"The last amount demanded, the five hundred thousand, is bigger money, but is it big enough?"

His eyebrows arched. "Meaning?" But he knew where I was going.

"Three-million-dollar homes, Leo, and all the guy wants is a sixth of the value of one house?"

"Half a million is still a lot of cabbages."

"Is it a lot of money to the Bohemian?"

"Dek, you're a dog chewing one meager bone to death. If the Bohemian's got money problems, he needs a lot more than a half million."

"That's what I'm starting to think, too. Maybe the relatively small amount of the money demanded exonerates the Bohemian—"

"Hallelujah."

"—and clears people inside Gateville as well. Because the half million is only a fraction of what any of those houses is worth."

"And that in turn leads you to . . . ?"

"Somebody from the past."

His eyebrows crept up another inch.

I asked again the same question I'd called him with a half hour earlier. "Tell me one more time how impossible it is to date the writing on those extortion notes."

"Pretty damned impossible. Pencil lead is graphite crystalline carbon with binders and hardeners. You can separate these components chemically to isolate the waxes, resins, and clays, but you need a known reference sample to date them. Pencil lead is very stable, unlike ink, which evaporates over time. So, without a comparison sample, pretty damned impossible."

"But the letters could have been written years ago?"

"Or yesterday."

"Stay with me on this, Leo."

"All right. Yes, the letters could have been written many years ago."

"That would explain the relatively small amounts demanded in the letters—the fifty thousand that was never arranged to be picked up, and the half million that was. Those demands were valued in 1970 dollars, because the notes were written in 1970."

"O.K."

"We've passed through dot-com times, Leo. Things have gone up. Why hasn't the guy upped the dollars to keep up with the times? Why hasn't he written new notes, used a library computer?"

"My point at the beginning." Leo shrugged. "Maybe the best we can assume for now is he's a guy who sticks to his plan."

"Exactly. Because he meticulously laid this whole thing out in 1970."

Leo watched my face and waited.

I set my coffee cup down on the steps. "What if he also buried the D.X.12 back then?"

He didn't react at first, not visibly, but I knew the signs: rock-solid stillness as his mind shot into warp speed, analyzing the permutations. Then the agitation, the twitching eyebrows, the tapping fingers.

He jumped up from the stoop and went down the six steps to pace on the sidewalk, his mouth struggling to verbalize what was flaring in his mind.

"Put there by a construction worker at the site," he said, looking up.

"Yes."

"Jeez, it's perfect." He grinned up at me like he'd discovered gold. "Fricking beautiful. The Gateville developers were paranoid about security from day one. Yet during construction, one of their workers was planting D.X.12 like a guy hiding Easter eggs, so he could come back, attach a fuse, and start setting off bombs. Fricking beautiful," he said again, still pacing back and forth. "They hired a fox, with bombs, to build the henhouse."

I looked down at him. "But why wait so long to put the plan in high gear? Why did he quit after the first little bomb at the guardhouse?"

He stopped pacing and looked up. "Cold feet?"

I shook my head.

"The ten grand was enough?"

"Not when he'd already written other notes demanding more."

He came up the stairs two at a time and sat down. "Then tell me," he said, watching my eyes, ready to play.

Even when we were kids, he'd loved the mental sparring. But this time, I was ahead of him. I'd spent most of the night on top of the turret, working my way through it. I might have been a little light on sleep, but I was rehearsed and I was ready. And I had a plan.

"Either we've got the world's most lethargic extortionist," I began, "taking decades to get his letters in the mail and do the crime, or . . ."

"Or?" Leo's black eyebrows tangoed on his forehead, prompting.

"Or the bomber has been away for a long time."

"Like where?" He leaned closer, almost leering.

"Like prison," I almost shouted.

Leo beamed. "Excellent. It explains the long lapse between the bombs. In 1970, the guy comes up with a plan. He writes the notes, plants the D.X.12, sets off the first explosion behind the guard-house, and collects ten thousand dollars. But that money is only supposed to be the first installment, the test run, the priming of the money pump. There's going to be more, a lot more."

"But something happens," I cut in, percolating with brilliance now. "He gets sent to prison for something else, and his big Gate-ville caper gets put on hold. Until recently, when he gets out and puts everything in motion again."

"Precisely." Leo nodded approvingly.

"The only thing I can't figure is, why bother with the old notes he wrote long ago? Why not punch out new letters, with bigger dollars, when he's using the computer to address the envelopes?"

"A trifling issue. You'll come up with an answer."

"So now," I charged on, "all we have to do—"

Leo held up his palm, his lips moist. "Allow me to speak for the great Sherlock. All you need do is assemble a list of the people who worked construction at Gateville, who then got sent to prison, and who recently got out."

I nodded quickly. Damn, I was good.

Leo smiled a particular half-smile, and the coffee in my stomach roiled. I knew that smile. It was his executioner's smile, given to those who'd overlooked something as they dared to match speed and wits with him. I'd seen it a hundred times, right before he tripped the blade.

He spoke. "Since at least half the contractors who worked at Gateville must have gone out of business by now, and the other half threw out their old payroll records decades ago, you will be forced to try to reconstruct employee names from interviews with hundreds of older people who may or may not remember who they worked with back then. If you skip lunches and don't sleep more than an hour a night, you ought to be able to come up with an inaccurate, incomplete, and completely erroneous starting list of candidates in four or five years."

The guillotine blade had plummeted, severing my empty head.

I started to open my mouth, to protest, but no words would come. There were no words; Leo was right.

"What do I do?" I finally asked.

"Go to the Bohemian. Tell him that the D.X.12 might already be in the ground. Tell him that no amount of security is going to keep the bomber out forever."

"I don't trust the Bohemian, not completely."

"Dek, you've got to abandon the deranged money manager theory."

"It's not that. It's that he knew the significance of the lamppost." I'd told Leo about the *X* erasures on the blueprints.

"And didn't tell you right away? That proves nothing. He's your client."

"He was around Gateville when it was under construction, and since then, he's had the only set of blueprints."

"Jeez, Dek. He's protecting his own clients. You've got to go to him, convince him to bring this to the Feds." Leo looked into my eyes. "You don't really believe he's involved, do you?"

"I like my recent parolee theory a lot better." I stood up. We walked down the steps, and I got in the Jeep.

Leo leaned close to the driver's window. His small, dark eyes were worried. "If that ground is laced with D.X.12, they're going to have to change the name of the development."

I waited.

"They're going to have to call it Bombville," he said.

I wasn't armed enough to spar with the Bohemian. I drove to the Maple Hills Municipal Building instead.

The big guy with the pocket rainbow of colored felt tips was alone in the Building Department, like before. Unlike the last time, though, it was early, only ten in the morning. He was still on the front section of the newspaper. He raised his eyes and scowled across the empty desks at me. "Back again?"

"I'm not here about blueprints this time," I said, fighting my own joy at seeing him. It's never manly to gush. "I need the names of the contractors that worked at Crystal Waters. They must have applied for permits."

"We don't keep permit copies that long."

"How do I get the names?"

His chair creaked. "Perhaps if you made an appointment."

I was short on sleep, long on cranky. "Do I go upstairs to the mayor's office to make one, or have one of the Board members at Crystal Waters make it for me?"

I'd pressed the right button. His huge hands dropped to the arms of the chair, and he started to push. It was like watching birth, the slow way he emerged from the oak chair. "Come with me."

I followed him as he lumbered through the empty office to a small file room jammed with mismatched tan, black, and gray metal cabinets. He squeezed down the center aisle and stopped next to a gray four-drawer file. Steadying himself with one meaty paw on top of the cabinet, he aimed his eyes down to read the labels on the drawers. "Open that one," he said, pointing at the bottom drawer.

I knelt and opened a drawer filled with black vinyl ring binders labeled with white tags. I pulled out the one marked PERMIT RECEIPTS. 1966–1980. I stood up and handed it to him. He set the book on top of the cabinet and began thumbing through the ledger pages.

"Here's the first entry for Crystal Waters," he said, pointing with a large thumb. It was the fifth entry on the 1969 ledger page, done in fountain-pen ink, and showed receipt of fifty dollars for a permit to demolish a barn. "This ledger will have the names of all the contractors who posted a bond for Crystal Waters."

We went back to the general office. He pointed to a vacant desk and shuffled, wheezing, back to his newspaper. I sat down, opened the book, and began making a list of every permit issued.

I closed the ledger at two fifteen. Maple Hills had done very well from the sale of permits. From the first demolition to the final posting for the electrician who'd installed the pump in the pond fountain, they'd collected permit fees from one hundred and seventy-two different contractors for the Gateville project.

I brought the ledger to the big man's desk and set it down next to his newspaper. He was on the classified advertisements, his day well over half done. He didn't look up when I thanked him and left.

One hundred and seventy-two contractors. Leo was right. It would be impossible.

# Twelve

I had two cups of machine coffee in the hall of the Municipal Building and went into the library to one of the computer stations. I logged onto the Internet and started searching the online yellow and white page listings for the names of the contractors that had gotten permits for Gateville. I searched by name, by geography, and by business type, when I could figure it from the name of the business. At five o'clock, I went out to the hall for more coffee. I'd gotten halfway through the list and had found current addresses for only twenty-eight of the contractors.

Twenty-eight live names out of eighty-plus. Too many were gone—out of business, reorganized into other businesses, or just plain vaporized—and that was for openers, as Leo had warned it would be. Of those still operating, it was doubtful any would have employees or records going back to Gateville.

I looked at my watch. Five fifteen. It was past midnight in Paris, too late to call, even if I did have a reason that would sound plausible. I finished my coffee and went back to the computer. Plodding was better than thinking.

I worked the rest of the evening and finished just before they

closed the library at nine o'clock. I'd found current addresses for
sixty-one of the one hundred and seventy-two names.

I drove back to the turret, microwaved something in a plastic
tray that didn't look anything like its picture on the box, and
looked at things I didn't care about on television. Sometime
around four thirty, I went up the metal stairs to my cot, which is all
one can do when one doesn't have a bed.

At six in the morning, fresh from ninety minutes' sleep, I made a
full pot of coffee, filled my travel mug, and went up to the roof to
clear my head and listen to the dawn. By eight, I was ready to talk
to the Bohemian. I called his office, got the machine. I tried his cell
phone, got his voice mail. It was just as well. I left a message that I
needed all the records he had on the contractors that had worked at
Gateville, pronto. I ended by saying I'd stop by his office at two
o'clock to look at them. Then I shut off my cell phone. I didn't want
questions.

At eleven, I grabbed my blazer, khakis, and a blue button-down
shirt and went to the health center. I said hello to the old boys
draped over the machines, ran six laps as well as anyone can who's
only gotten ninety minutes sleep and has the coffee trembles to
prove it. After I showered, I checked my phone for messages. The
Bohemian had called. He sounded subdued. He said he'd have the
records as I asked, at two o'clock.

I swung through McDonald's on my way to the Eisenhower for
a large coffee and a Big Mac. Big Macs are good for road grub because they pack so many basic food groups—proteins, carbohy-
drates, and special sauce—into one pucklike cylinder that, if
handled gingerly, is ideal for driving. Midday traffic was light
enough to dodge most of the potholes that could launch the coffee,
and I got to the Bohemian's building at ten to two without a drop
of coffee spilled and just the merest orange hint of special sauce on

my shirt sleeve. I parked, slipped on my blazer, crossed the street, and rode the elevator up.

The tanned blond was gone. In her place, the dour Griselda perched, sucking the light out of the reception area like a black hole in space. She looked up as the elevator doors opened, resisted the urge to throw herself at me in frenzied abandon, stood, and motioned for me to follow. The office was quiet, hushed like a place abandoned by people gone to the funeral of a child. She opened the door to the small conference room, told me the Bohemian would arrive shortly, and left without the offer of coffee or a magazine. I didn't mind. The wait would give me a chance to study the lagging dog in the English oil painting, for what it was seeing that I could not.

I didn't have much time to study. The Bohemian and Stanley came in a few minutes later, each carrying two yellowed cardboard file boxes. They set them on the credenza against the wall.

"Excuse our tardiness, Vlodek." The Bohemian brushed his hands against the sides of his trousers. "We had to go pick these up. One of the developers' widows had them in the attic of her garage. These are the last records of Safe Haven Properties, as you requested, and without question. Now, if you please," he said as he and Stanley sat down, "tell us what this is about."

"I think Crystal Waters was laced with explosives when it was under construction. I think D.X.12 has been buried there, at the Farraday house, underneath the old school bus shelter, and in other places we don't know about, since 1970."

The Bohemian's face remained impassive; we could have been discussing the weather. But Stanley's face had turned crimson, and beads of sweat sprouted on his forehead, big, like raindrops on a waxed car. He reached in his pocket for a handkerchief.

Neither of them looked surprised.

"Why do you believe this?" the Bohemian asked in an even voice.

"Because you believe it."

His face stayed expressionless, his eyes fixed on mine. A hell of a poker player, I would have bet.

"And because it fits the facts," I continued. "Old paper, most likely with old writing on it. A type of explosive that hasn't been available since then. And old dollar values: the fifty thousand, even the half million you just paid. Not huge dollars by today's standards, but big bucks in 1970. But mostly," I said, looking right back into the Bohemian's unblinking eyes, "I believe it because you believe it."

"Suspected," he said then, without hesitation. "No, even that's too strong a word. We've had an irrational fear of it, like a nightmare."

"Yet you did nothing for all those years."

"What would you have had us do, Vlodek? Dig up all of Crystal Waters on an irrational fear? Send everyone into a panic, launch a thousand lawsuits, ruin the developers and the people who bought the homes, and then probably find nothing? We paid the ten thousand dollars in 1970, and he went away. Don't say we did nothing. There was nothing to do."

Stanley put away his handkerchief and leaned toward me from across the table. "We thought it was over long ago, Mr. Elstrom. Like you, we thought it could have been a construction worker, but there had been a thousand men at Crystal Waters. As for him burying D.X.12 throughout the place . . . it was too farfetched to consider. How could we have found it, or him, without throwing everything at Crystal Waters up for grabs?"

"Stanley, you didn't even try."

The Bohemian knocked his knuckles on the table twice, quick, sharp. "No need. The man went away."

"He left behind stashes of D.X.12."

*"We don't know that."* The Bohemian's eyes were shiny with anger. He took a long breath. "What we do know is that our predicament today is the same as it was in 1970, except that our fi-

nancial risk has gone up. Today, the homes at Crystal Waters, with the common acreage, the community house, and the other amenities, are worth collectively over one hundred million dollars. Dollars that will be gone forever if there is public speculation that explosives are buried at Crystal Waters."

"So you sit back and hope the man will stay away more decades, now that he's been paid?"

"It's what happened the last time," the Bohemian said.

"It's time to go to the Feds."

"With what?" The Bohemian waved his hand at the yellowed boxes of records stacked on the credenza. "Do you really think the authorities will have time to sift through all those records? And what would they be looking for?"

"The name of an old worker, recently paroled after spending the last thirty-five years in jail."

The Bohemian leaned in. "You think his name is in those records?"

"If your bomber is one of your old construction workers, then the name of the company he worked for probably is. But if the bomber is somebody else . . ." I let it hang.

The Bohemian took it. "You mean if it's one of the Members, or myself, or Stanley here, or even you, Vlodek, then the search through those old records will be pointless?"

"I think it's probably pointless anyway," I said. I took out my list of contractors and slid it face up to the center of the round table. "One hundred and seventy-two contractors paid for permits to work at Crystal Waters. I found current addresses for only sixty-one of them. More might exist under changed names, but it's a safe bet most are out of business. We'll never get a complete list of the men who worked there."

"It's a place to start," the Bohemian said. He looked at Stanley. "Can you get information on recent parolees from your old police buddies?"

"I'd have to go to Chief Morris."

"Be discreet. Tell him we've received some vague threats that we'd like to investigate ourselves, and remind him of our generosity with his charitable efforts."

"Will do, Mr. Chernek."

The Bohemian looked at me. "How about it, Vlodek?"

I turned to Stanley. "Is there any way to start searching for the D.X.12?"

"There's ground-penetrating radar," Stanley said. "Law enforcement uses it to locate all kinds of things buried beneath the ground. But it's nondiscriminating. It shows shapes and masses that could be anything: buried bricks, solid refuse, pipes, whatever."

"Would it have shown the D.X.12 buried beneath the bus shelter lamppost?"

"As a separate shape, maybe, if it was buried alongside the lamppost base. If it was buried directly beneath the base, then maybe not."

"And the Farraday bomb?"

Stanley shrugged. "The same. The radar might have picked it up if it was buried alongside the foundation, but no way if it was inside the cement, or inside the house." He turned to the Bohemian. "The problem is the radar doesn't tell us what is under the ground, only its shape. We would have to dig down to examine each shape we pick up. We could end up digging up the whole community."

"And find most of it," I said.

They both looked at me.

"How will you ever know if you've found it all?" I asked.

"He's got a point, Mr. Chernek," Stanley added quickly.

"Check out the feasibility of it, anyway," the Bohemian said to Stanley. "It's worth trying, especially since it doesn't require the police, and we can pass off any digging as electrical or sewer work."

The certainty was back in his voice; the captain was back at the helm. He turned to me. "So we're back to those boxes. What now?"

Once again I marveled at the smooth way he was sidestepping my insistence on bringing in the Feds.

"Find the bomber."

The corners of his mouth turned down. "Vlodek—"

I cut him off. I'd been Vlodeked enough. "You can't do this yourself. Ground radar won't find all the D.X.12; your security won't keep your man out forever. Eventually, he'll be back, and he'll find a way in. You have to find out who he is before he does that, and that means going to the police. Let them go through the records."

"Is there any harm in us conducting a preliminary search first? The police can only benefit from our efforts."

"How much time are you thinking?"

"With my staff somewhat diminished, say a month."

"Today's Wednesday. Friday afternoon, at whatever point we are in those records, I'm going to the Feds."

We started right away. The Bohemian and Stanley sorted through the old invoices, waivers of lien, warranties, and receipts, calling out the names of the contractors. I made the notes, comparing the names with those on my list, and wrote down the kinds of work each contractor had done. It was slow, tedious work, but as the Bohemian said, we had to start somewhere.

By seven o'clock that evening, we'd gotten through three of the four boxes. The Bohemian sent Griselda out for sandwiches, and we continued working. At nine thirty we closed the last box. Adding the contractors that hadn't needed permits increased my list to a total of two hundred and forty-nine names.

The Bohemian leaned back in his chair. "Not all of these would have had the means and opportunity to plant multiple explosive."

"We have to rank them by the access they had," I said.

Stanley glanced at his watch.

"Time to leave, Stanley?" the Bohemian asked.

"I think I better."

"Go ahead. Vlodek and I will finish up. We'll reconvene here to-morrow morning, say at eight."

Stanley said good night and left.

"Stanley's wife is not well," the Bohemian said. "Some minor neuroses and a couple of dependencies. They lost their son a year and a half ago. They have a neighbor who stops in when Stanley is at work, but the neighbor works nights, and Stanley must be home with his wife."

I wondered if there was anything that pulsed in Gateville that the Bohemian did not know about.

We worked through my expanded contractor list, highlighting with yellow marker the ones we guessed might have had the opportunity to plant explosives at the guardhouse, the Farraday home, and the bus shelter lamppost. Our prime candidates were contractors that had reason to be working in the ground—road installers, cement workers, landscapers, electricians, plumbers and sewer outfits—but there were dozens of other potentials as well.

I stood up to stretch. It was eleven o'clock, and I was starting to suspect the kitchen hardware installers and the interior decorators. "According to the dates on these records, Crystal Waters must have been one huge beehive, crawling with workers."

The Bohemian set down his fountain pen. "It was. Because all the houses went up at the same time, only contractors large enough to handle several structures at once were used."

"Why was that? Why didn't the developer treat the project like other residential projects: sell the lots individually and build the houses one at a time, according to the purchaser's specifications?"

The Bohemian smiled, but it didn't reach to his eyes. "Security. Crystal Waters was always about security. The plan was to build the houses all at once, then lock out the world. If the houses were built one after another, the project would have gone on much longer. Workmen would have been coming and going for years, and there would be no chance for tight control until the last house was finished." He shrugged at the irony of it.

We finished the revised contractor list at midnight. By our estimate, at least one hundred and six contractors had had opportunities to plant multiple bombs at Gateville. The Bohemian said he'd have the list researched for current addresses by the following morning.

He leaned back in his chair and laced his fingertips together behind his head. "Let's say we get lucky and we find a just-paroled ex–Crystal Waters worker and the police capture him with D.X.12 dust on his fingers. Say he confesses and tells us where he buried all the D.X.12, and we go and dig it up. Could we be sure we're safe then?"

I shook my head.

# Thirteen

As arranged, we were back in the Bohemian's conference room the next morning at eight. As I'd come in, I passed a young man leaving the office, carrying a cardboard box filled with desk items and pictures in frames.

The Bohemian wore a crisp, muted glen plaid suit with a soft beige shirt and a perfectly knotted, tiny-figured maroon tie. With his silver hair, glowing tan, and sparkling teeth, he was burnished and polished like a man who'd won the lottery for the second time. Except for his eyes. They looked haunted.

Sitting next to him, Stanley fidgeted in his rumpled security uniform like he'd slept in it. I'd been on the roof all night. I felt like Stanley looked.

The Bohemian tapped a thin stack of stapled papers with a different fountain pen than the one he'd used the day before. Today's pen was fat, like a torpedo, with an iridescent blue barrel and a cap that looked like solid gold.

"I had Buffy come in early to run these contractor names against the State of Illinois active database. She also searched nearby states for the same names, in case any had moved."

"Who's Buffy?" I asked.

"My secretary."

Startled, I laughed, and then said, "Fatigue," to cover it. That the dour Griselda was named Buffy went beyond misnomer; if she'd been a product, it would have been felonious false advertising. I needed sleep.

The Bohemian slid one set of the stapled copies across the table to Stanley, the other to me. "Of the one hundred and six contractors we deem to be candidates, fifty-eight are out of business. The forty-eight actives are asterisked, split twenty-four to a page."

Each of the two pages had a double column of names, addresses, and phone numbers. Stanley scanned both pages. "I'll check out the second page, you take the first," he said to me.

"Will you have time?"

"Stanley will have to make the time," the Bohemian answered sharply, then forced a smile. "Excuse me, I'm beginning to agree with you, Vlodek. This looks hopeless. Too many of the contractors have gone out of business, their worker rosters forever lost to us. Of the ones still operating"—he tapped his set of the copies—"you can bet most of their records will be long gone as well. All of which makes finding our man, assuming he even was one of the workers at Crystal Waters, almost impossible."

"You've just made the argument for turning this over to the Feds right now," I said.

The Bohemian nodded.

Stanley looked up from his list. "Where's the harm in checking these first?" He turned to the Bohemian. "If we get nowhere, we'll go to the Feds."

"Nowhere or not, we go to the Feds tomorrow, Friday, at four," I said.

"Agreed," the Bohemian said.

"What about that list of parolees?" I asked Stanley.

"Chief Morris said he'd fax it here this morning."

The Bohemian leaned toward Stanley. "What did you tell him?"

"Like you said, that we were receiving minor threats, and we suspect a worker from long ago."

"He didn't make the connection to the Farraday explosion?"

"He doesn't want to make that connection, Mr. Chernek. Chief Morris is very appreciative of Crystal Waters's past support. If he has questions, he won't risk asking them if he doesn't have to." Stanley went out to check on the list of parolees.

The Bohemian and I sat for a few minutes, listening to each other breathe. It was like straining to hear water drip. After a few minutes, I said, "Maybe we'll get lucky, find somebody who remembers something."

The Bohemian looked at me. "Do you really think so, Vlodek?"

"Not a chance in hell."

We went back to silence.

Stanley came back with a stack of photocopies. "I had Buffy make a dozen sets for each of us. That way, we can leave the list at the companies if needed." He handed one stack of sets to me.

I scanned the list. The parolees were listed alphabetically, along with their ages.

"I masked out the names of the releasing institutions, so nobody can tell this is a parolee list," Stanley said.

"We're only interested in men old enough to have been at Crystal Waters." I flipped through the pages. Ignoring the younger parolees still left a few hundred candidates. It looked futile. I stood up, anxious for the next day and a half to be over, and looked at the Bohemian. "Tomorrow at four o'clock."

He met my eyes and nodded.

Stanley followed me out the door, and we rode down in the elevator together. We walked to my Jeep.

"We can't give up on this, Mr. Elstrom."

I leaned against the fender. "You don't think we need the Feds?"

"Maybe. But they won't come running. They're being pulled

every which way in these times. Better we do the spadework and bring them something they can get their teeth into quickly."

He was probably right; suddenly I was too tired to know. There had been too many nights of too little sleep, even before the mess at Gateville started. I unlocked the Jeep and sat with the key in my hand, watching him as he walked across the parking lot to the baby blue Crystal Waters station wagon. His head was down and his shoulders sagged. He looked like a fat, balding child, about to cry.

Of the twenty-four contractors on my list that were still in business, two were pavers, two were landscapers, three were plumbers, and one was an electrician. The remaining sixteen were a hodgepodge of other things. All had been paid at least five hundred dollars at Gateville, which meant, by our guess, they'd been there long enough to plant explosives in multiple locations.

I pulled a metro map out of the glove box and circled the locations of the companies on my list. They were scattered all around Chicago and its suburbs. The closest, something called The Tillotson Partners, was less than a mile away.

I drove south through the old factory district. Cement mixers, flatbed trucks loaded with lumber, construction vans, and pickups clogged both sides of the dirt-crusted old street, reducing it to one lane. Huge, bright banners hung on half of the old factories and warehouses, advertising residential lofts starting at four hundred thousand dollars per unit. ONLY A FEW LEFT, many read, and I didn't doubt it. Chicago was full of people ready to plop down big scratch to look like they were starving artists. It wasn't for me, and not just because I didn't have the four hundred thousand dollars. The closest I'd ever gotten to art was a paint-by-number canvas of an owl an aunt had thrown away out of sheer embarrassment. Even as a child, I'd had difficulty operating inside the lines.

The rehabbers had not yet gotten around to the ancient, soot-stained building that housed The Tillotson Partners. There was no elevator, and my footsteps echoed loudly on the linoleum steps, nicked and scuffed dull from decades of commerce.

The gray-haired lady behind the scarred wood desk on the third floor told me they made signs. Interior and exterior. Road signs, street signs, and washroom signs. That's all they'd ever done since 1956, she said: make signs. She'd never heard of Crystal Waters, but she thought it quite possible they'd made the lettering on the brick wall and the fancy, filigreed iron posts and name signs for Chanticleer Circle. She did not know if the company kept old payroll records. The woman who did the payroll wasn't in; she only came in twice a month. I left my card and asked that the bookkeeper call me. As I went down the stairs, I wondered how the developers of Gateville had chosen the name, Chanticleer Circle, for the project's only street—and, for that matter, why they had bothered to erect signs at all. When there's only one street, and it's a circle, there's not much potential for confusion about where one is.

In the Jeep, I checked the Bohemian's master list. Safe Haven Properties had paid Tillotson forty-eight hundred dollars back in March of 1970, a month before the guardhouse explosion. That was at the end of the project, when the paving was done and the grounds had been smoothed over and landscaped. Still, Tillotson had had access, and nobody would have questioned them digging holes. I put a question mark next to Tillotson and pulled away.

If even the signage installer was a potential, the hours until the next afternoon, at four, were going to be the most futile of my life.

I hit two more places—a plasterer and a roofer, neither with records or recollections—before my stomach reminded me I'd been up for hours and had never had breakfast. I pulled into a true Chicago-style hot dog stand, authentic right down to the flies and the red-and-yellow-striped awning, and scanned the menu painted on the flaking plywood for quick, morning food that would be easy on a nervous gut, like scrambled eggs and whole wheat toast. They didn't have that, so I ordered a hot dog, French fries, onion rings, and a diet Coke to neutralize the calories, and ate off the fender of the Jeep, standing up.

The hot dog had two peppers, plump, fresh green ones. For as long as I could remember, Kutz offered only one, a shriveled, brown little thing that regular customers, when they forgot to tell him to hold it, threw into the bushes so they wouldn't have to look at it. I'd always suspected Kutz offered only the one tiny pepper because he knew his customers would toss the grizzled thing anyway, and, rodent lover that he was, he didn't want to cripple the tender stomachs of the rats that foraged in the hard dirt of his dining area with too many peppers.

I finished greasing my palate, got in the Jeep and spent the rest of the morning and all of the afternoon working my way west, paralleling the Eisenhower Expressway. I stopped at an outfit that made planters, geese, and ducks out of cement and, after them, a drain-tile manufacturer, a curb installer, and an asphalt seal coater. None had people who remembered the Gateville job; none had payroll records from back then. But all had had access inside the gates, and none could be ruled out. As with the companies that morning, there was no point in leaving the list of parolees.

Nobody knew anything; not anymore.

I got to the first plumber on the list just as he was closing up. He was outside his storefront, a block from the expressway, fumbling with a metal accordion security fence. He was about sixty, with a three-day beard stubble, gin on his breath, and a case of the shakes. We talked on the sidewalk as his trembling fingers struggled to snap the padlock. He'd installed the underground sprinkling system at Gateville with three other fellows but hadn't seen them in decades. He made a quick show of looking at my list of parolees, but his eyes kept straying to his watch. He was late for a tavern. He finally got the padlock snapped, told me he had to leave, and took off down the sidewalk as fast as he could aim his wobbling legs.

I scratched him off the list. If that man had just pulled five hundred thousand dollars out of a Dumpster behind Ann Sather's, he'd never have opened his storefront again. He would have stayed home, curled around a bottle, and drunk his way through as much of the money as possible before the reaper punched his ticket.

It was five thirty. I got in line outbound on the Eisenhower and called the Bohemian to report I had nothing to report.

"No likely suspects?"

"Most of them were likely suspects. All had access to the grounds. All could have done a little extra digging and dropped devices into the dirt. The only one I can scratch is the plumber."

The Bohemian sounded tired. "Are we wasting our time?"

"Yes, along with wasting your money. But if we're getting you closer to calling the Feds tomorrow, it's progress. Have you heard from Stanley?"

"He visited two of his names before he had to get home. He got nowhere, as well."

"I'll start up again first thing in the morning, but it's going to be the same, so use this evening to convince yourself this thing is too big for us."

"That's what I told Stanley," he said.

# Fourteen

The first of the two landscapers was a mile and a half north of the turret, on a side street off LaGrange Road. It was just getting light when I pulled into the gravel lot Friday morning. I parked between a flatbed truck loaded with balled shrubs and a rusty black Chevy Nova that had been old twenty years before.

The owner was behind the wood trailer office, making marks on a clipboard as two Mexicans loaded evergreens onto another flatbed truck. He was in his early forties.

"Sure, I remember Crystal Waters. I was a kid, but I worked on the job with my dad and the crew. There were workers everywhere. It was a big deal for my dad, getting hired to work on a major site like that one."

"Do you still have records from that job, employee lists?"

He looked at me, reappraising the story I'd given him. I'd said there were sewer leaks at Crystal Waters and I was looking for anyone who might know about changes to the original blueprints. That didn't explain wanting employee rosters, and he'd caught it. "Employee lists?"

"We think there were deviations from the sewer plans that

might have caused you to change your own ground work. We're hoping some of your old employees would remember."

He didn't believe me. I wouldn't have, either.

"We don't keep payroll records that long."

The dim bulb that's loose-wired in my head flickered weakly as I realized my mistake. Landscapers don't always keep names. Some of them hire workers for cash, undocumented people up for the summer.

He put down his clipboard. "We've got nobody here from that long ago, except for me." He made a laugh with his mouth. "But I was more interested in Little League than landscaping in those days."

He walked me around front to make sure I got back in the Jeep. He probably didn't figure me for Immigration and Naturalization, because my story was too cheesy, too full of holes, but he knew I wasn't telling the truth. I gave him one of my cards. It has my name, the word RESEARCH underneath, and my cell phone number. I asked him to call if he remembered anything.

As I pulled away, I looked in the rearview mirror just as he dropped my card into the trash barrel.

The electrical contractor worked out of a whitewashed converted gas station in a rundown section on the western edge of Chicago, next to Oak Park. I pushed open the peeling green wood door and stepped into the dank dark of what had once been the gas station office. An old man sat behind a dented metal desk, reading a tattered copy of *Popular Mechanics* in the dim light of a gooseneck lamp. He put down the magazine, pulled his feet off the desktop, and smiled up like he was grateful for the interruption.

I skipped the story about sewer leaks and just said I was trying to track down people who'd worked at Crystal Waters.

"I remember that job." He offered me coffee from a scratched aluminum Thermos. I shook my head. He poured some for himself into a clear plastic cup and went on. "Never worked in a place so fancy. I was hired at the last minute to wire the marble fountain in the pond. Job only took two days."

I remembered the Bohemian's comment about hiring only big contractors to work at Gateville. "Weren't you a little small for a project like Crystal Waters?"

"You bet," he laughed. "Those projects always go to the big boys. I've always been small time, adding outlets in somebody's home, putting in patio lights, or some such. That, and fixing electric motors." He pointed at the doorway to the old auto service bay. I looked, and saw shelves piled high with dozens of small, oily black motors and dusty spools of colored wire.

"One of the main electrical contractors at Crystal Waters had a problem at the last minute," he continued. "Somebody quit sudden or something, just as the job was almost finished. They called me, on the hurry-up, to finish the wiring to the fountain so they could get the final city inspection and people could start moving in. I figured they got me out of the yellow pages," he said, pointing to a wood sign on the wall: A-1 Electrical. "My name's Ziloski, so I go with A-1. I get a lot of calls because I'm the first name in the book."

As he talked, I turned to look again at his inventory of electrical motors and coils of colored wire. Something about them nagged at me, a question I should know to ask, but I couldn't think of it.

"Need a motor?" Ziloski chuckled, his voice nudging me. "I got plenty."

I laughed at that and asked him more questions to keep him talking. I wanted time to think of the question I couldn't grasp.

"I never worked around buildings so posh," he said again. He sounded like someone who'd caught a glimpse of a movie star as he described the fountain, the houses, and the expensive, mature trees that were planted to make the development look like it had been there for years. The details were as fresh in his mind as if he'd seen them yesterday.

I was only half-listening; my mind was still clutching for the question that would not come. I gave up, finally, after an hour of jawing, and left him to his ragged magazine, rusted motors, and dusty coils of colored wire. I doubted he'd been at Gateville long enough to do much of anything, but I had to give him a question mark on the list because I didn't have solid reason to cross him off.

I visited another landscaper and then one of the generic names that turned out to be a fertilizing operation. Neither seemed a likely candidate, but each had had access. I gave them angry question marks, too. I was getting nowhere.

I went east, then north up Western Avenue, to the second plumber on my list. I pulled off the street in front of the white frame building and parked between two vans.

"I need some help with a plumbing project you guys did in 1970," I said to the black-haired man working at a cluttered desk in the paneled front office.

"Warranty ran out yesterday," he said over his reading glasses. Then he laughed. "Which project?"

"Crystal Waters, in Maple Hills. Is there anybody here who worked on that job?"

"I did, start to finish. Over a year."

I looked at him more closely. I'd thought he was in his early forties when I walked in, but the lines around his eyes made him older than that. He could have been at Gateville.

I didn't bother with coy. "There have been a couple of recent disturbances that we think might date back to the construction of the development."

"The house that blew up earlier this summer?"

"No, not that."

"They're thinking someone planted explosives in the plumbing when that house was being built?"

I looked out the window. He was reading me like I had a digital display wired on my forehead.

He whistled. "I'll be damned," he said, not at all bothered by my lack of a response. "We had ten, fifteen guys on that job, all told. Had the contract for the rough and the finish plumbing for all the houses. Mister, that place was crawling with all kinds of workers, so it could have been anybody, not just plumbers. Unless you're telling me you're sure the explosives were planted in the plumbing?"

"I'm not talking about explosives."

"Bet your ass you're not," he grinned. "Well, hiding explosives on that job would have been easy enough. There was so much going on, nobody would have paid attention. That jerkweed Maple Hills building inspector sure wouldn't have caught it. He didn't look for much except where the doughnuts were."

"Have you got employee records from back then?"

"You think we might have made a note in somebody's file: 'Good worker, but plants bombs?'" He waited for my laugh and then said, "We keep good records, but only for seven years."

I showed him the list of parolees. "Any names look familiar?"

He took ten minutes to examine the pages before shaking his head. "None of these were ours."

"Do you remember anything unusual about any of your men from back then, like someone who acted strange, or was mad about something?"

"Mister, I remember something unusual about most of the men who worked for me, then and since. Crystal Waters was a long, dirty job. There was mud everywhere because everything was tore up. Contractors were trying to get all the homes done at once, so there was lots of push to get things done on schedule. Job like that, at any one time, half our guys would have been pissed off at something. But mad enough to plant bombs? Not likely."

On my way out, I asked him to keep what we'd talked about quiet, because a lot of it was speculation. He said he would, and I believed him. But as I closed his door, I realized I wouldn't have minded if he used a megaphone to shout the story up and down

Western Avenue. It would chase the people out of Gateville, out of harm's way.

It was noon; four hours until the Bohemian was to call the Feds. I stopped at Kentucky Fried, skipped the fried, had the grilled, fooled no one. I ate at a counter by the window and watched the cars buzzing by. Reds and blues, greens and yellows. Cars of all colors, like the spools of wire at A-1 Electric. Like the snakes writhing in the firelight in the dream I'd been having.

I understood.

I left the food. I got in the Jeep and hurried back down Western, bits of Kentucky poultry stuck like grit to the dry roof of my mouth.

"Change your mind about buying a motor?" Ziloski smiled from behind the desk at A-1 Electric, setting down his magazine.

"Have you ever wired outdoor lampposts?"

"Only a couple thousand," he said.

"Is there much to it?"

"Like wiring a lightbulb." He blew the dust off a pad of paper, stood up, and came to the counter. "Wiring anything is simple: one wire in, one wire out." He drew a circle on the sheet of paper. "That loop is called a circuit. A lightbulb, a lamppost, don't matter which, interrupts the circuit—fits itself into the circle." He drew a lightbulb on the line that made the circle. "There's your lamppost."

"You just need two wires to hook up a lamppost?"

"Basically."

"Could you need more?"

"Sure, if you were using the lamppost electrical box as a kind of connecting point for other circuits."

I told him I had to go to the car to make a call. Stanley wasn't in; one of the guards said he'd gone home early. But the Bohemian was in his office.

"I want the ground under the lamppost dug up right away. Can you arrange that?"

He didn't ask me for a reason. The tone of my voice must have been enough. He put me on hold for the five longest minutes of my life, then came back on. "It'll be done within the hour, Vlodek."

I told him I'd call him later and hung up. I went back inside A-1 Electric and gave Ziloski a hundred dollars to follow me out to Gateville.

A security guard stood talking with the same two workmen who had been there the day of the blast. Next to them, a fresh hole had been dug at the base of the lamppost. As Ziloski and I walked up, I paid particular attention to the second workman, the one who'd said nothing the first time. The Bohemian's man. He avoided my eyes.

I looked down into the hole. The multicolored wires that had lain spilled at the bottom, like snakes of all colors, were now bundled and wrapped neatly with tape.

"Is Stanley here?" I asked the guard.

"Still home."

"His wife?"

The guard nodded, then pointed at the hole. "How long will you need this open?"

"Not long," Ziloski said.

I'd told him to just look, and tell me what he found when we were alone. Now, he knelt in front of the lamppost and, from a small tan canvas tool bag, pulled out a screwdriver and removed the access plate from the base. He used a penlight to peer inside the base cavity. After a few seconds, he reattached the plate and stepped down into the shallow hole.

I asked the guard if he'd been on duty the day the lamppost got blown over. He nodded.

"Did the blast knock out any other electrical fixtures in the development?"

The guard shook his head. "Just this light."

I thought back to what Ziloski had told me about wiring. If the lamppost had been used to route wires to other fixtures, then those would have been knocked out as well. But that had not happened. Just the one lamppost had gone out; only this one lamppost had been wired with something special.

The guard and I made small talk for several minutes as Ziloski picked at the dirt around the wiring going into the base of the lamppost. He separated two loose strands of wire that were capped with little red plastic cones, then looked up. "Who reconnected the wiring?" he asked the guard.

"The same electrician who does all the outside stuff for Crystal Waters."

Ziloski nodded and climbed out of the hole. "Best get back to the shop," he said to me.

"You can fill in the hole," I told the tall workman.

"You sure?" He grinned. "Someone else might want a peek to-morrow or the next day."

I smiled back. "Be no big deal to dig it up again, right?"

His grin widened. "No problem at all."

I walked Ziloski back to his truck.

"Tell me what you saw."

"What are you looking for?"

"Just tell me what you saw."

"There's singe marks on the underground conduit pipe where the wires come out, like there was a fire recently. Whoever recon-nected the wiring did a professional job, good splices, everything taped. The connections are all shielded, and on the wires they didn't reattach, the ends are all tightly capped and taped."

"Everything's normal?"

"Whoa, I didn't say that. Those wires they didn't reattach bother me. There's at least one extra pair of wires running close to that lamppost that don't belong there. Jobs like Crystal Waters are bid, and usually go to the lowest bidder. Laying in extra wires jacks up the cost, and I just can't see why those wires are needed."

"There used to be a school bus shelter there. Maybe they were for that?"

"Those extra wires are too thin, more like doorbell wire, not thick enough to carry juice to lighting. Like I said, the ends were singed, like they were burned off. They were the ones capped recently, so, for sure, now they're doing nothing. Makes no sense, why those thin wires were put there in the first place."

I called the Bohemian from the Jeep and told him what was in the ground.

# Fifteen

The Bohemian called back in two hours. By then, I was back at the turret, sitting on the bench by the Willahock, staring at the sky to the west, tensed for the first flash of yellow from the mother of all explosions.

There were no Vlodeks this time. "We're set to meet at five thirty."

"That's the soonest?"

He swore. "That's two hours from now. I've been on the phone since you called, conference calling with Chief Morris and some guy named Till at the Bureau of Alcohol, Tobacco, Firearms, and Explosives. A.T.F. is not pleased."

"Are you evacuating?"

"I recommended that to Bob Ballsard."

"What did he say?" I remembered Ballsard. He was the chairman of the homeowners association. I'd met him at the Crystal Waters Fourth of July party the previous summer, the annual event the association held to let the Members think they knew the names of their neighbors. Ballsard was a nervous, rabbity little man, a partner in his father's law firm. He had a deep tan and had worn

Topsider shoes, no socks, and a yachtsman's cap festooned with a battery-powered flashing American flag. And he had big, Teddy Roosevelt teeth. As he made party talk with Amanda, I became transfixed by those big teeth. They seemed too square to be natural, and I wondered if he'd had them specially made for clamping onto halyards or lanyards or whatever sailors call those ropes that make sails go up and down.

"Bob was noncommittal," the Bohemian said. "He'll be at the meeting this afternoon."

"He's got no choice. He's got to clear the place out."

"See you at five thirty," the Bohemian said, and hung up.

I didn't want to kill another hour watching for the sky to blow up, so I headed to the health center, did laps, then took a long shower. None of it helped. Getting on the expressway I was just as twitchy as I'd been earlier.

On the Eisenhower, the slow-motion horror of the day continued to unfold. An avocado-colored refrigerator had fallen off a truck onto the middle lane, backing up traffic for two miles. The world was full of threats. I got to the Bohemian's office fifteen minutes late.

Griselda Buffy was not pleased with my tardiness. "Everyone's been waiting," she said through the dark maroon paint that made her mouth look like a wound. She led me to a different conference room.

This one was much larger, with blue striped wallpaper and a silver coffee service shining on a sideboard. It was a room for the reading of big money wills.

Several men sat on dark blue leather chairs, around the long mahogany table.

"Vlodek," the Bohemian said from a chair on the left side of the table. He didn't bother to force a smile.

Stanley Novak sat two places to his left, a vacant chair in between them. Stanley's face looked dry and immobile. I had the fleeting thought that he might be in shock.

The man to the Bohemian's right, sitting at the head of the table, looked up from copies of the extortion notes spread out before him and nodded. He was in his late fifties, had wiry gray hair cut short, and wore a brown suit. He looked me up and down like he was measuring me for a uniform.

"Vlodek, this is Agent Till of A.T.F.," the Bohemian said.

Agent Till stood up to shake hands. He was shorter than he seemed sitting down, no more than five-seven or -eight, and stocky. He looked like he could wrestle crocodiles. And win.

"And the chief, of course," the Bohemian finished.

Chief Morris of the Maple Hills police, red faced, wearing a tan sports jacket and the kind of blue tie they give to tollbooth attendants, sat across the table from the Bohemian. He was also in his late fifties. He nodded but didn't bother to get up. I'd met the chief when I'd gone to Village Hall to purchase an auto license. He must have heard the counter clerk repeat my address, because he came bounding out of his office to introduce himself. I thought it odd, the chief of police introducing himself to a car license applicant, and realized, reluctantly, that it had everything to do with Crystal Waters and not the subtle sophistication of my voice.

"As soon as Bob Ballsard arrives, we'll begin," the Bohemian said. Agent Till sat down and went back to examining the photocopies of the two notes. I took a chair on the chief's side of the table.

No one spoke. It was like we had arrived early for a wake and were waiting for someone to finish powdering the guest of honor and wheel him in.

Bob Ballsard, chairman of the Board of Members of Crystal Waters, and future inheritor of great wealth, breezed in at five o'-clock. He wore summer-weight gray slacks, a navy blazer like mine but undoubtedly acquired at five times the cost and most certainly without any trace of ketchup on its sleeve, and a white shirt with a green tie that had little sailboats on it. He caught me leaning to take a discreet look at his shoes. He was wearing polished penny loafers, not Topsiders, and I was relieved to see he had on socks. He acknowledged me with a frown and a narrowing of his eyes. To the others, he offered a perfunctory apology that meant nothing of the sort, ignored the chair between the Bohemian and Stanley, and went down to sit at the foot of the long table.

Agent Till unstrapped his wristwatch and placed it in the center of the table in front of him. "Mr. Chernek has advised me of a developing situation at Crystal Waters." His voice was raspy and had the hard edge of Chicago's south side. "Before I proceed, I must tell you that for now, my role in this matter is strictly advisory. This matter is still under the jurisdiction of Chief Morris."

Everyone looked at Chief Morris. Morris looked at the A.T.F. agent and cleared his throat. "That's mostly a formality, though. A.T.F. will assume control of this case?"

"If the situation later warrants." Till turned to the Bohemian. "Let's start with a summary of where we are now, so we're all singing out of the same hymnal."

The Bohemian began with the letter that came in 1970, prior to the guardhouse explosion, and the subsequent letter and ten-thousand-dollar payment. He then moved to the two recent letters, the bombings of the Farraday house and the lamppost, and the five hundred thousand in cash left in the Dumpster. He ended with my discovery, the previous afternoon, of the extra wiring underneath the lamppost. He did it all in ten sentences.

Till looked at me. "And from this you've concluded . . . ?"

"The bombs in Crystal Waters are wired to one or more remote locations. The bomber triggered the Farraday house and the lamppost from someplace else." I paused and then said it: "The bombs are all wired together. He can flip the remaining switches at one time, to send all of Crystal Waters up in one huge fireball."

"Jesus," Chief Morris said next to me, but everyone else was silent. The Bohemian, Ballsard, and Stanley had known since I called the Bohemian that morning. Stanley grabbed for his handkerchief anyway. The Bohemian and Ballsard sat like granite.

Till turned to the Bohemian. "To date, there have been just the two payments made?"

"Correct," the Bohemian said. "Ten thousand, back in 1970, and then five hundred thousand last Sunday night."

"It didn't occur to you to inform us before last Sunday night so we could monitor the drop site?"

"We were hoping that, if we paid him, he would go away like the last time." The Bohemian's face was expressionless.

Till turned to scan the faces of everyone else at the table. To the Bohemian, he said, "Your man came back. He will come back again. The only way to stop him is to catch him. That's why it's a damned pity nobody was watching that drop site."

I cleared my throat. "I was."

The room went quiet again, but this time it was as if the air had been suddenly sucked out of it. The Bohemian and Stanley looked away, but the eyes of the others were hot on my skin.

Till looked at me. "You were there?" he asked in a slow, deliberate voice.

"In a garage across the alley."

"Jesus, Elstrom—" Ballsard muttered.

Till cut him off. "Let him continue."

I took them through the kids passing the basketball, Stanley putting the bag of money in the Dumpster, the arguing midnight lovers, the garbage truck arriving at dawn, and my futile search for the money. To me, my voice sounded normal enough, but I felt like I was wearing a clown suit and a red rubber nose.

"No chance the garbage men hauled it off?" Till asked.

"More and more, I'm thinking that could have happened. I think they tossed the top bag from the Dumpster into the truck before I got to them."

Till studied me for a minute and then said, "How long were you asleep?" The contempt in his words cut like a razor through a rotted peach.

"I took every precaution. I sat tilted—"

Till shook his head abruptly. "You fell asleep." Dismissing me, his eyes turned to the Bohemian, then to Ballsard, Stanley, and back to the Bohemian. "You've all been cute, keeping this to yourselves. What you've done with your five hundred thousand is give your bomber a taste for easy money. Next time he'll want a million plus, guaranteed."

Ballsard made a noise like something was stuck in his throat. "We can't come up with that."

Till ignored Ballsard; he wasn't done with me. "What exactly was your role supposed to be in this?"

"I was hired to examine the notes."

"You're a document examiner?"

"I provide that service. I brought the notes to a well-regarded document specialist."

"He's not much of anything, according to the *Tribune*." Chief Morris jerked his thumb at me as leaned across the table toward Stanley. "You brought in this jamoke without bothering to contact us?" It was theater, and everybody knew it. Morris didn't want to touch the Gateville explosions; he wanted to ride in parades and pose for the *Assembler* next to new squad cars. But Morris was right. I was too obviously a mistake.

The Bohemian spoke up, to cover both Stanley and Ballsard. "For the record, Chief, it was I who insisted on pursuing the investigation privately."

"Let's move on." Agent Till held up a copy of the contractor list. "We do have a lead. An electrician, no?"

"Likely as not," I said. "Anybody else stringing wires in an electrician's trench would have been noticed by the electricians. And stopped."

Till set the list back on the table. "There were five electrical outfits working at Crystal Waters, all of which are still in business. How many have you interviewed, Elstrom?"

I'd told him about hiring Ziloski to look at the lamppost. Stanley said he hadn't gotten around to his four.

"The chief and I will get to them," Till said. He looked down the long table at Bob Ballsard. "There's one more thing. You've got to evacuate."

Ballsard's face flushed red, like it was the first time the idea had been raised.

"Get everybody out of Crystal Waters," Till prompted, his eyes fixed on Ballsard.

Ballsard sputtered. "I don't see—"

"Got a wife, Mr. Ballsard? Kids?"

"Yes, but—"

"They at home now?"

"Actually, they're at my parents'—"

Till nodded, the corners of his mouth turning down. "Get everybody out. I can't insist, because I have no standing right now, but if turning one switch can send your whole development into the sky, you're fools not to evacuate."

Ballsard's eyes were wild as he looked toward the Bohemian.

'You've got to do it, Bob," the Bohemian said.

"When word gets out—"

"I understand, but Agent Till is right. You must get everyone out."

"I'll take it to the Board," Ballsard said.

"Do it this evening, Mr. Ballsard." Till picked up his watch and strapped it on his wrist. "That's it, then. The chief and I will work together, with A.T.F. in an advisory capacity. Mr. Ballsard will inform his Board of Members that Crystal Waters must be evacuated. We will reconvene as the situation warrants." Till stood and started for the door. Chief Morris scrambled to follow him. Ballsard, looking dazed, stood up then and also walked out, his lips tight over his Teddy Roosevelt teeth.

I started to get up, too, but the Bohemian motioned for me to sit back down.

"I wouldn't want to be Bob Ballsard tonight," the Bohemian said.

"I wouldn't want to be Bob Ballsard any night," I said.

"Vlodek—"

I held up my hand. "Why the hell didn't he run out of here like Paul Revere, to alert everyone at Crystal Waters to get out?"

"He has considerations," the Bohemian said.

"Bullshit."

"The Members are not as resilient as you, Vlodek. They were not schooled in bouncing up and starting over, like you did. They would not know to bathe at a local health center."

It was a small thing, but startling. "How do you know that?"

"Stanley apprised me of your status." He shook his head. "Enough of that. How do we progress?"

"We're out of it," I said. "Chief Morris has the case, but that's nominal. A.T.F. has the scent; they'll follow it."

The Bohemian shook his head. "Only until the next rumor of a terrorist threat aimed at a downtown skyscraper. Then we go on the back burner. No, Vlodek, we must pursue this investigation ourselves. Stanley, do you agree?"

"Absolutely, Mr. Chernek."

"How, Stanley? You know law enforcement. A.T.F. has the databases, field agents, labs, and big-time experience. Things we don't have."

"Maybe, Mr. Elstrom, but like Mr. Chernek says, we're just one terrorist alert away from being put on hold. You saw the way Agent Till was reluctant to commit to anything, how he wanted the chief to be in charge. Agent Till can't commit resources to a threat against a gated community full of rich people, especially since what's been destroyed is an empty house and a lamppost. Think what would happen if the papers picked up on that, what they would say about Agent Till nursemaiding a place like Crystal Waters when he should be focused on the airports, the railroad stations, the skyscrapers downtown. No, we've got to stay on this ourselves, like Mr. Chernek says."

"So you both believe we should continue our own interviews?"

They nodded.

I pulled out the contractor list the Bohemian had revised. "Do either of you remember anything about these electricians? Any problems, even little ones?"

"I just wrote the checks," the Bohemian said. "The Safe Haven partners would have dealt with any problems."

"I've been thinking of something this morning, Mr. Elstrom." Stanley started drumming his fingers slowly on the tabletop. "At the tail end of the project, one of the electricians didn't show up to wire something, and everybody was worried the final occupancy permits wouldn't be issued on time. They had to scramble to get somebody else to finish the work."

The Bohemian shook his head. "I don't remember."

"Would it have had to do with wiring the fountain?" I asked Stanley.

His fingers stopped drumming. "Could be."

"Ziloski, the electrician I brought to look at the lamppost, told me that's why he was hired back then, to finish wiring the fountain for somebody who hadn't shown up."

Stanley nodded. "I remember the electrician going missing, and wondering if he might have had something to do with the bomb. But I called his employer and they said he had a family emergency, so I dropped it."

"Do you remember his name?"

"James, I think. James something. But like I said, he came up clean."

I picked up my contractor list. "Do you remember which company he worked for?"

"It was so long ago, Mr. Elstrom. And like I said, it was a dead end."

"You looked for the man's name on the parolee list?"

"I didn't recognize any of those names."

"Keep trying, Stanley. We're chasing straws in the wind."

Stanley reached across the table for my copy of the contractor list, circled two names, and gave it back. "You check those electricians. I'll check the other two."

We left the Bohemian sitting in his grand conference room and rode down in the elevator together and went to our cars.

The sun was going down as I got off the expressway. I didn't want to eat alone. I didn't want to think alone. I swung by Leo's. His Porsche was parked at the curb in front of his mother's bungalow.

"Want to go get something to eat?" I asked through the screen when he came to the door. Then I noticed the silvery, geometric-patterned shirt and the light green slacks. Dress duds. "Going out, or merely planning to change a tire on a dimly lit road?"

"I just dropped Ma at church for Friday night bingo. Endora and I are going to the movies." He opened the door and stepped out onto the concrete porch. He studied my face in the glow of the yellow bug light. "You all right, Dek?"

"Peachy. Why do you ask?"

"Because you look like shit. When's the last time you ate?"

I thought back. "Lunch, but I left most of it. I'm on a new diet: the Bad Nerves Diet. I'm going to write a book about it and get rich."

He turned around and held the door open for me. "You hit the jackpot tonight, pal: pork, sauerkraut, and dumplings. A Polish Happy Meal." I followed him into the kitchen.

He pulled a big plastic salad bowl out of a cabinet, opened the refrigerator, and filled the bowl with the leftovers. He stuck a fork and a knife upright, like two flagpoles, into the big chunk of pork and handed the bowl to me. It must have weighed five pounds, and it was still warm. "Mind if we sit outside? You're such a pig, and I won't have the time to hose down the kitchen after you're done." He grabbed two bottles of Pilsner Urquell out of the refrigerator, and we went outside to sit on his front stoop.

He opened both beers and set one on the cement next to me. "Now tell Uncle Leo what's ailing you, but talk straight ahead, toward the street. I don't want your food on this two-dollar shirt."

I ate and told him about the extra wires under the lamppost and the meeting with A.T.F. at the Bohemian's. When I told him my theory that all the D.X.12 in Gateville was wired together, he set down his beer bottle so hard I thought I heard a crack.

"One switch blows it all away?"

"Could be."

"Why hasn't he threatened that, then?"

"I think he's playing with them, stringing them along, one explosion at a time. A cat with a mouse."

"Or because he thinks he can extract more total money if he does it a chunk at a time." Leo looked off down the street. "At least you've passed it off to the Feds," he said.

"I'm still on it. Stanley remembered part of a name from 1970, one of the electricians. The Bohemian wants Stanley and me to chase it down, paralleling Chief Morris and Agent Till."

"That's probably wise," he said, taking a pull on the Urquell.

"No, it's not. Using Stanley and me is like using Laurel and Hardy. I'm not equipped for it, and Stanley is supposed to be spending his time watching security at Gateville. Besides, his wife is sick, and he gets called away."

"What's the harm in you poking around, too? Worst case, you generate some billing that buys you hot water for the turret, unless you actually enjoy going to the health center and getting naked with winos?" His eyebrows cavorted on his forehead.

I laughed, for the first time in what felt like forever. Leo Brumsky, with his crazy shirts, pastel pants, and furry eyebrows, always found a way through the cloud to the lining.

He grinned and went on. "Talk to coppers, they'll tell you: The damndest things can pop up out of nowhere during an investigation. Everybody's just got to keep plugging."

I set the bowl of food on the step. It was still over half full. "It's so amateurish. People can die, Leo, unless this thing is handled right."

"As you said, A.T.F. is on the job. As for you, do your best. Continue on, as this Chernek wants. And don't discount amateurs." He checked his watch and stood up. "You've been fed. I'm late." He ducked into the bungalow and came back with a sheet of aluminum foil. "You can have the remaining pounds for breakfast."

We walked down the stairs to the curb.

"What theater are you going to?" I asked.

He launched his caterpillar eyebrows into a crazed dance that would have made Groucho Marx squirm with envy.

"The drive-in."

"You're a perv, Leo. What's playing?"

"It doesn't matter. It makes me feel young," he said as he got in the Porsche.

"And Endora?"

"She feels really young." He smiled out the window, twisted the key, and drove away, leaving me with a blast of German exhaust, a double entendre, and a bowl of cooling pork.

# Sixteen

"Two young boys from the A.T.F. took our old payroll files first thing this morning," the woman behind the counter at Universal Electric said with an exaggerated southern drawl. She was in her seventies but still fighting. She'd dyed her hair orange and drawn eyebrows to match on her forehead. She wore a low-cut leopard print dress, tight.

I checked my watch. "It's Saturday morning, only nine fifteen."

Her perfume was strong. The kind, I imagined, that came in barrels.

"It's the early bird gets the worm, honey. They was here at eight sharp." She leaned over the counter to give me a glimpse of wrinkled breasts. "What's this about?" she whispered, although we were alone in the tiny office. "Those two A.T.F. boys were as tight-lipped as lockjawed sparrows. They showed me a list of names and asked if any had worked here. I said no. Then they demanded our old payroll records, gave me a receipt, and took off with not more than two peeps."

I looked around like a spy about to pass a government secret.

"They're looking for a guy who bombed a draft office in 1970. They think he was working for you at the time."

It was a good lie. She brightened, keeping the breasts on the counter.

"Which project?" she asked, looking up to make sure I was looking down.

"Crystal Waters."

She nodded.

"You would have been way too young to have been working here then."

She dropped her voice even more so I'd have to lean closer. "I was a mere slip of a girl, you understand, too young to be working legal, but I was here then."

I feigned surprise. "Ma'am—"

"Call me Willadean, Honey."

"Willadean, that certainly is a shock. Do you remember anybody named James who would have worked on that job?"

"James, James . . ." she pursed her orange lips and lifted off the counter. "First name or last name?"

"I assume it's a first name."

She started to shake her head, then stopped. "Could it have been Jaynes, Michael Jaynes?" She spelled the last name out. "Him I remember."

"How's that, Willadean?"

"He was a strange, strange man. Wild man with a beard, and full of anger. I remember Mr. Davis, he was the owner then, having to tell Michael time and again to keep his political views to himself. Said he was agitating the other men and Mr. Davis didn't want the work slowed down from arguing politics and all. Michael was always nice to me, though."

"When did he leave here?"

"That's the thing I remember: He just up and disappeared sud-

den one day. I can't recall the specific day, but I do remember there
was much consternation about what might have happened, like
whether he'd been in an accident or been mugged or something.
Mr. Davis phoned the rooming house where Michael was staying,
but they didn't know anything. They said his stuff was still in his
room. The men working with him didn't know anything, neither.
It was a mystery all around. Mr. Davis held onto Michael's last paycheck for a while but finally had me forward it on."

"To where?"

"To the personal contact he wrote on his application, of course."

"You wouldn't still have that application?"

"Probably was in the box with the other payroll records I gave
to them young boys from the government."

"And that last canceled check?"

"They was young boys from the A.T.F. They didn't know how to
ask things of a lady."

"You've still got it?"

"Oh, I still got it, honey." She leered across the counter.

I tried to leer back. "For sure, but I meant that last canceled
check."

She cocked her hip and wiggled her finger in a come-hither gesture I'd seen once in a beach-party movie made a few years before
I was born. She led me to the back warehouse, walking in front of
me so I could admire the shifting tautness of the leopard fabric
from behind. As we moved between the skids of cartons, one of the
degenerates that lurks in my brain struck up the strains of Maria
Muldaur singing "It Ain't the Meat, It's the Motion," complete with
a bump-and-grind drum roll that kept time to the clicking of
Willadean's red high heels on the cement floor.

She stopped at the back wall and pirouetted. "The bank records
are up there," she said, pointing one arm and both leopard-covered
breasts at a pile of cardboard boxes high on a storage rack. The

boxes were neatly labeled. "Whatever you want, just grab it," she said, taking a half step toward me.

I don't scamper—I'm too big—but at that moment, I was as sprightly as a pup chipmunk as I hopped up onto the skid of electrical cables below the cardboard boxes. I pulled out the box labeled CANCELED CHECKS, 1970–1979 and jumped down, clutching the box like a shield. I carried it to a nearby workbench. Willadean unfolded the top flaps and went through the rubber-banded bundles of bank envelopes inside, extracting several.

"You said he would have disappeared in April of 1970?"

"Yes."

"Then we would have sent out his last check in June or July, and it would have come back processed in August or September." She opened several of the envelopes and fanned through the green payroll checks inside, finally extracting one. "Here it is," she said, handing it to me.

It was an ordinary check, dated April 25, 1970, made out to Michael S. Jaynes in the amount of $116.74. I turned it over. A woman's hand had endorsed it first with Michael's name, then with her own underneath, "Pay to Carlinda State Bank. Nadine Reynolds." The Carlinda State Bank of Carlinda, California, had rubber-stamped it beneath her signature.

"You wouldn't know what relationship this Nadine Reynolds had to Michael?" I asked.

"Only that she must have been the contact listed on his employment application. I don't recall whether the form said she was his wife, his mother, his sister, or anything."

"There must have been an address for her, to send the check?"

"On the application in the boxes them boys took."

We walked back to the office, her leading, me a safe five paces behind. She made a copy of the check for me and promised to send another to the A.T.F. agents who'd been there that morning.

"I'm here every day except Sunday, honey, but my nights are free," she told me at the door.

I told her she could count on me being back, sure as a bee sniffs honey on a dewy rose. I didn't know whether that was possible, but Willadean liked it and smiled an orange smile.

It was ten thirty. I drove east to the other electrical contractor Stanley had given me to check. The owner, about seventy, came out of his office mad and said he'd told "the authorities" who'd come that morning that he didn't have time for such crap, and besides, who saves payroll records from that long ago, anyway? I agreed with him and left.

I called Agent Till from the Jeep. His message tape said he was gone for the weekend. I told his voice mail about Michael Jaynes and Nadine Reynolds and said one of his junior agents would be receiving a photocopy of the canceled check. I asked him to get back to me on Monday morning with the address for Nadine Reynolds shown on Jaynes's employment form.

I spent Saturday lunchtime at the Rivertown Health Center. I ran twice as far as my previous record, breathing through my nose to chase away the sticky scent of Willadean the Electric Lady. She'd seen me as ripe game for her lacquered wiles, and I needed to get younger, quick.

Agent Till called at two fifteen that afternoon. "Who's this Michael Jaynes?"

"Your message machine said you were gone for the weekend."

"Your government never rests. What do you know about Jaynes?"

"Only what your boys could have found out for themselves. He was outspoken politically. He vanished around the time of the guardhouse bombing, leaving behind his clothes in his rented room. His last paycheck was forwarded to a Nadine Reynolds, apparently to an address shown on the employment application your people picked up. I'd like that address."

"We'll check it out."

"Can I have that address?"

"Why?"

"Anton Chernek wants me to run a parallel investigation."

"Why the hell would he want that?"

"In case you get distracted with terrorists."

"I don't want to keep you awake, Elstrom. We'll check things out," Till said, and hung up.

Rivertown hasn't had a public library since Lyndon Johnson was president, so I drove to the one in Maple Hills and Yahooed, Googled, and Lexis-Nexised on one of their computers the rest of Saturday afternoon. Once again, I scared myself at the information that's floating out in cyberspace. Pressing the right Internet buttons gets directory listings for anybody in the country who has a published telephone number. Pressing others gets ages, high schools, spouse's names, aerial photos of their neighborhoods, and maps to their houses. And that's all for free. Spending a little money gets credit reports, divorce histories, and a lot of other information that shouldn't be so easily available. The Internet has taken the wear off gumshoes, and replaced them with calloused fingertips. If Sam Spade, Philip Marlowe, and Sherlock Holmes were sleuthing today, they'd have squinty eyes from staring at computer screens, and carpal tunnel wrists from too many hours spent banging on a keyboard.

There were twenty-four Nadine Reynoldses listed on the Internet, ranging in age from twenty-six to eighty-one. None of them lived in California, but that didn't rule anything out. Nor did the ages. They could be the daughter or the mother of the person I was looking for. I printed the list and drove back to the turret.

I started telephoning the East Coast numbers. The first six weren't home. I left messages saying I worked for an estate attorney, which was true enough—the Bohemian did estate work—and asked for return calls to my cell phone. I counted on greed to make them overlook the fact that they couldn't call it collect.

Nadine Number Seven was home. She'd spent her entire life in Canton, Ohio, and had never heard of a Michael Jaynes. I kept calling.

At six thirty, I took a break for dinner. I microwaved the last pounds of Ma's pork, kraut, and dumplings and took it to the city bench overlooking the river. After I ate, I fell asleep, sitting up, like an old rummy with a wine load. At seven thirty, I went up to the turret for more telephoning and talked to Nadines Sixteen, Eighteen, Twenty, and Twenty-one, all in the West. All were wrong. During the evening, three of the earlier Nadines for whom I'd left messages called back. Each said she'd never heard of a Michael Jaynes, and each hung up the instant I said there was no potential for inheritance. I made my last call, to Nadine Twenty-four in Eugene, Oregon, at nine o'clock. She wasn't home.

I was at a dead end, except to wait for a few return calls. The A.T.F. would be tracing Michael Jaynes and Nadine Reynolds through the federal database. Things were happening, but for me, there was no place to go. All I could do was sit on the sidelines and wait for the phone to ring.

I parked in the La-Z-Boy and ate a jelly doughnut and watched microscopic men play baseball on my little T.V. The players looked like gnats, flitting around on the tiny screen. And sometime in the middle of the night, after the baseball game, the seventies sitcom reruns, and the junior college broadcast of introductory economics, I fell asleep.

Five Nadines called by nine thirty on Sunday morning. Two of them tried very hard to convince me they had a distant relative named Michael Jaynes who, for sure, would have remembered them in his will. After I was certain each had never heard of him, I said I'd called for help with his burial expenses. Both hung up without getting my address for their Christmas card lists.

At eleven, the Bohemian called, sounding out of breath. "Your cell phone has been busy all morning. Don't you have a second landline, a regular home number?"

I told him I only had one cell number, one computer line, and one mouth, and some considered that last a blessing.

He didn't voice his agreement. "What did you say to Agent Till yesterday afternoon?"

I told the Bohemian what I'd told Till about my visit to Universal Electric, Michael Jaynes, and how I was trying to track down Nadine Reynolds. "I asked Till for Nadine Reynolds's address from Jaynes's employment application."

"Do you think our bomber is this Michael Jaynes?"

"It's worth checking out. What's going on with Till?"

"He's riled. He's called a meeting for tomorrow morning at the Maple Hills police station."

"Because of me?"

"He's angry that I want you to keep investigating, but the meeting is about Bob Ballsard. He won't evacuate."

# Seventeen

The Maple Hills police station occupies a redbrick building designed to look like something in Colonial Williamsburg. Parking is in back, because nobody in eighteenth-century Williamsburg parked cars in front.

I got there a half hour early and waited in the painted cinder-block hall, reading public notices about lawn-sprinkling restrictions while I drank vending-machine coffee from a paper cup that had a losing poker hand printed on it.

Stanley arrived at quarter to ten, holding the door open for Bob Ballsard. Stanley's pale blue uniform looked crisp, but the skin on his face sagged like it was falling off of its own weight. Ballsard wore one of his blue blazers, a yellow tie with blue anchors on it, tan trousers, and polished boat shoes with no socks. He looked like he was going to a dockside tent party at the Chicago Yacht Club.

They paused in the hall.

"Elstrom," Ballsard smiled nautically, "the chief invited you?"

"Actually, it was Agent Till. Seems he's angry at you and me."

His lips closed around his teeth, choking off the smile. I

couldn't tell if he was mad at Till's impertinence at being angry or because of the indignity of being lumped in with me.

"We'll see who's angry at whom," he said. He marched down the hall with Stanley following a half step behind.

The Bohemian arrived five minutes later. He was impeccably dressed as always, but there was a tight look to the skin around his eyes. The days were not being kind to the Bohemian. We walked together into the police department conference room.

Agent Till sat hunched forward at the end of the narrow folding table, his watch unstrapped and lying on the fake wood-grain table top. He was murmuring something to a red-faced Chief Morris, who sat to his left and looked like he would rather be anywhere but in that room. At the other end of the table, Ballsard and Stanley sat like two spinsters at a rock party, not speaking. Till gave me a quick, annoyed look as the Bohemian and I sat down. He repositioned his wristwatch a quarter inch to the left in front of him and began.

"Gentlemen, we need to get some things straight, starting with the fact that Chief Morris here is in charge of investigating this case." Next to him, Chief Morris shifted gingerly in his chair like he had stones in his underwear. "We need all the leads we can get, but the chief, and I as necessary, will chase them down. Outside help is not needed." Till aimed his eyes at me. "Am I being clear, Mr. Elstrom?"

"You bet."

"That said, tell us how you came across the name of Michael Jaynes."

"Actually, it was Stanley. He remembered that at the time the guard shack blew up, there had been a problem with one of the electric contractors. A supervisor had not shown up to do some final wiring, and there'd been concern that it would delay the issuance of the occupancy permits. Stanley wondered if the man's absence was tied to the explosion. He checked it out, found noth-ing. We thought it would be worth a second look. I found the con-tractor, Universal Electric, and asked about him. They remembered sending on his last paycheck, a copy of which you are getting in the mail."

"Like Mr. Elstrom just told you," Stanley said, "I checked with Universal Electric right after the guardhouse exploded. They told me Michael Jaynes had a family problem and had quit his job. Now, I know they lied about that because they didn't want any trouble getting final payment, but back then, I couldn't see any connection between Jaynes and the bombing, so I dropped it."

Agent Till reached in his shirt pocket for reading glasses, slipped them on, and opened a manila folder. "I don't know that he is much of a lead, but Michael Jaynes is interesting. He had an or-dinary boyhood in Santa Rosa, California. Only child, average stu-dent, ran track in high school. Went to U.S.C., dropped out at the end of his freshman year. Got drafted, Vietnam, 1965–66. Re-upped, took another tour over there. Wounded in a firefight, two Purple Hearts, got out in 1968. Got hired by Universal Electric. Good worker, they made him a supervisor. He was in charge of the Crystal Waters project until April 22, 1970, after which he didn't show up." He looked at us over the top of his reading glasses. "Ac-cording to his Army 201 file, he did advanced classes in demolition after basic training." Till put down the folder and looked at the Bo-hemian. "Any chance you could pinpoint the day back in 1970 that you dropped the ten grand behind the restaurant?"

"I could check the old records to find out when the developers withdrew the money."

"No need, Mr. Chernek," Stanley said. "I remember. It was the night of April 22. It was Earth Day; there were protesters all over Chicago that evening. I was worried I wouldn't get through all the traffic tie-ups."

"Jaynes disappeared the next day." Till looked at Stanley. "Yet you say you saw no connection?"

"Not after Universal Electric explained it as a family problem." Stanley dabbed at his forehead with a handkerchief.

Agent Till looked at Stanley for a long minute before he turned back to his folder. "As I said, gentlemen, Mr. Jaynes is an interesting man. He has not been seen, or heard from, since. No G.I. Bill applications, no claims for Army medical, no filing of income tax returns. For all intents and purposes, the man known as Michael Jaynes disappeared from the world when he quit Crystal Waters, the day after ten thousand dollars was left in the Dumpster."

"He changed his name and disappeared," the Bohemian said.

"And that's consistent with the facts," Till said. "*If* it was Jaynes who blew up your guardhouse in 1970, he extorted your money and high-tailed it out of here. His parents were dead, he wasn't married, he didn't have any kids we know of. He saw a chance to score, took it, and vaporized."

"All for the huge sum of ten thousand dollars," I said.

"Ten grand was a lot of money back then," Till said.

"Not to a guy who had bigger plans. We don't have the 1970 letters, but Stanley and Mr. Chernek think the notes they received this summer are identical—same pencil lettering, same paper. It's not that much of a reach to think he wrote those back in 1970, too. And as we know, those demanded fifty thousand, and the five hundred thousand Stanley just paid."

Till shrugged. "He got scared after the guardhouse, so he took the money and ran. Change of heart. It happens."

"Come on, Till. It takes him all those years to get to thinking of the painless way he scored the ten grand, of the plan he put in place back then, of the notes he wrote, and don't let us forget all that D.X.12 he planted in the ground, before he decides to come back for another helping?"

Till looked at me over the top of his reading glasses. "Your point?"

"Our man never planned to quit at ten thousand dollars. It was a test run, just for openers. Then something stopped him, caused him to abort the plan. That's the key. Find what stopped him all those years ago, and you'll find your man."

"Like from this?" He held up some white sheets of paper. "Your fabled parolee list?"

"Just because he isn't on the Illinois list doesn't mean the idea's not worth trying. You can do parolees for the whole country."

"We did. Too many names to chase down."

"What about Nadine Reynolds?"

Till looked at me, his face momentarily blank. "Who?"

"The woman Michael Jaynes listed as a contact on his employment application. I called you for her address."

Till nodded and flipped through his file folder. He came to a photocopy. "Nadine Reynolds. General Delivery, Clarinda, California. I forwarded an interview request to our San Francisco office, asking them to check her out."

"That's it? You forwarded a request?"

He took off his reading glasses. "Between us, the F.B.I., and local and state cops, we get hundreds of reports of terrorist sightings, bomb threats, and what-have-you, every day. Some days it seems like every Jordanian cabdriver, Egyptian flight student, and Saudi college kid around Chicago is reported doing something suspicious. Our reality is we have to check them all out. To say we're short-staffed doesn't cover the half of it." He rubbed his eyes and looked around the table. "Do I believe there's a real threat at Crystal Waters? Yes. Does it rank with the other threats we get every single day, the bomb threats against big buildings, somebody overhearing something on the train about a plan to poison the water supply, or the hourly incidents at Milwaukee, O'Hare, and Midway airports? Maybe. I don't know. Without concrete evidence linking these notes"— he tapped his manila file—"to the two explosions you've had this summer, I'm limited in what I can do."

"What about ground-penetrating radar?" Stanley asked.

Till shrugged. "You can hire private contractors, if you want to waste the money, but my guess is that G.P.R. will never find it all. I certainly can't provide federal resources for that."

The Bohemian spoke. "Then what are you telling us? We're not to chase down our own leads, yet you're too busy to offer us help?"

"I'm telling you to quit being such damned fools," Till snapped. "I don't want you chasing down anything, making things worse, like your man Elstrom might have done last Sunday night." He looked around the table. "Have any of you considered that Elstrom was spotted and scared away the bomber from the pickup? And that now the money is rotting somewhere, buried under tons of food waste and household trash, while your bomber is angrily planning something worse?" He glared down the table at Bob Ballsard. "But even more, I want you to quit being negligent with human lives. What is it about evacuation you don't understand? You might have bundles of D.X.12 wired together all over your little community, wanting just one spark to turn you all into ash. And don't tell me about your security; it's for shit. Get the people the hell out of Crystal Waters."

Till grabbed his wristwatch from the table, jammed it in his suit coat pocket, and stood up. "I'm done. Any questions, direct them to Chief Morris." He turned quickly and left the room. Chief Morris got up before anybody could ask him anything and followed Till.

"Bob—" the Bohemian began, but Ballsard, red faced, was already marching out of the door. Stanley made a move to follow him, but the Bohemian motioned for him to stay.

"We must trace this Nadine Reynolds on our own," the Bohemian said to both of us.

"You just heard what Till thinks of that," I said.

"I also saw him fumble the lead about Nadine Reynolds. The man has too much on his plate."

I looked at Stanley.

"Stanley has other commitments, Vlodek. You have to be the one to go to California to find Nadine Reynolds."

"Chances are, she's long gone," I said.

"What other leads do we have?"

"Till said he forwarded the information to the A.T.F. office in San Francisco," I said. "He'll follow up."

The Bohemian nodded, watching my eyes.

The clock ticked on the cinder-block wall.

"Surf's up," I said.

# Eighteen

"How are you going to start?" Leo yelled into the phone.

I pressed the cell phone harder against my ear. I was next to a window at an unoccupied discount airline gate at Midway Airport, trying to get away from yelling kids, hysterical parents, and the bobblehead on the loudspeaker, so in love with his own voice he'd been paging the same guy for the past half hour. I like discount flyers; they're cheap, and they take off the same day they're scheduled. But sound bounces around their end of the concourse like monkeys banging on drums, and it's always tough to talk on the phone. I moved behind a vacant check-in counter and crouched down.

"Say again, Leo."

"Do you have a plan?" he yelled.

"Drive up to Clarinda, ask at the bank, start trolling the town looking for people who know her."

"Why fly all the way to California? Hire a local. Or better yet, why not have A.T.F. do it?"

"That's what I told the Bohemian. He doesn't want to wait. Since Nadine Reynolds is our only lead, he wants me out there,

Johnny on the spot, to pursue it right away. Besides, A.T.F. is easily derailed these days, getting tons of threat alerts."

"At least the Gateville people are no longer buying the idea that the matter's over, since the payoff's been made."

"No. Now they're realizing that if getting five hundred large is that easy, this Michael Jaynes, or whoever, is coming back for more. What scares me is he'll blow up something else first, to get us frantic before he sends another note. Next time he goes for a million, the A.T.F. agent said."

The bobblehead was back on the P.A. system, this time with four new names.

"I told you, Dek," Leo said when he heard the bobblehead pause for air.

"Told me what?"

"Told you you'd get lucky with a lead. I just didn't think it would be this quick."

"Or this good. A bona-fide link to a name."

The boarding call for my flight came over the loudspeaker. I told Leo I had to go.

"Dek?"

"Yeah?"

"Don't let the California beach babes touch your privates."

I laughed, sort of.


If I'd owned a surfboard, I would have been angry I'd packed it. San Francisco Airport was cold, fifty-five degrees, and rainy when my flight landed at three that afternoon. I took the shuttle to the car rental building and stood in line at Avis. When it was my turn, I told the blond lady I wanted a convertible. It's been raining for days, the lady said. They had plenty, Mustangs and Sebrings. What did I want? I said red.

I snailed north on 101, one more clot in the afternoon rush hour. To the north, San Francisco was invisible in the soup. After an hour, and maybe ten miles, 101 dissolved into a maze of city streets. I kept on for another ten minutes, following the traffic and looking for a gas station to ask for directions, when the Golden Gate Bridge came out of the mist like a ghost ship, not gold at all but a rusty red-orange, almost the same hue as Willadean the Electric Lady's hair.

I drove across the bay, into the green haze of hills in Sausalito and Mill Valley. By now, the traffic had thinned and the rain had stopped. It was six thirty. And it was California. Fifty-five degrees or not, I pulled over, dug a sweater from my duffel to put on under my windbreaker, slipped on my Cubs cap to alert the Californians I was a tourist, and dropped the top of the Sebring.

I cut west, over to Highway 1, the old two-lane blacktop that chases the crags of the California coast. The airline magazine said it was all hairpin turns and switchback curves, offering views of protected land and undeveloped shoreline that were not to be missed. The airline writer was no romantic, but she was right. I got stuck behind two flatbed produce trucks lumbering through gear changes and a vanload of gawking tourists, their heads stuck out their windows like pigeons begging for peanuts, and I didn't mind at all. In the mist, the rock formations down in the froth along the shore looked like herds of prehistoric dinosaurs, hunkering down in the shallow waters for the night.

The road curved inland, and I drove through farmland that looked like Iowa until it curved back again to the sea. I got to Bodega Bay at dark. Clarinda was due north, and Santa Rosa, boyhood home of Michael Jaynes, was east. I opted for neither and pulled off in front of an old frame motel right on Bodega Bay.

While the dark-haired teenaged girl processed my credit card, I thumbed through a guidebook for sale on the counter. It said that Bodega Bay was the film site of Alfred Hitchcock's *The Birds*. I remembered three scenes in the movie: a house that was attacked by birds, a school that was attacked by birds, and a café where a tweedy old lady, who resembled a bird, opined that doom was in the offing. The guidebook said the house had been extensively modified with plywood by Hitchcock and had never been a recognizable tourist site once the plywood was removed; the school wasn't in the town at all, but several miles to the east; and the café had been expanded so often it no longer looked like the place in the movie. Welcome, film buffs, to Bodega Bay, site of *The Birds.*

The girl handed me my room key and told me that the restaurant across the street would close in half an hour. I have that kind of face; it always looks hungry. I left my bag in the car and ambled across Highway 1, deserted now, in the dark, of trucks and tourists. The restaurant was old and paneled and apparently had not been featured in *The Birds,* but it was serving sea bass and lime pie, and I had both, with coffee, although it was late for caffeine, past ten o'clock. I was the only customer, and the waitress, a nervous woman without much of a smile, left me alone. At eleven, having successfully fended off starvation for another night, I walked back across the highway. My room was old enough to have windows that opened all the way, and I fell asleep listening to the water lap at the pier pilings, remembering another such place, on an inlet off Lake Michigan, where Amanda and I stayed once when we were married.

I was up at seven the next morning, but that was Chicago time. It was only 5:00 A.M. in California, and the roosters in Bodega Bay were still chilling in their rooster haciendas. The restaurant across the street was open, though, and as I went to a booth, I eyed the lime pie sitting in the glass case. There was plenty left—my piece last night was the only triangle missing—and fruit is always good for breakfast. But it was a new day. I had whole-wheat toast and black coffee and felt the leaner for it. I did get a slice of the pie to go, though, in case I got stranded in the desert, should a desert appear along the ocean coast highway.

I walked back to the motel. As I paid my bill, I asked the counter clerk about Clarinda.

"Not much there," she said. "Mostly it's a hub for practitioners of the therapies."

"Therapies?"

She walked around the counter to the tourist brochure rack, picked out a directory the size of a small phone book, and handed it to me. "They're all in here. Whatever problems you're having with your aura, your pet, your living room furniture, or if you just want to get more intimate with your plants, these people can take care of it." She smiled a good, sane smile. I thanked her for the book and walked out.

The sun was brightening the sky behind the rolling hills to the east. No rain today. I put the top down on the convertible and drove out of Bodega Bay, site of the film *The Birds*.

Highway 1 was still empty of tourists and truckers. Clarinda was less than an hour away, even if I poked along, so I drove slow, and stopped at most of the observation points to watch the rising sun color the monstrous stone humps in the water first red, then orange, then yellow. I lingered at one particularly spectacular vista, listening to the ocean pound below, watching the colors of the coast change, second by second, before my eyes. I forced myself to remember the wires under the lamppost, and how likely it was that others just like them connected dozens, maybe hundreds, of high-yield explosives throughout Gateville. It seemed impossible that something like that could exist on the same planet that offered the beauty I was seeing along the California coast.

Even with poking along, I got to the brown molded plastic sign welcoming me to Clarinda at eight thirty. The town was a hundred yards up, not much more than a wide place in the road, with a green two-island BP gas station, a small general store, and, fifty yards past those, a long white frame building with green shutters and another molded plastic sign, also brown, saying it was the

Clarinda Inn and Convention Center. I swung into the B.P. and filled up. The young girl inside was Asian and didn't understand English. She gave me correct change for my twenty, but when I asked her about the Clarinda State Bank, she giggled and tried to give me the key to the men's room. I smiled back and left.

The gravel lot in front of the Clarinda Inn was empty except for a rusted old Plymouth Reliant and a faded tan Volkswagen Microbus that looked straight out of the sixties. The bus was painted with red flowers and round blue peace symbols and had a POLLU-TION—IT'S EVERYBODY'S WORRY sticker on the back bumper. I'd seen television images of the sixties, of dark swooping helicopters, bright flashes of ground fire, and men running with stretchers in Vietnam; of girls flashing their fingers in a *V,* for peace, as they put daisies into rifle barrels held by stiff-faced, trembling National Guardsmen; and of hippies, rolling down the road in Volkswagen buses adorned with flowers and peace symbols. Apparently, some were still rolling, and one had rolled to a stop right in front of the Clarinda Inn. I parked next to it, stepped around the oil it was leaking, and went in.

There was no one at the desk. The sign above the dining room entrance said to seat myself, so I did, at a small table by the window that looked out over Highway 1 and the ocean inlet just beyond. Only two of the other tables, both by the window in the long, dark hall, were occupied. A young girl, fresh-faced without makeup and wearing a red-checkered apron, came over. "Breakfast?" she asked.

"That would be great." I was thinking of scrambled eggs, crisp bacon, and hash browns. Surely no one would count the dry piece of whole-wheat toast I'd had earlier as anything but a crouton.

"Coming right up," she said, and left.

I sat and looked out the window while I waited for her to bring a menu.

There were four middle-aged women at the next table, dressed to varying degrees in faded denim and flowery blouses. None wore much makeup. As they chatted, first one, then another would get up and go to a small table in the corner, to return with a glass of cranberry juice. Being tack-sharp from the top-down drive in the morning air, I looked around and noticed the coffee was kept elsewhere, on a sideboard, alongside glass pitchers of orange juice. I got up and poured myself a cup of coffee.

In a few minutes, my waitress returned, carrying a plate. She set it down in front of me. It held two little stacked pancakes, topped by a lone, shrunken raspberry.

I smiled up at her. "I haven't ordered yet."

She looked at me as though I'd said I left my lunar orbiter idling on the roof. "You said you wanted breakfast, sir."

"I don't recall ordering this." I looked down again at the two tiny cakes and the puckered berry. If they continued to serve food that looked that small, they ought to start using smaller plates.

"We don't cook to order," she said. "We offer one entrée for breakfast. Today, it's granola cakes with raspberry."

I caught the singular on "raspberry." "I'll eat it," I said. California was making me healthier by the minute.

She left, and I ate the poor raspberry in one bite, sparing it from further isolation atop the two griddle cakes. I cut the pancakes into tiny squares to make them last and looked out the window while I ate.

"I'm thinking of getting into reflexology," one of the women at the next table said, as she returned with another glass of cranberry juice. Either my hearing was improving in the California air or the conversation at the next table was getting louder. The woman speaking was pretty in a natural way, blond hair with streaks of gray, and a rose blush on her cheeks. "Things are becoming so competitive, I can't just do aromatherapy and massage. I've got to find another niche to survive." I snuck a peek at the other three women at the table. They were nodding enthusiastically in agreement.

Another of them, this one red-haired, drained her glass with a flourish, got up, and walked over to the corner table for a refill. I wondered again why they kept the cranberry juice on one table, the orange juice next to the coffee on another. Then again, I was in California, and perhaps that was explanation enough.

I looked around the room. The only other occupied table was shared by a bearded fellow with a ponytail and an overweight girl in desperate need of a bra. They were also drinking cranberry juice. I caught my young waitress as she walked by. "Why do you keep the cranberry juice on one table and the orange juice on another?"

She looked where I was pointing. "Oh, no, sir, that's sherry. We serve it during afternoon tea, but it's there all day."

"How convenient," I said, sneaking another glance at the blond-gray lady at the next table. The rose blush on her cheeks had deepened. Nothing like a little toddy to give a glow first thing in the morning. I turned back to the waitress. "Can you tell me where the Clarinda State Bank is?"

"There's no bank in Clarinda. I've lived here all my life, and there's never been a bank in Clarinda."

"Might there be someone here who's been around longer?"

"I'll ask," she said, and bustled off.

"I try to build up slowly, ease in the ecstasy with my fingers," the red-haired woman at the next table was saying.

"Absolutely," the blond-gray lady with the flushed cheeks agreed, bobbing her head. Or maybe it was that her head was wobbling. "Building for the whole hour is the only way."

When I was in high school back in Rivertown, the hookers who worked the parking lot behind the bowling alley had a different name for it, but they built ecstasy with their fingers, too. They didn't go slow, though; they went real fast, and they only charged five bucks, less if they wore gloves. And it didn't take an hour, not with high school boys.

"You were inquiring about the bank?"

The man had come up behind me so quietly I hadn't heard him.

I looked up. He had a full gray beard and was wearing a white chef's jacket and hat. "Yes. I'm looking for information about the Clarinda State Bank. It was here in 1970."

"Indeed it was, though it wasn't much of a bank. It closed sometime in the midseventies, torn down for that gas station." He gestured out the window at the B.P. and smiled. "You can see Clarinda isn't really ripe for commercial development."

"Is there a city hall, or a telephone company office? I'm looking for someone."

"Might I inquire who?"

"Nadine Reynolds. She used to live here, or at least bank here."

"Can't say as I know the name."

"Is there anyone in town who might have known her?"

"There's old-timers around, but they're mostly retired loggers or sixties people farming little plots up in the hills." He didn't pause to explain what kind of crops "sixties people" would be growing in small plots in the hills. "Your best bet is to go across the street, ask at the post office."

I looked out the window. All that was across the street was the little general store.

"It's got postal boxes inside," the chef said. "Ask Betsy, she runs the place. She might remember your Nadine Reynolds."

The waitress brought me my check. Eighteen bucks, which was nine bucks a cake if they threw in the raspberry gratis. Of course, that included all you could drink of the sherry. I left twenty-two dollars on the table and walked outside, a healthy man.

The sign on the store said it opened at ten, leaving me an hour to kill. I got in the car and drove north a couple of miles, but there was nothing there but more hills and craggy cliffs. I pulled off at an observation point and leafed through the therapist directory I'd picked up in Bodega Bay.

The counter clerk at the motel had been right: There were advisors, therapists, and counselors peddling every kind of assistance,

from tantric sex instruction, avatar training, and radical forgive-
ness to polarity therapy and shamanic counseling. I didn't understand any of it; the ailments that were plaguing people in Northern
California had not yet struck Rivertown. One ad in particular
caught my eye. Some fellow was offering help in "Getting Right
with Your Colon," which sounded like it might be popular as a
postlunch seminar topic outside Kutz's Wienie Wagon. I tossed the
directory into the backseat and drove back to Clarinda.

A tall woman with braided gray pigtails was hauling out wire
display racks from inside the store. I pulled in and parked.

"I understand this is also the post office," I said from the convertible.

"It is." She set down a round contraption full of T-shirts on
hangers.

I got out, followed her inside, and helped her carry out a rack of
brightly colored inner tubes.

"Inner tubes?"

"The Russian River is great for tubing," she said. "Can I help
you find something?"

"I'm looking for a Nadine Reynolds, used to live around here."

"Still does," she said, disappearing into the store. She came out
with a shelf rack stacked with beach towels. "She in some kind of
trouble?"

"I need to talk to her about an insurance matter."

She nodded, satisfied.

"But Nadine Reynolds still lives here?"

"Think so." She paused. "Still gets mail, mostly junk, ten, twelve
times a year."

"Where does she live?"

"Don't know. I've never seen the woman. Her mail comes general delivery. I hold it until Lucy comes in."

"Lucy?"

"Lucy Vesuvius. When she walks down for her mail, she always asks if there's anything for this Nadine Reynolds and says she'll bring it up to her. Got a letter in there right now for Nadine."

"Do you have an address for Lucy Vesuvius?"

"She lives up in the hills, Runnelback Road."

I pulled my cell phone out of my shirt pocket. "May I use your phone book?"

"Pay phone's inside." She turned from straightening the T-shirts on the round rack and saw the cell phone in my hand. "Those things don't work around here," she said. "Too many hills, not enough towers. The Zen folks say that's the natural order, the hills keeping cellular out. Me? I'd like to have one. Anyway, Lucy doesn't have a phone, regular or cellular. If you want to talk to her, you have to go on up."

She grabbed a small brown paper bag from a stack on a seed table and sketched a map. "I expect she's at home. Lucy doesn't seem to get around much, except for a hike down here once, twice a month for provisions."

"What does she do?"

"She's one of them in touch with her inner spirit. Sometimes I think I'm the only one's got a toe in the real world around here." She paused. "You sure this Nadine isn't in some sort of trouble?"

"No. Why do you ask?"

"Because I been running this place for twenty years, and excepting one other guy, you're the only one's asked for Nadine Reynolds."

Good news, I thought. Till had mobilized one of his San Francisco agents. "The other fellow, was he a government type, in a suit, came up in the last day or so?" I asked.

She laughed. "Not hardly. First off, he calls, never comes here. Second, he sure doesn't sound like a government man. He's a little too soft-spoken, a little too polite. He always asks if I know how Nadine's doing. I always tell him what I just told you: I don't know her, but somebody comes down periodic for her mail, so she must be doing all right. I always ask if I can pass on a message. He says no, and that's pretty much it until he calls again a few months later."

"How long has he been calling?"

"Ever since I've owned the store. When I see Lucy afterward, she always gets real excited about it and promises to tell Nadine right away."

"This caller, he doesn't leave a name?"

"Sure he does. Michael. His name is Michael."

"Michael Jaynes?"

"He never has said his last name, but Lucy seems to know who it is."

"I think I'll head up there," I said, starting for the car.

"Hold on a minute." She went into the store and came out with a small packet of mail. "Might as well bring the mail up, if you're going up to see Lucy." She handed me the rubber-banded bundle.

I opened the car door and set the mail next to me on top of the bag map. "Where I come from, they're not this trusting with the mail," I said.

"Neither are we, but you have a good face."

"An honest face?"

She shook her head and laughed. "No. More like it's too confused to be dishonest."

I smiled with her at that, then drove away.

A half mile up into the hills, I pulled over and slipped the rubber band off the mail. A letter-sized white envelope, computer addressed to Nadine Reynolds, was in the middle of the packet. The address was printed in the same font as the summer's two extortion letters, and it had been postmarked from the same Chicago zip code, the day after the money was left in the Dumpster behind Ann Sather's restaurant.

If my cell phone worked, I would have called Till.

# Nineteen

As the crow flies, Lucy Vesuvius's place was no more than two or three miles from the store in Clarinda. But if the crow used Betsy's paper-bag map, following the same twisting, rutted dirt and stone roads that I did, it might still be hopping on its tiny, clawed feet. The squiggly lines Betsy had drawn on the map were accurate enough, but she'd used no street names, because there weren't any. Instead, she'd noted landmarks at intersections, like "Red Barn, Part of Roof Missing," or "Fallen, Rotted Tree." It must have been years since she'd been back up in those hills. The red barn had collapsed; I drove past the rubble twice before I thought to get out of the car to check the heap of boards for flecks of red paint. The fallen, rotted tree was gone, too—dinner, most likely, for a previous generation of termites.

The little cottage was so densely nestled in the woods that I drove past it three times before I spotted the painted plaque nailed to a tree. It had a picture of a volcano erupting, with READINGS lettered underneath a mountain. Vesuvius. Cute.

I parked as far as I could get off the narrow, one-lane dirt road and walked through the trees. The tiny house wasn't much more than a shack. It had been painted lavender, with darker purple and red trim, but now most of the paint was off, and black mildew covered much of the exposed gray wood. Spindly trees grew right up to the cracked cinder-block foundation. The front door had moss on it and looked to be swelled shut from moisture. I knocked anyway, several times, but there was no answer.

I walked around to the back. There was a small, sunlit clearing behind the house, planted with irregular rows of a hodgepodge of different plants and bushes. I recognized tomatoes, a row of something low to the ground that could have been strawberries, and, in the center of the plot, several tall pointy plants that might have been destined to be smoked rather than eaten. At the opposite end of the clearing, a woman in a faded pink sundress and a tattered straw hat, unraveling at the brim, was bent down, tending a row.

"Hello," I called.

She looked up. Her mouth moved, but I couldn't hear her. I walked closer.

"Hello," I said again.

The freckled face under the unraveling hat was in its late fifties or early sixties, wrinkled and worn by the sun, but she had a child's smile, wide-eyed and full of innocent delight.

"Lucy Vesuvius?"

"That's me," she said, straightening up. She stuck out a dirty hand. I shook it. It was calloused and rough. "Forgive me, I forgot I had an appointment."

"We haven't. I just took the chance you'd be home."

"You from the welfare?"

"No, ma'am."

Her eyes got narrower. "I didn't figure you were. It's been years since I applied. What brings you here, then?"

"I brought your mail," I said, handing her the small bundle with the letter to Nadine Reynolds on top. I watched her face.

"I don't know why Betsy down at the store bothers," she said, holding out the packet far enough to see without reading glasses. "All I ever get is catalogs for stuff I don't—"

She stopped suddenly, and her fingers tightened on the white envelope with the Chicago postmark. She slipped it out of the packet, slit it open with a grimy fingernail, and pulled out a sheet of folded white typing paper. A twenty-dollar bill fluttered to the ground, but she didn't seem to notice. She was too intent on the white sheet of paper. She held it up against the sun and turned it over, looking for writing. The paper was blank. I had the feeling she no longer knew I was there.

I bent down to pick up the twenty-dollar bill and held it out to her. "I wonder if you can help me."

Slowly, she lowered the blank piece of paper. Her eyes were unfocused, like her mind was a million miles away. Then she smiled and took the twenty. "I get so little mail. Come inside and we'll have peppermint tea. It's the least I can do for you driving up my mail."

I followed her to the back step of her fading lavender cottage. "Please remove your shoes," she said, pausing to kick off her sandals. "Keeps the karma in balance." She dropped the blank sheet of paper and the envelope into a plastic tub filled with old catalogs and opened the back door.

Lucy's tiny kitchen was a war zone of clutter. Pots, pans, and metal utensils, some rusted, lay nestled on the shallow counter beneath sagging chipped-enamel cabinets.

She moved to an indoor hand pump set into the counter, next to the sink. "Just take a minute," she said, working the pump until water came out. She filled a dented copper teapot and set it on a narrow two-burner propane stove that could have been scavenged from an old house trailer. She scratched a wood match against the underside of the counter, held it to the burner until a flame caught, and set the kettle on to boil.

"Take a seat," she said, waving the match. She came over to the two scratched white-painted wood chairs by the stained oak table and pushed aside a few red clay pots so we'd have room for our tea. We sat down.

"You didn't tell me what brings you all the way up here." She smiled at me across the corner of the tiny table, smoothing the wrinkles on the lap of her sundress.

"Nadine Reynolds."

Her mouth held the shape of the smile, but the life went out of it. It was like a switch had been closed, shutting off the animation to her face. She looked at me with frozen eyes.

"Obviously, you know Nadine Reynolds." I gestured toward the backyard. "That was her mail you opened out there."

The teakettle started to whistle. She didn't move; she continued to sit, paralyzed, oblivious to the shrieking steam for several more seconds until, at last, the sound got through. She pushed herself up from the chair like she had arthritis and shuffled the three steps to the stove. Slowly, she filled two silver tea balls with dried leaves from a mason jar, dropped them into white china mugs, and added boiling water from the kettle. She brought them back to the table and sat down with a sigh.

"I grow my own tea," she said in a faraway voice. "Peppermint's my favorite."

"Nadine Reynolds?"

She looked down and pulled at the little chain holding the tea ball in her cup. "You from the police?" she asked without looking up.

"No, ma'am."

"You'd have to tell me if you were law enforcement, right?" she said. Her eyes were still down.

"I suppose I would, but I'm not."

She raised her head then and looked at me. "Nadine Reynolds has not been here for a long, long time."

"She still gets mail here. Money."

"Nadine Reynolds was a confused young woman, a girl really,

filled with love and uncertainties about her fellow man. Nadine could not live as she had."

She stopped.

I waited.

"Drink your tea," Lucy Vesuvius said after another minute. She took a small sip. Some of the life was coming back into her face. "Peppermint's at its most exhilarating when it's hot."

I took a sip. She was right; it was exhilarating. Of course, after one slice of dry wheat toast and two granola hotcakes topped with an orphaned organic raspberry, beef broth could have sent me to the stars in ecstasy.

"Nadine Reynolds," I said again.

"What do you want with her after all these years?"

"I'm not looking for her. I'm looking for someone she knew. Michael Jaynes."

"Michael?" All the dullness was gone from her voice now. "Has he sent you?"

"Do you know where Michael is?"

"Have you seen Michael?" She leaned forward in her chair.

I shook my head. "I'm trying to find him."

"Why?"

"Something about insurance on an electrical contracting job he worked on a long time ago. Do you know where he is?"

She looked down as her fingers strayed to her dress pocket to touch the twenty-dollar bill. Then her eyes moved up to my face.

"A long, long time ago," she said, "when things were very confused, there was a war that no one wanted. It was a time of upheaval, a time of fear. Our own police, supposedly sworn to protect, had turned on us. Some people left the country, to Canada, to Europe. Some put their heads down and endured, praying the horror would pass. And some, like Nadine Reynolds, protested peacefully. Nadine had grown up privileged, in Ohio. She came out here to college, to Berkeley. There she met a group of peace-seeking people, and she lent her presence to those who were trying to convince the politicians that what they were doing in Vietnam was wrong. But some of those gentle people had lost their way, too. They did things they shouldn't have done, things they couldn't see were just as wrong as what they were protesting against."

Lucy Vesuvius got up, went to the stove, and held up the dented kettle. I shook my head. She poured more hot water into her cup, brought it back to the table, and watched the steam rise for a minute before continuing. "One night, the little group that Nadine had joined set off a small disturbance, a little explosion in the middle of the night, when no one was supposed to be around. Underneath a police car, just an empty police car, behind a police station." She shook her head, still looking down at her tea. "There was a girl, come to see a rookie cop on his break. She was out in back, waiting in the parking lot. She got hit by a tiny part from the car. Just a bit of the outside mirror, the paper said, but it was enough to blind her." Lucy raised her head. Her eyes were wet. "Don't you suppose everyone knows that wasn't supposed to happen?"

"I'm not here about that."

She pulled a piece of paper towel from a roll on the table and dabbed at her eyes.

"It was Michael who built the bomb?"

She shook her head, hard. "No. Like Nadine, he had no idea the others were planning a bomb. It scared him. It made him angry. He was just home from Vietnam. He'd seen the horror, the wrongness of violence. All he wanted was for others to see that, too. But in the end, the people who'd built that bomb were no better than the people they were protesting against. That's what war does, Michael said: It infects everybody."

"And after the police car blew up?"

"The ones who'd set the explosive took off, shocked and scared by what they'd become. Nadine dropped out of school, came up here."

"What about Michael?"

"He'd learned electrical in the Army and went down to L.A. to work construction. It was no different down there. The craziness was everywhere, and it wore at him like an infection. He told Nadine he was going to check out the heartland, the Midwest, to see if things were less agitated there." She blew her nose with the paper towel. "They were going to get married, you know, Michael and Nadine. But too much had happened. They were both changed people. He took off, and she stayed up here, out of touch with it all, hoping Michael would come back and they could rebuild what they'd had. He never did come back."

"But he calls."

She shook her head. "He never did come back."

"Betsy down at the store said he calls every few months."

Lucy shook her head again.

"And he sends her money."

She dropped her eyes, and her hand moved again to the pocket of her sundress.

"That twenty was from Michael, wasn't it?"

She raised her head. "No telling. There's never a letter."

"Why doesn't he write?"

She twisted the piece of paper towel she had in her hand. "What's there to say?"

None of it was making sense. "Is he running? Are the police looking for him for that car bombing?"

"I told you, Michael wasn't involved. When he went down to L.A., he kept on using his right name. If they'd been looking for him, they would have found him easy enough."

"Then why doesn't he write? Why send money with no letter?"

She managed a small smile. "He's been doing that since he left. The message doesn't have to be in words."

"In 1970, his employer sent his paycheck here, after he quit working for them."

She closed her eyes and smiled, thinking back. "For sure, that was strange. The check came with a note saying Michael had listed her name as somebody to contact. Nadine cashed the check and put the money in a cigar box. The money is still here." She dabbed again at the corners of her eyes with the piece of paper towel. "Can you believe, still here after all this time, waiting for him?"

"You have no idea where he is?"

She forced a tight smile and looked right into my eyes. "I wouldn't tell you if I did."

I stood up. "Thank you for the tea."

"Thank you for the mail."

I walked around the table and let myself out the back door. I sat on the stoop to put on my shoes. After a glance backward to make sure she wasn't watching out the window, I fished the blank piece of paper and the envelope out of the plastic tub and stuffed them in my pocket.

I drove back south through Clarinda. The V.W. bus and the faded Reliant were gone from the Inn, their people fortified for another day. After a few miles, I pulled off at an observation point, got out my duffel, and wrapped the envelope and the sheet of paper inside a clean shirt. It was a long shot, but all there had been was long shots. Maybe A.T.F. could find a fingerprint on the sheet of paper.

I watched the waves pound the big rocks down below and thought about Lucy Vesuvius. I'd believed her when she told me that Michael Jaynes, service-trained demolitions expert, disillusioned war protester, skilled electrician, and authentic angry man, had taken off for the Midwest long ago. I'd believed her when she said he never wrote, just sent the occasional ten- or twenty-dollar bill wrapped in blank paper. I'd believed her when she said she'd never tell where he was, whether she knew or not.

And I believed she hadn't seen him, at least not recently. From the way she tore at the envelope I'd brought, she was too hungry for news of him.

It was that envelope that nagged the most. I couldn't figure the twenty-dollar bill she'd just received. It was such small change, enough only for a few groceries. A ten or a twenty might have been all he'd been able to spare in the years past, but now he had half a million, enough to stuff an envelope full of hundreds. But the en- velope I'd brought her, postmarked after the money pickup, had contained only another twenty.

Till's people would have to get on it. I picked up the cell phone to call him. The display still read NO SERVICE. I set it down on the seat, started the Sebring, and drove on.

My phone started chirping with message alerts two miles south of Bodega Bay. I was on the inland stretch then and pulled off on a gravel road next to a horse farm. I punched in my voice mail code. There were seven messages from Leo and four from Stanley.

I got Leo on his cell phone.

"Where the hell have you been, Dek?"

"Surfing, beach parties, hot tubs with implanted California girls—"

"Anton Chernek was arrested by the F.B.I. yesterday afternoon."

I stared at the corral across the road. The horses had stopped moving.

"Dek?"

"I heard you. F.B.I., not A.T.F.?"

"F.B.I., Financial Crimes. One of Chernek's clients accused him of stealing from her account. What's interesting is that the story is on page three of today's *Tribune*, which means the reporters have been tipped there's more than what's in the ink. Embezzlement cases usually are reported in the metro or business sections. So there's more news to come."

"Any mention of the problem I'm working on?"

"None yet."

I stared at the horses.

"Maybe you were right, Dek. Needing money bad enough to embezzle from clients might have made the Bohemian desperate enough to extort money from Gateville."

# Twenty

Stanley had been frantic when I called him from California, insisting I return immediately. "Santa Rosa, Michael Jaynes, give all that to Agent Till," he'd said, breathing hard into the phone. "I need you here."

I caught the next flight back to Chicago and landed at nine fifty that night.

Even without his pale blue uniform, Stanley was easy to spot in the crowded terminal. He was pacing back and forth by the entrance to the parking garage, his lips moving silently. He looked like a man trying to talk himself into a heart attack.

"Thank God you're back." He moved to take my duffel. We tugged; I won, and hung on to it as we moved up the walkway to the garage.

"Boy, was I glad when you called," he was saying. "I didn't want to keep leaving you messages, but the Board is expecting me to handle it all." He spoke in a rush, like there were a thousand words in his mouth, each fighting to get out first.

He led me down one of the aisles to the blue full-size Chevy van with the wheelchair lift that he'd driven to Ann Sather's restaurant. We climbed in, and he started the engine.

"I told Mr. Ballsard we've got to stay on our guard, but he's not listening. He thinks it's over."

"He thinks it's Chernek?"

Stanley nodded. He threw the van into reverse, took his foot off the brake, and gave it too much gas. The van lurched backward, cutting off an S.U.V. creeping toward us, looking for a space. The driver hit the brakes, honked, and shot his fist out the window, a finger in the air. Stanley, oblivious, jerked the shifter into drive and punched the van forward.

"Slow down, Stanley, and tell me what you know."

"I don't know squat." In the halogen lights of the garage, his knuckles were white on the wheel as he steered the big van down the tight curve of the exit ramp. "Just that Mr. Ballsard seems so sure it's over."

At the bottom, he shot across several lanes without looking, rocking to a stop at an open pay gate. I told him to pull over after he paid, so we could talk. And live. He steered off to the side and put the van in neutral.

"Start with what you heard from the police."

"Mr. Ballsard got a heads-up from Chief Morris that the Feds were going to arrest Mr. Chernek on a charge of embezzlement."

"Who made the charge?"

"Miss Terrado. She used to live at Crystal Waters with her parents. She sold the house after they died." He reached for a folded newspaper on the floor between the front seats and handed it to me. "This morning's *Tribune*. It says Miss Terrado is accusing Mr. Chernek of stealing two hundred thousand dollars from her accounts by putting it into a phony investment."

"Could it be true?"

He shrugged. "I wouldn't know about things like that."

"Take a guess."

"We should get going. I need to be home." He put the van into drive and pulled out of the garage exit. I held my questions, deciding my chances of survival were greater if I didn't interrupt while he drove.

He didn't speak again until after he'd turned onto Fifty-fifth Street. "You can imagine, in my job, I hear stuff." He sounded reluctant, like he felt he was ratting out his own brother. "Most of it's baloney, just gossip, but did you notice the empty desks at Mr. Chernek's office?"

"Hard to miss. I heard he was losing clients, and that his staff was leaving, but I also heard that's normal when the stock market is rocky."

"I've been at that office plenty, Mr. Elstrom, and I can tell you, there used to be people crawling all over those offices, crowding the aisles." He looked over at me. "You notice his reception room?" The van drifted toward the shoulder.

"Watch the road, Stanley. Yes, I noticed."

"Anybody ever waiting when you went in?"

"I came late in the day, both times."

"Doesn't matter. That reception room used to be packed with people waiting to see Mr. Chernek or one of the associates. No more. And then there's the mail."

"The mail?"

"You know we inspect the mail at Crystal Waters? Examine the envelopes, and irradiate anything that looks suspicious?"

"For anthrax?"

"That, and other stuff. We got a service that picks up every day, nukes anything we don't like the look of. I can't help noticing a lot of the Members have started getting envelopes from new investment companies like Paine Webber, Salomon, Merrill Lynch. Places that do what Mr. Chernek does. And people from those places have started coming to Crystal Waters for appointments at night, too, with the Members that used to use Mr. Chernek."

"People blame their investment advisors when their portfolios tumble. They look for a change." I shifted on the seat to look at him. "Do you really think losing clients gives Chernek a motive for extortion?" I remembered when I'd asked the same question of Leo.

Stanley kept his eyes straight ahead, his mouth closed. He wasn't ready to take that step. But his silence was loud.

I turned back to look out the windshield at the taillights speeding past Stanley's now-sedate thirty-five miles an hour. We drove in silence for several minutes until he turned north toward Rivertown.

"What am I going to do, Mr. Elstrom? What if Mr. Ballsard is wrong, what if it's not Mr. Chernek, what if there's another bomb?"

"Have you talked to Till?"

"All this just happened yesterday afternoon."

"Call him. Ask if we can come in for an update."

"Then what?"

"That depends on Till. Where's Chernek now?"

"I suppose at home." Stanley pulled up in front of the turret. "I almost forgot. How was California?"

It was only that morning that I'd drunk peppermint tea with Lucy Vesuvius. It seemed like it had been a year ago.

"I found Nadine Reynolds. She goes by the name Lucy Vesuvius now. Michael Jaynes has been sending her bits of money ever since he left California in 1970, but she says she hasn't seen him."

"Do you believe her?"

"There's more. The lady at the store in Clarinda told me that a man named Michael, or somebody else, calls every few months, inquiring about Nadine Reynolds. Lucy didn't admit that."

He cut the engine. "What do you mean, 'or somebody else'?"

"Something about the Michael Jaynes lead doesn't add up."

"Like what?"

"I don't know, Stanley."

"So you think it could be Mr. Chernek, too?"

I opened the van door, grabbed my duffel, and got out. "I think your bomber could be Michael Jaynes. And yes, it could conceivably be Anton Chernek. But I also think it could be Bob Ballsard, some other Member, or anybody else who's gotten into Crystal Waters in the past few months. So I also like 'or somebody else.' Call me when you get us set up with Till." I gave him a wave as he started the engine and pulled away.

I pulled out my mail from the tin box, unlocked the door, and went in. The turret smelled like the inside of a varnish can. I opened a couple of the slit windows, turned on a fan, and ate a peanut butter sandwich standing up while I read through my mail. An unstamped City of Rivertown envelope smelling of coconut was under the electric bill. On city stationery, Elvis had written, "Absolutely no pink roof will be allowed," and had drawn two quick circles around the rendering of the turret in the upper right-hand corner. I wadded it up and threw it toward the garbage can. I missed.

With the Bohemian a suspect, and Ballsard convinced the matter had ended, I was probably out of a job. Maybe that was a good thing.

I finished the sandwich, washed my hands twice to get rid of most of the smell of coconut, and went up to the third floor. As I opened windows, I noticed a dark sedan parked down on the street, in the shadows past the streetlamp. Lovers, I thought, watching the submarine races on the river.

I needed that kind of youth, that kind of optimism. I sat on the cot, threw my clothes toward the chair, and dropped my crowded head onto the pillow. I'd had too much to think.

Till's office was on the fourth floor of a beige box on South Canal Street in Chicago. Stanley and I were escorted to a beige conference room at the end of a beige hall at ten the next morning. A splash of real color in that place probably would have caused a stampede.

Till was already there, in his brown suit. "Tell me about Nadine Reynolds," he said, his face its usual scowl.

I'd put the blank sheet of paper and the envelope addressed to

Nadine Reynolds in a plastic bag. I set it on the table.

"She was Michael Jaynes's girlfriend when he took off for the Midwest late in 1969. Ever since, I think he's been sending her small bits of money in envelopes like that one. Notice the postmark and the computer font."

He held the bag up and examined the envelope and the blank sheet of paper. "She says these are from Michael Jaynes?"

"She likes that idea."

"Never a letter?"

"Just a blank piece of paper, like that one, wrapped around the money."

"You believe her?"

"About that part, yes, but she says she hasn't seen nor spoken to him since he left California."

"You don't believe her about that?"

"The lady at the general store in Clarinda told me a guy named Michael—he doesn't leave a last name—calls every once in a while, asking about Nadine Reynolds."

Till straightened up in his chair. "What did this Lucy say about that?"

"She didn't. She just shook her head."

"And that was enough to stop you from asking anything more?"

"Nadine changed her name to Lucy Vesuvius years ago. She's been living the hippie dream in the hills north of San Francisco since Michael Jaynes took off, giving card readings, getting by with a small garden, probably growing her own weed. I don't think she's seen him since. If they'd been communicating, he'd know about her name change. He wouldn't be sending cash to her, or calling the local store asking about her, using her old name."

"Why does he send her money?"

I shook my head. "She doesn't question. She's just grateful."

"For a ten or a twenty?"

"For the contact."

"Did she say why he's hiding?"

"I didn't tell her he disappeared. She said they were both on the fringe of a group that set off a bomb that blinded a bystander, but she swears neither she nor Michael was involved, and that Michael didn't go into hiding."

"What else did you learn from Lucy Vesuvius?"

"She grows her own tea."

Till smiled a little twitch of a smile. "What kind?"

"Peppermint."

"Did you get high?"

"Not that I noticed."

The little smile disappeared. "Then how can you believe Michael Jaynes has had no communication with her other than to send her bits of money, or to call once in a while, asking somebody else about her?"

"I didn't say I believe anything. I said she believes it."

"Did you stop to think maybe he's sending her some sort of prearranged signal?"

"Send your own guy to interview her, Till. Someone more cunning."

He shrugged. "She said all the payments have been postmarked from Chicago?"

"Just like that one," I said, pointing to the envelope in the bag.

"I don't suppose you thought to get that twenty he sent?"

"I thought fingerprints on paper money . . ."

"It would have been a remote chance, but it would have been nice to try. I'd feel a lot better if we could tie Michael Jaynes to these with a fingerprint." He tapped the plastic bag containing the blank sheet of paper and the envelope.

"What about Chernek?" I asked.

Till leaned back and clasped his hands together behind his neck. "Chernek's not my case. That's F.B.I."

"Come on, Till."

He dropped his hands. "I've been briefed, that's all. Over the past year and a half, the value of the funds Chernek manages for his clients has declined substantially. A big chunk of his client base left him to go to other money managers. His business is down, he's lost many of his associates, he's having personal money problems. And he likes to live big. Nice office, nice house, nice things. So when one of his clients contacted the Bureau, accusing Chernek of diverting funds, they looked into it. Funny accounting gets immediate attention these days. And the Bureau saw enough to get a warrant for his arrest."

"You had nothing to do with that?"

"Ask me what you really want to know, Elstrom. Ask me if Chernek's money problems give him a motive. Only an idiot wouldn't see that. And though I'll deny it, it's why we grabbed him as quick as we did. If he's got potential, we need him neutralized."

"He's out on bail now?"

"They had him less than two hours. The kind of connections he's got, they did real good having him that long." He turned to Stanley, who hadn't said one word so far. "What's going on at your end?"

"Mr. Ballsard will be the chief contact for the investigation instead of Mr. Chernek."

"I meant about evacuating Crystal Waters."

"I don't think Mr. Ballsard has made up his mind."

"Jesus, Novak."

"I'll tell him you're concerned, Agent Till."

Till leaned forward in his chair. "Tell Ballsard to quit dodging my calls, or I'll have him brought down here. Tell him Chernek's arrest means nothing. He must get his people out of Crystal Waters, send them to their summer homes or wherever people like that go, until we know what we're doing. Tell him if he doesn't get those people out of there, I'll call the press and spread the word like I'm ringing a bell."

Perspiration beaded across Stanley's scalp.

"You don't think it's Chernek," I said to Till.

Till turned to look at me. "I'm ruling nobody out."

"Then why don't you act like it? Don't you think you should be investigating anybody who's had access to Crystal Waters in the last six months?"

"Like the people who plant the shrubs and cut the grass?"

"Among others, certainly."

"I work with what I've got, Elstrom."

"We'll still pursue Jaynes?" I said.

"You mean the A.T.F. should still pursue Jaynes."

"Exactly."

"Our computer artist is doing an aging of his Army photo, to get some ideas of what he might look like now. We'll send it to San Francisco and to our offices in the Midwest. They'll send it on to electrical suppliers and contractors. Maybe we'll shake something loose."

"Like you did with Nadine Reynolds?"

Till stood up. We were done.

"I think Mr. Chernek is an honorable man," Stanley said.

"One can hope," Agent Till said.

In the elevator, I told Stanley I was finished with the case.

He was surprised. "Why?"

"I've been working for Anton Chernek, who is now a prime suspect. You've got the attention of the F.B.I. and A.T.F. They need to check out this Michael sighting, sweat Lucy like I can't. And they need to open up the investigation, start considering others beyond the missing Michael Jaynes and Anton Chernek. I can't do any of that, Stanley. It's got to come from A.T.F."

"I'll talk to Mr. Ballsard. I need you to stay involved."

"Ballsard and I . . ."

"I'm sure he no longer thinks about last Halloween. Let me talk to Mr. Ballsard."

In the parking lot, he told me he'd be in touch.

. . .

I called Leo from the car and suggested fine dining at Kutz's. The coarse onions Kutz dropped like carpet bombs on his hot dogs would scour away any lingering effects of the California granola cakes with raspberry. And I wanted to bounce an update off Leo's head.

Traffic outbound on the Eisenhower was light, and I got from downtown Chicago to Kutz's while the line of construction workers and truckers was still a dozen deep outside the order window. I parked at the far end of the lot to wait for Leo and fell asleep.

Stan Getz's saxophone backing Astrud Gilberto woke me up. Leo had pulled up next to me, wearing a Panama hat and the kind of big plastic sunglasses they give to old people after cataract exams. In his enormous purple Hawaiian shirt, he would have looked like a retired jeweler who had wandered away from an assisted living facility in Miami Beach, except that he was driving a brandnew Porsche Carrera convertible with the top down.

"How many miles did last year's Porsche have on it, Leo?" I asked out the open window of the Jeep.

He grinned up at me. "Fifty-four hundred. But Endora saw this color and said I ought to snap it up before they discontinued it."

I stepped down from the Jeep and walked around Leo's new car. It was silver, with a pinkish cast to it. I looked at Leo, still seated behind the steering wheel, in his ridiculous straw hat and black septuagenarian sunglasses and smiled.

"Endora said I'd grow to love the color," he grinned.

I nodded. One of the many reasons I liked Endora was that she melded her eccentricities with Leo's, encouraging Leo to be Leo, only more so. If that meant a pink Porsche once in a while, so be it.

Leo was buying, so I ordered two hot dogs. "My billing client may go under indictment, so you might have to feed me until I collect Social Security," I said as we waited by the window.

"Makes sense." Leo slid the sagging tray carefully off the

counter and carried it to a table in the shade of the viaduct. "Tell me what you learned about Michael Jaynes," he said, shooing away a pigeon and sitting down.

"Don't you want to talk about the Bohemian?"

"In due time. First Jaynes." He picked up a hot dog.

"He calls."

That stopped him. He set down the hot dog.

I told him about Nadine who became Lucy Vesuvius, about the random arrivals of the ten- and twenty-dollar bills over the years, and about the man named Michael who called the store in Clarinda every few months.

"No telling, though, whether it is your Mr. Jaynes?"

"Nor, if it is, if he ever gets up to Lucy's place."

"There's never a letter with the cash?"

"And such a modest amount, at that."

Leo took a bite. "Meaning?"

"Meaning once again this case is defined by 1970 dollars. Dollars that don't make sense."

Leo's eyebrows inched up from behind his cataract glasses, waiting.

I went on. "I believe the money demands—the ten thousand, the fifty thousand, the five hundred thousand—were written back then."

Leo nodded. "You've said that."

"Why use those old notes at all, Leo? Why not write new letters—letters demanding much larger dollars?"

"You've said that, too." He started on his second hot dog.

"Then there's the money Nadine's been getting all along. Ten or twenty bucks would have bought a big bag of groceries back in 1970, but it's not even a tank of gas today."

"It's all he can spare."

"*Could* spare, Leo. The last envelope was postmarked three days after the half million was left behind Ann Sather's. If Jaynes had just come into half a million dollars, wouldn't he have stuffed a lot more into the latest envelope?"

Leo's dark eyebrows were all the way up now, poised just under the brim of his straw hat. "Unless?" he prompted.

"Unless the bombings are not about money at all."

# Twenty-one

I called the Bohemian's office from Kutz's parking lot. Griselda
Buffy answered the main line, put me on hold, and, in less time than
it should have taken, came back on and told me Mr. Chernek would
see me whenever I could make it. I told her I could make it right
away. I hopped on the Eisenhower for the third time that day and got
down to the Bohemian's building in the same time it took to chew a
roll of Tums.

I stepped around a young man in a too-tight dark suit studying
the building directory in the foyer, punched the elevator button,
and rode up.

The reception area was empty. I sat on one of the creased green
leather wing chairs and picked up a two-week-old issue of *Business
Week*. Several subscription cards fell out. Two weeks old, the magazine hadn't been touched.

Fifteen minutes passed. The phone didn't ring; no one came
through the reception area. The only sound came from the grandfather clock in the corner, slowly ticking as if it were fighting the
loss of each minute.

I got up and opened the walnut door to the general office. No typing on keyboards, no opening of drawers, no talking on telephones. The office was dead, like a bus station in the middle of the night after the last bus has pulled away. I walked down a row of empty cubicles to the private offices in back.

Griselda Buffy stuck her head around a filing cabinet, her face startled. In that morgue, I must have sounded like a brass band.

"Mr. Elstrom. I didn't know you were here."

"There's nobody up front."

"I'll tell Mr. Chernek you've arrived."

She went down the corridor, tapped on a door, and went in. I looked around. The secretarial desks were deserted, cleared of papers and pencil cups like the cubicles. The doors to the private offices along the back were closed. I wondered if Griselda Buffy and the Bohemian were the last ones there.

The door down the hall opened. Griselda stepped out and motioned me to come to the Bohemian's office.

"Vlodek," he called out while I was still five feet away, rolling the vowels in his usual robust way. When I walked through his doorway, though, I almost stopped at the change in his appearance. His bronzed country club tan had gone pale, and the white collar of his apricot shirt lay loose around his neck. He sat behind an enormous paneled walnut desk, in a high-back burgundy leather chair that looked too big for him. It had only been three days since I'd seen him, but he looked like he'd shrunk in that time.

"Please, sit," he said. Cardboard file boxes, some with their lids removed, were stacked on the floor and on the four guest chairs. Opened manila folders were spread everywhere. I took two boxes off one of the side chairs, set them on the floor, and sat down.

The Bohemian set down the sheaf of papers he was holding and looked at me across the desk.

"Tell me what's going on," I said.

I thought I saw a faint tremor in his big hands as he folded them on his stomach. "I am accused of stealing from a client, to cover the losses I, and my other clients, have suffered from my poor investments. And, though I have not as yet been accused of anything more, the losses also give me an excellent motive to set off bombs and extort money from Crystal Waters."

"What have you told the F.B.I.?"

"The truth, Vlodek. My accuser, Miss Terrado, suffered losses in her portfolio as a result of my advice. That I do not deny. But so did many other of my clients, as well as many of the people who work here, including myself. I admit I am guilty of not being able to predict the future, but all of Ms. Terrado's investments have been intact; none have been removed from her account. The records will prove that."

"Did you show those records to the F.B.I.?"

"I have not been given the chance. One would assume they would have wanted to review my files before they launched a grandstand play like a public arrest. But they did not."

"Because they like you for the Crystal Waters explosions."

"Yes. They need a suspect on hand, in case another house blows up. I'm available, here and now, unlike our elusive Mr. Jaynes. And because of my undeniable market losses, I do have cause for a motive. Unfortunately, since this is a criminal matter, my lawyers and I don't get to depose my accuser, the government, or their source, the troubled Miss Terrado. I've got to be tried to fight back."

"Tell me about Miss Terrado."

"I have not as yet been formally terminated as her advisor, which is her true goal, so I can't tell you everything, but since the woman is ruining me, I feel I am entitled to certain liberties. She has been liquidating her inheritance to the tune of a million a year, most of which goes for powder for her and her friends to put up their noses. The last asset she's got is the trust account her late parents set up for her with me, with me as administrator. She left that for last because she knew I'd fight her wasting it away, but now she has no choice. She needs the money for her addictions, so she's got to get me off the trust. So she accused me of pilfering. When I'm removed from overseeing her account, the trust reverts to her control, and she can sniff herself into oblivion."

"But you say your records will exonerate you."

He waved at the boxes of files stacked around his office. "That will be in a year or two, in pretrial, when the government is forced to examine my evidence. Unfortunately, the news of my being cleared will be buried in the back section of the paper. By then, I will have long since been ruined." He managed a smile. "I guess I don't need to tell you how this feels."

If it was performance, it was masterful, especially the part that played on my own dissolution. But I liked the idea better that he was telling the truth.

His eyes locked on mine. "They must be convinced I have no potential as a suspect at Crystal Waters. How was California, Vlodek?"

I told him about Lucy Vesuvius, the long-ago police car explosion, and the most recent twenty-dollar bill in the envelope.

"You say Michael Jaynes calls every once in a while?"

"The woman at the store said whoever calls leaves just a first name, and that it is Michael."

The Bohemian's face had regained some of its old healthy color. "That's good. He's taking big chances, keeping up with those calls, now that the bombings have resumed. If we could just get Till to set up a trace on that store phone."

"What's Michael Jaynes been hiding from? Blowing up the back wall of the guardhouse in 1970? You told me it was never reported to the police. Why would he hide?"

The Bohemian shrugged. "Jaynes doesn't know we didn't report it. Or maybe he did something else that caused him to hide all these years."

"I don't buy it."

"What are you saying?"

"I'm not sure Michael Jaynes is involved anymore."

His face flushed suddenly. "Why the hell would you think that?"

"As I told Stanley and Till, a guy who's just scored a half million dollars doesn't keep sending a twenty to an old girlfriend after he's hit pay dirt. He sends more."

"I need Michael Jaynes, Vlodek." He leaned across his big desk. "He disappeared right after the guardhouse in 1970. He didn't pick up his last paycheck. Both actions are consistent with him grabbing ten thousand dollars in extortion money and then taking off."

"Maybe he wrote the notes, planted the D.X.12, and blew up the guardhouse, but he's been gone for too long. I think he collected the money in 1970 and disappeared for good. Changed his name, kept his nose clean, the works."

"Then who is sending the notes and setting off the D.X.12?"

"Someone who wants us to think he's Michael Jaynes."

"Someone else picked up the ball and is running with it?"

"Yes," I said.

"Who?"

"Could be you."

"Shit." He spun his chair to look out the window. The back of his neck was red. After a minute, he spun around. "You find Michael Jaynes."

"I don't know how."

"Learn."

"A.T.F. is involved. They can do more than I can."

"Not for me, they won't."

"They will, if it gets them the truth."

"Find Michael Jaynes, Vlodek."

His phone rang, loud, like an alarm inside a drum. He picked up the receiver, spoke into it, and started shuffling through the folders on his desk. I told him I'd get back to him and went out.

Griselda Buffy sat typing at the reception station, perhaps trying to make the place sound less like a tomb. It wasn't working.

I went down the elevator and crossed the street to the lot. Just as I started the Jeep my cell phone rang.

"How's Chernek?" Till said.

I switched off the engine and looked around the parking lot.

"Crown Victoria, last aisle by the bushes, closest to the street." I picked out the dark green car parked in the shade. "Stick your hand out the window and wave."

I did. A hand waved back. Till was in voice contact with the driver of the green sedan.

"I have a unit by the door on the other side of the building, too," Till said.

"Was that your young man in the ill-fitting suit in the lobby when I went in?"

"Cheap suits are all we can afford on government pay."

"I thought you were too short-handed for Crystal Waters."

"The lads in the two units are rookies on stakeout training. Sitting in hot cars watching doors is the real work of the A.T.F."

"You really think you'll get something that way? He'll spot you."

"He already has. We made sure of it."

"You want him to know you're watching?"

"We like to intimidate. If he's our man, it might prevent him from setting off another bomb. Of course, we've got two other suspects."

"Two others?" I was surprised. "Jaynes and Chernek. You've only got two suspects, total."

"There's you. That's three."

My throat went too dry to fake a laugh. "Me?"

"You work for Chernek."

"Damn it, Till."

"You've got motive, too."

A nerve tingled behind my eyes. He wasn't kidding.

"What motive, Till?"

"You hate rich folks. You married one of them, moved into her fancy house at Crystal Waters, nobody made you feel welcome. Almost right after, you got your face plastered all over the papers for manufacturing evidence, you lost your little business, and now you'd not only shamed your wife, her important father, and your new neighborhood, but you'd bankrupted yourself as well. You were broke. Your wife dumped you, took off for Europe, but let you stay in her house for a month. You sat and drank and plotted revenge. Somehow you'd heard about the bombing of the guardhouse. You got hold of some D.X.12 and a few sheets of old tablet paper. You got creative. You wrote notes, planted a few bombs, before they threw you out, drunk, last Halloween."

"What about the wiring that connects everything together? When did I do that—at night, wandering around drunk?"

"I don't need to put it all together, Elstrom, not yet. It's enough that you interest me."

"Like Jaynes and Chernek?"

"They interest me. But you I really like."

"You've got two suspects."

"Three, Elstrom, and one of the primes hasn't been heard from in thirty-five years. That leaves Chernek, the man with the gold-plated motive, and he's real smart. And you. Not so smart, but still with motive and means."

"I can't believe your gut is telling you it could be me."

"My gut, Elstrom? You know how on T.V., after the second commercial, the wise cop sits on the edge of a desk in some gray squad room, rubbing his belly, shaking his head, and saying, 'My gut tells me . . . ,' and then he names the bad guy?"

"The famed lawman's intuition."

"It's bullshit. My gut's like my ex-wife, been lying to me for years. The times my gut told me I know something, it turns out it's wrong. The only time my gut is right is when it tells me it's hungry, and then I dump chili in it and it shuts up. The rest of the time I ignore my gut and plod."

"Sounds like real law work, Till, pursuing me because you need to plod."

"It's what I can do, Elstrom. It's what I can do."

"What are you doing about Michael Jaynes?"

"Two agents interviewed Lucy Vesuvius this morning. She insists she hasn't seen him."

"What about setting up a trace from that pay phone in Clarinda?"

"And have a man monitoring the line for the next few months, ready to jump on a phone conversation that might be too quick to trace?"

"How are you going to find him?"

"He's disappeared for too many years. If he's not dead, he doesn't want to be found, and he's been damned good at staying hidden. I can't pull agents off other cases for some nut-cake manhunt, but I didn't need to. I had you to chase that wild goose, Elstrom, and you got nowhere. Unless . . ."

He paused, baiting me.

I bit. "Unless?"

"Unless there was nowhere to get to. Maybe you were just trying to fool us all with this Michael Jaynes stuff."

"It's a wrong bet to concentrate only on Jaynes. But you can't forget about him, not if your only other suspects are Chernek and me."

"What do you suggest?"

"Start looking at everybody who has had access—"

"Manpower problems," he said, cutting me off. "What other bright ideas have you been percolating?"

"Those computer-aging photos you said you were going to do."

"You see those things work on T.V.?"

"And at the movies. I bone up on investigating technique in all kinds of places."

"They never work, you know. Too many variables in a person's appearance."

"Why don't you try?"

"They're done. We used Michael Jaynes's Army picture, added a bunch of years, then did four more with baldness, large weight gain, the beard the woman at Universal Electric said he had, and a mustache. I sent them to our branches yesterday."

"And they'll send them to electrical contractors?"

"When they can. Maybe you could get your rich friends at Crystal Waters to blanket electrical firms, too. There's two hundred right now sitting in an envelope in our lobby with your name on it. Come pick them up." He hung up.

Till was too twitchy for me to figure. He was firing blindly in all directions. I would have been all right with that, thinking it might shake something loose, except that one of the places he was aiming was at me.

I pulled out of the Bohemian's parking lot, my eyes in the rearview mirror. Nobody followed me. Maybe Till was just jerking me around about being a suspect.

I drove east the few blocks into downtown, parked in the short-term garage, and went into the A.T.F. offices. As Till had said, an envelope with my name on it was at the first-floor reception desk. I pulled one sheet out.

There were six images: an Army photo and five computer renderings created from it. When he'd enlisted in the Army, Michael Jaynes could have been anybody's fresh-faced boy next door: big smile, round baby features under the Army buzz cut. The computer shots aged him, but in each he still looked harmless, like the guy down the block, in plaid shorts, who cuts his grass every Saturday afternoon before going inside to pop the tab on a brewski and watch the ball game. I slid the sheet back in the envelope, went back to the Jeep, and oozed into rush hour on the Eisenhower Expressway.

Just past Austin Boulevard, the outbound traffic loosened up and I spotted it hanging back, three cars behind, in the far outside lane. Another dark Crown Victoria, this one blue. I changed lanes;

they did, too, maintaining the three-car gap. I sped up; they stayed with me. I slowed down; they backed off. They must have picked me up outside the A.T.F. offices.

I stayed in the outer lane until just before Harlem, then cut left through a hole in the left two lanes, shot up the inside exit, ran the red light at the top of the overpass, and swung right. They might have been rookies, but they were good enough behind the wheel. They swung left across all the traffic, too, and made the exit without drawing a single horn.

I went north, then west on Lake Street. A couple of times, I turned off onto the side streets, but that was just for sport. By then I was sure. They stayed with me all the way to the turret, not bothering to do much to conceal themselves. I got out of the Jeep and walked to the door. They parked a hundred yards down, just off Thompson.

I tried to not think about being under surveillance. I nuked three Lean Cuisines and watched crime shows on my mini T.V. I didn't learn any useful investigative techniques, but at nine o'clock I did remember the piece of lime pie I'd gotten in Bodega Bay. I found the Styrofoam container nestled in my still-unpacked suitcase. The pie was warm and had congealed into a kind of lime mash embedded with sodden specks of crust that had become mostly indistinct, like the information in the Gateville investigation.

I ate the pie and went up to my cot. Before I turned out the lights, I looked out the window. The dark Crown Victoria was still there, in the shadows past the streetlamp.

# Twenty-two

It rained the next morning, so hard the water streamed into the turret like the Devil himself was up dancing on my roof, aiming a pressure hose at the cracks in the tar. The five-gallon pickle buckets I'd scavenged from the deli couldn't catch it all, and for three hours, I raced the rain, emptying old varnish cans, a plastic wastebasket, and the pickle buckets out of the top-floor windows like a third-world washerwoman. Each time, I was tempted to wave a long finger at the boys in the Crown Victoria.

Stanley called late in the afternoon. By then the rain had stopped, though water was still dripping in.

"Mr., Mr. Elstrom—" Stanley started, began again, stammering so badly I cut him off.

"Let me guess, Stanley. Ballsard thinks the matter is over."

"He feels the A.T.F. will keep a close watch on things, and besides, we paid the demand and should be left alone now, anyway."

I asked the question only to hear how he was going to dodge it: "He's not going to evacuate Crystal Waters?"

"You wouldn't believe the extra security we hired. More than when you were last here."

"He's taking a big chance."

Stanley breathed heavily into the phone. "Like I said, with the A.T.F. hunting for Michael Jaynes and watching Mr. Chernek, Mr. Ballsard feels the matter is under control."

I wondered if Stanley knew I'd been added to Till's list. "And if it's not Jaynes or Chernek?"

Stanley paused. "I agree with you about Mr. Chernek. But this Michael Jaynes . . ."

"What if somebody else is doing this? Somebody you're not searching for?"

"Michael Jaynes is sending money to Nadine Reynolds from the same Chicago zip code as our bomb threats."

"A ten- or a twenty-dollar bill?"

"It was all he could afford, Mr. Elstrom."

"He could have sent more after he picked up the half million behind Ann Sather's."

He didn't say anything. I was a broken recording, playing in an empty room.

"You've got to clear out Crystal Waters, Stanley."

"Mr. Ballsard feels—"

I gave it up. "I got some computer-generated renderings from A.T.F., showing what Jaynes might look like now. At least see if you can send them out to electrical contractors."

"I'll pick them up."

"I'll drop them off. I'm going to be out there anyway. It's too late today to call Amanda in Paris, but tomorrow I'm going to get her to authorize me to supervise the removal of her artwork. The bomber hasn't gone away, Stanley, and she needs to get her stuff into a bonded storage house until things are safe again at Crystal Waters."

I looked up at the water dripping from the ceiling. Just a drop every few seconds was all, now.

"Stanley?" I asked after a minute.

"Yes, Mr. Elstrom?" His voice sounded far away.

"I'll let you know when I'll be out with people to pick up her art."

I didn't hear him say good-bye but supposed I'd missed it. I clicked off my cell phone and looked at my Timex. It was just after four o'clock. I called Leo, got him at home. He gave me the name of a firm he used to transport and store valuable art. I called Amanda's answering machine in Crystal Waters, knowing she checked every day for messages, and asked her to call me. Then I hung up the phone and told her I missed her.

I'd been too tired to squint at my tiny T.V. and had gone to bed at nine thirty, thinking of ways to fool myself into sleep. Nothing worked. Too many dark shapes crawled in under my eyelids, each of them carrying bombs. I got up at two forty-five in the morning, made coffee, and took my travel mug up to the roof.

I had just taken a second sip of the coffee, trying to think of nothing at all, when the ground flashed below and blinding light shot up into the sky like a million-watt strobe. I dropped out of the chair, onto the gravel roof, pulling my forearms over my head to shield my eyes from the glare. A roar came then, a big ripping boom that shook the turret. Crazily, I heard my stainless travel cup bounce hollowly some place far away. I pushed down flat against the roof and crab-crawled across the stones to the trapdoor. I found the handle, lifted the door enough to squeeze through, twisted, and dropped through the opening, feet first. I missed the ladder and fell to the floor, pain shooting up from my knees. Miraculously, I stayed on my feet. I reached for the pull rope and tugged the trapdoor closed to the harsh white of the sky outside.

I circled my arms to stay on the ladder down to the fourth floor, rang the metal on the circular stairs as I ran down to the third. The inside of the turret was bright from the fire outside the windows. The cell phone was by my cot, someplace. I got down on my knees, flailed at the floor for my phone. Found it, punched 911. A woman answered instantly, told me they'd already gotten a report. Units were on the way. Anybody hurt? Told her I didn't know, the blast was outside. Go down to the basement, she said, away from another explosion. There was no basement, but there was no time to say that. I clicked off, ran down the next two floors, and out the door.

The shed was a flaming skeleton. All of the siding was gone; the few remaining wall studs stood spindly and black in the orange inferno. Two Rivertown ladder trucks came racing off Thompson Avenue, sirens screaming, just as the uprights collapsed into the pile of burning rubble. What had been a garage-sized shed was now a small bonfire of boards. Start to finish, it hadn't taken five minutes.

Firemen jumped off the trucks, making for the hydrant. A Rivertown fireman with a shield on his helmet came over. There was no hurry now; there was nothing left.

"This place yours?"

I nodded.

"What happened?"

"I don't know. I was on the roof when it exploded."

"On the roof at three in the morning?"

"I do that sometimes."

"The building just exploded?"

"It was just a shed," I said, to say something. My mind was a few feet away, starting to poke at the idea that someone had just tried to kill me.

"What did you have in there?" Behind him, two firemen trained a single hose on the fire.

"Rats. And some half gallons of paint, a can of turpentine, a push lawn mower, a long wood ladder."

"Enough paint and turpentine to set it off?"

"I don't think so."

"We'll be in touch." He turned and walked over to the firemen hosing the fire.

In the shadows, out of the way, Till's two men leaned against their Crown Victoria, watching. One was talking on a cell phone. I wondered if he'd been the one who phoned in the first report.

The fire trucks left at five. I went back inside and lay on the cot, trying to slow my heart by telling myself the explosion had been just a message, nothing more.

Someone pounded on my door at six fifteen. I went down and opened it. It was Agent Till.

I stepped outside. Two men in olive drab padded bomb suits, looking like 1950s television spacemen, poked through the black rubble, gathering bits from the ruin of the shed. Farther down, the Crown Victoria was gone.

"Looking for D.X.12?" I asked.

Till nodded and turned to watch the men.

"When you find it, what conclusion will you draw?"

"That, I do not know."

"I was up on the roof when the thing went off."

He turned back to look me. "Are you one of those guys that likes to watch, Elstrom?"

I stared at him. "I might have been killed."

"Don't be melodramatic." His eyes went back to the men in the bomb suits.

"Then what do you call that explosion, Till?"

"A diversion, to get the scrutiny off you. An attempt against you must then point to somebody else, mustn't it?"

"You're saying I set this off?"

Till shrugged. "Maybe not. Maybe this was just an accidental loss of inventory, some unstable shelf stock of yours that got a little too unstable."

"What did your stakeout boys see?"

"Your inside lights going on a few minutes before the explosion." He looked at my eyes. "And nobody going in your shed."

"It was put there while you were tailing me elsewhere. I'm threatening someone."

He nodded. "Perhaps, Elstrom. Perhaps."

Amanda's home answering machine was full, probably from the messages I'd been leaving all morning. She wasn't answering her cell phone either, though it was only late afternoon in Paris, and caller I.D. would have told her it was me.

She was avoiding me. Somebody—Stanley, a Fed, a Maple Hills cop, maybe even Till himself—had gotten to her, had told her about the explosions at Gateville, and now, the one in my shed. Whoever had called her might have greased it up, saying I wasn't really under suspicion, but they would have let the link dangle, about as subtle as a helicopter hovering over a lawn party, impossible to ignore. Whoever called would have suggested it was best for her to avoid all contact with me until things settled out. I didn't blame her. After my Halloween escapade, and now explosives in my storage shed linking me to Crystal Waters, I wouldn't have talked to me, either.

I passed the middle days of August in a void, isolated from any contact with the Gateville investigation.

I gave up trying to call Amanda. After learning of the potential bombs at Gateville, she would have flown in from Paris, removed her artwork, and gone back. That she hadn't called when she'd been home told me all I needed to know about what must be running through her mind.

Agent Till wouldn't take my calls, either. He must have found D.X.12 in the remains of my shed, because the surveillance on me continued. At no time was I more than a hundred yards from a Crown Victoria, and that was fine. I'd gotten myself to believe the bomb in my shed was a message, not a serious attempt on my life. I didn't understand the message, though, and until I did, I wanted a couple of Till's young men, with their fast feet and semiautomatic weapons, nearby.

I didn't try to call Stanley, and I didn't expect him to call me, not after a chunk of D.X.12 had gone off in my shed. I mailed him Till's composites of Michael Jaynes and assumed he'd sent them out to anybody he thought might be helpful.

The Bohemian took my call, but I only called once, and that was because he was technically still my client. I told him about the D.X.12 explosion in my shed.

"That makes me a suspect now, too," I said.

"You need Michael Jaynes as much as I do, Vlodek."

"Maybe it's not Michael Jaynes."

"Then who, Vlodek?" he shot back.

"Someone who benefits by shifting the suspicion to me."

"Like me?"

When I didn't answer, he swore and hung up.

I tried to play those days light under the constant surveillance, show Till's boys that I couldn't possibly be a bomber. Mornings, I worked outside, cutting up the rubble of the shed, filling a large Dumpster with the remains of the charred wood, exploded paint cans, and odd bits of trash I'd never bothered to throw out. It was hot that August, and the work was deadening, but the sweating passed the time as, down the street, Till's boys watched from a dark Crown Victoria.

Lunchtimes, when he was in town, Leo and I met at Kutz's. I arrived as the head of my very own two-vehicle parade, and Leo thought that a stitch. He told Kutz the guys in the dark sedan were Secret Service, there in case the president of the United States needed my advice on a moment's notice. That didn't impress Kutz, but he was delighted that the young suits always brought big appetites—and rarely made it five feet before bobbling their overloaded, springy plastic trays upside down onto the dirt. Those were good days for government reorders at Kutz's Wienie Wagon.

222          Jack Fredrickson

Afternoons, I'd take the boys on a field trip to the health center, waving at them as I ran my circles. Then we'd troop back to our cars and drive to the turret so I could work indoors and they could watch my front door.

It worked for a time, but after two weeks of long days spent wondering whether a new bomb was coming to take down the turret, of not hearing Till call to report he was closing in on a suspect other than me, of never sleeping more than two hours at a time, and trudging up to the roof to watch the sky to the west, my fingernails began to itch.

Then it rained.

It came blowing and pounding one night, too much to catch in buckets and pickle pails. It poured in from the roof and ran down the limestone walls, to pool temporarily on the fifth floor, until, building pressure, it cascaded through the floor to the floor below. I emptied and mopped and swore all night.

The next morning, when the sun at last came out, I strung up my undies and called the roofer and gave him the go-ahead. I still didn't have a permit, but that only sweetened my rage. I needed a roof, but after two weeks of waiting for Gateville, I needed the gut-emptying release of outright conflict even more.

I made sure to be working outside, two days later, when the roofing crew arrived. It took just seventeen minutes for Elvis to storm over. His skin had worsened.

I told him I was having the roof patched, not replaced. He demanded entry. I told him to get a warrant. He told me he didn't need one. I blocked the door. And so it went, on and off, for three days, while from above, the roofers tossed bits of my old roof from the top of the turret. They were ridiculous, those outdoor arguments in the hot August sun, but good for his complexion. By the time the roofers were done, his skin had noticeably improved. And I had gotten a few solid hours where my stomach wasn't queasy, worrying about Gateville.

. . .

Till finally took one of my calls toward the end of August.

"I take it you found D.X.12 residue by my shed?"

"We're still analyzing."

"Have you tried to find out who might have put it there?"

He chuckled softly into the phone.

I asked other questions. He was polite. Yes, he'd sent out the computer pictures of Michael Jaynes. No, he'd not gotten any responses yet. Yes, it was conceivable there were other suspects, but Chernek and I remained the primes. No, he had no one else specifically in mind. Yes, the best course was to evacuate Crystal Waters. No, he couldn't enforce that. And no, he couldn't comment on the Chernek investigation; it wasn't his case.

"Bullshit to all of that," I said.

"Absolutely," he said.

And the last days of August dribbled away slowly, like water down a clogged drain.

Until early in the morning of August 30.

# Twenty-three

They were battering down my front door, BAM BAM, BAM BAM, fast and loud in a one-two tattoo. I rolled off the cot, onto the floor, came awake. BAM BAM, BAM BAM, the pounding was closer now, as if men in heavy boots had gotten inside and were charging up the stairs, but it was the turret echoing, the metal stairs reverberating in sympathetic vibration with the timbered door.

The sky was black outside the slit windows. I rubbed at my eyes. The big red digital letters on my clock said it was three in the morning. Down below, the pounding went on: BAM BAM, BAM BAM. I grabbed my jeans and yesterday's knit shirt from the chair, pulled on my Nikes, and ran down the stairs.

"Stop it!" I yelled through the door. I swung it open and switched on the outside light.

Two fresh-faced young suits stood under the light, looking like choirboys hawking chocolates to send their youth group to Salt Lake City to sing in the nationals. Except it was three in the morning. And they were holding A.T.F. photo I.D.'s.

"He's here, sir," the blonder of the two said into a cell phone. He listened, nodded, and clicked the phone off with his thumb. "Please come with us, Mr. Elstrom."

I took half a step back from the glare of the outside light. They both stepped forward.

"Am I being arrested?"

"Agent-in-Charge Till instructed us to bring you to Crystal Waters."

The air went out of my lungs. "What happened?"

"Please come with us, sir," Blonder said.

They walked me to the Crown Victoria. The other agent, the one with darker hair, opened the back door for me, and I got in. They sat in front. As Agent Blonder twisted the key, I started pressing with questions. Without turning around, Agent Other cut me off, saying their instructions were merely to drive me to Crystal Waters. Agent Till would speak to me there. We sped out of the dark of Rivertown in silence.

I didn't have to wait the whole ride. I saw it in the sky above the ridge from two miles away: a bright red glow pushing at the black of the night like blood spilling into ink. I thought of yelling at the agents to tell me what was going on. But I didn't. I knew. And as we got to the top of the ridge, I saw.

Flames punched high into the sky from inside the walls of Gateville, looking from the top of the ridge like a bonfire for giants. A hundred flashing red and blue lights, some still, some moving, ringed the inferno, down Chanticleer and out onto the highway. Fire trucks, ambulances, and police cars.

The inside of the Crown Victoria went white as headlamps came racing up from behind. A siren screamed. Blonder jerked the wheel and skidded onto the gravel shoulder as the fire truck raced past us. A hundred yards ahead, a Maple Hills police officer, lit up like prey in the glare of the fire engine's headlights, yanked a wooden barricade out of the way a fraction of a second before the truck flew through.

Blonder checked his rearview mirror before pulling cautiously back onto the road. Holding his I.D. out the window, he coasted down to the police officer and stopped. The cop examined it in the glare of his flashlight and waved us through. Blonder drove the rest of the way down the hill hugging the shoulder, and pulled off the road two hundred yards short of the marble pillars. He shut off the engine.

Fire seemed to engulf the entire western half of Gateville. Flames shot up fifty, one hundred feet, spiking jagged yellows and oranges high into the air. I looked for the greatest concentration of flames, the highest density of flashing red and blue lights.

It was right where Amanda's house was.

I pawed the door, fumbling for the handle. It was locked, from the front seat.

"Let me out," I yelled.

Blonder started to say something, but a diesel fire truck pulled up next to us, blocking out his voice. I slapped at the window button. It was shut off, too.

"Let me out," I shouted. I pressed my face against the glass, straining to see past the police cars and ambulances parked on the highway, past the uniformed police officers, white-shirted E.M.T.'s, and others in civilian clothes standing frozen on the blocked-off highway, watching the sky burn inside the wall.

The fire truck pulled away.

"That's my wife's house," I yelled.

Blonder turned. "No, sir, that's the house across the street from your ex-wife's." He opened the driver's door and got out. Other shifted on the front seat so he could watch both me and the conflagration outside. They weren't going to let me out.

Blonder crossed the highway and walked up to a Maple Hills policeman standing by the gate. Another Maple Hills officer sidled up to join them, his right hand resting lightly on the pistol holstered by his side. Blonder said something to the first policeman;

the officer touched the tunic radio clipped to his epaulet and spoke into it. A minute later, the officer motioned for Blonder to go in.

Just then, a sudden gust of fire shot up, and for an instant, the very top of the dark gray roofline of Amanda's house stood bright in silhouette against the orange sky, a few hundred feet from the center of the fire. I took a breath, relieved. The air coming in from Agent Other's open window in front was acrid and stank of a chemical fire.

I leaned forward on the backseat and tried to sound calm. "Can't you tell me anything?" I asked Other.

Other didn't take his eyes off the fire across the highway. "Agent Till called for us to pick you up and bring you here."

"How about we get out and stand by the car?"

He grunted a no. I gave up and watched the flames poke at the sky. For thirty minutes, they raged higher and higher, showing no signs of diminishing. Then Agent Blonder came out of the entrance, crossed the street, and opened my car door.

"Agent Till would like to speak with you now, sir."

I went with Blonder across the closed highway to the gate. The Maple Hills officer stood aside, and we went in.

To the right, both sides of Chanticleer Circle were lined, bumper to bumper, with fire trucks, ambulances, Maple Hills police cars, and two dark Crown Victorias. We moved down the center of the street, past the lot where the Farraday house had been, to the curve.

To the left, a dozen firemen in yellow slickers wrestled big tan hoses like giant pythons, aiming streams of water into the flaming pile. The roof and the walls were gone, but I remembered the house. It had been one of the largest in Gateville, a redbrick, gray-roofed Victorian, with at least five bedrooms, a four-car garage, and a solarium off to one side. Now it was a mound of burning wood and smoking bricks.

People from the surrounding houses stood on their lawns, watching the firemen and the police. One pointed at me.

Farther around the curve, Amanda's house loomed in the glare of the fire, pulsing red from the flashing lights sweeping across its arched windows and massive walnut front doors.

Agent Till, wearing khakis and a beige button-down shirt, stood with Stanley Novak on Amanda's driveway. They were talking to a dark-haired young man in a Crystal Waters security uniform. Though the August night was hot, superheated by the fire, Stanley wore a flannel shirt. He looked cold.

Till spotted Blonder and me and motioned for us to come up. Stanley's eyes never left the face of the young security guard. Till turned back to the guard. "Tell me again," he said.

The young guard rocked on his feet, side to side. "There was no warning. One minute everything's quiet as a graveyard, the next second there's a fireball in the sky, followed by a huge boom."

"You're certain nobody ran out just before the explosion?" Till asked.

"Not through the main gate," the guard said. "And we've got four men on perimeter, watching the walls. They didn't see anybody, either."

Till turned to look at the fire across the street. "Damn it."

"At least no one was hurt," Stanley said.

The guard turned to look at him, his eyes wide. "The family was home, Mr. Novak."

Till spun around. "You said the house was dark."

"I meant they were asleep," the guard said.

Stanley's pale face froze in the flash of the red lights. "No. Check the sheet. They went to Door County for the week, left us a phone number for their place up there."

The young guard shook his head. "They came back, Mr. Novak. The father, the mother, and the two little girls."

"Impossible," Stanley said. "I made my last round at eight. They weren't home."

"They got back a couple hours after you left. One of the girls had the flu, so they came home early." The young man's mouth trembled, and he looked away.

Stanley stared at the guard and then made a horrible churdling noise from deep in his throat. He pushed past me to run to two paramedics standing next to an idling ambulance.

"Did you get them out?" he screamed, grabbing one E.M.T. by the shoulders. "Did you get them out?"

The medical technician jerked his arms up and grabbed Stanley's wrists, yelling back that there was no chance of survivors. Stanley struggled, unhearing, trying to wrest himself free of the man's grip. Suddenly, he sagged and fell to his knees. "Shit, shit, shit," he sobbed. "Shit, shit, shit."

I ran over to him and put my hand under his elbow. "Come on, Stanley." I tried to pull him up. He was dead weight.

Till and Blonder came over and, together, we half-carried, half-dragged Stanley away, down Chanticleer toward the guardhouse. He fought us, incoherent, alternately mumbling, then yelling for someone to go into the rubble. At the guardhouse, the guard at the console helped us get Stanley to his desk chair in the back office. Till and I sat down in the metal side chairs across from the desk. Blonder stood in the doorway, right behind me.

Stanley slumped in his chair and looked, unseeing, across the desk.

"Stanley? What did you mean about the family being not supposed to be home?" Till asked.

Stanley's face tightened. He turned and reached for a clipboard hanging on the cinder-block wall behind him, moving his arm like it weighed a hundred pounds. "We have this sheet," he said in a slow, dull voice. He took the clipboard down and dropped it onto the black plastic desktop. "The Members tell us when they'll be gone, so we can keep extra watch . . ." His voice faltered.

"They were dead at the first blast, Stanley," I said. "The paramedics couldn't have done a thing."

Stanley looked out the window, towards the inferno at the west end of Chanticleer Circle. His face was slack, devoid of expression. "Bastards," he said.

I looked at Till, wondering if they had somehow learned that more than one person was involved. Till's face was a blank.

"Let's give him some time, Elstrom," Till said, standing up. I followed him out of Stanley's office. He led me to a quiet space by one of the pillars. Blonder came along, five feet back.

Till turned around. In the glare of the entry lights, I wondered how old he really was. Whatever his age, by the depth of the lines etched in his face, the years had been hard. I didn't want to imagine what it must be like, trying to sleep with a head full of crazies carrying bombs and guns. It took far less than that to send me up to the roof of the turret in the middle of the night.

"Where were you last night, Elstrom?"

"Asleep. Ask your boys."

Till looked past me at Blonder. "You think he was asleep?"

"Come on, Till."

"I don't know, sir," Blonder responded. "Mr. Elstrom spends a lot of time on his roof in the middle of the night, and we can't really see him up there. He could have been awake."

"Watching the sky, waiting, Elstrom?"

"Jesus, Till."

"But he'd been inside all night?" Till asked, still looking at Blonder.

"There's only the front door. We had that covered," Blonder said.

I stepped in front of Blonder so Till would have to look at me. "What are you saying?"

Till looked at me. "Like I told you before, motive and means. You've got both. You're broke. You have a real attitude about this place. And you were left alone in your ex-wife's house for almost a month before getting tossed out. You had plenty of time to plant a few bombs."

"We've done this before, Till. It's just as weak the second time around."

He shrugged.

"That's why you brought me here?"

"It's not just my gut that likes you, Elstrom. My head does, too."

Blonder's breath tickled the hairs on the back of my neck. He'd moved closer, ready to snap handcuffs on me. I moved a step to the side.

"You're grasping, Till. You can't find Jaynes, you can't make a case against Chernek, you won't look for anybody else, so you're aiming at me."

"You really like Jaynes for this, Elstrom?"

"I don't know."

"Chernek?"

"You're blowing smoke on him, trying to force a motive."

"So who fits better than you, Elstrom?"

Behind me, Blonder exhaled softly.

"Maybe the missing man," I said. "The one we don't know about. The one who got in here tonight."

Till watched my eyes. "There was another note, came day before yesterday. Two million."

"They'll never pay two—" I stopped. "It arrived the day before yesterday?"

He nodded slowly, his eyes still locked on mine.

"When was the payment supposed to be made?"

"Four days from now, Sunday night."

"The note arrived day before yesterday, and the bomb goes off tonight? He didn't give the Board time to pay."

Till nodded. "Bingo, Elstrom. Ballsard called me two days ago, screaming, said they'd just received another note, this one demanding that two million be left next Sunday, same place. Ballsard said he couldn't pay, not two million."

"So what was the plan?"

"We were going to surround the drop site, try to grab him."

"There was no way for the bomber to know you weren't going to pay."

"Bingo again." Till's eyes were hot on mine. "The bomber couldn't know he wasn't going to get more money—"

I finished it for him: "—unless he was connected to the investigation."

"Bingo for the third time, Elstrom. You've got all the answers, and that brings us right back to you."

"I didn't know about the new note, Till."

"Unless you sent it."

"Even if I had, I couldn't have known Ballsard wasn't going to pay."

"You could have had ways."

"Why did you pull me out here, Till?"

"I wanted to watch you watch the fire." Till turned to look up Chanticleer. There were only flashing red and blue lights now. The yellow glow from the flames was gone.

"Bingo your ass, Till."

Till smiled.

over the image on the screen. "His name is Michael Jaynes, he is sixty years old, and we believe he may have information about the explosions at Crystal Waters. We don't have a current picture, only an old Army photo, which we have used to prepare several views of what he might look like now. We are asking anyone with any information to call us or the Maple Hills Police Department."

"Any other suspects?" one of the reporters shouted.

The screen flashed back to the lectern. Till was looking right into the camera, like he was looking right into my eyes.

I squeezed the little television with both hands, as if I could keep the screen from showing the photo the *Tribune* had taken of me during the Evangeline Wilts trial. "Don't do this, Till," I heard myself say.

Till paused and then said, "None at this time." He shifted his eyes from the camera lens—and from me. I breathed and relaxed my grip on the television.

"What else can you tell us about Michael Jaynes?" the early morning man from the local Fox affiliate asked.

The cameraman widened the view to include the area to the side of the lectern. Chief Morris, wearing a tight uniform, was standing a full step back and off to the side from Till.

"Unfortunately, very little," Till said. "He was an electrician who worked on the construction of Crystal Waters. We believe he may have gained information back then that pertains to the current situation."

"You're going back to 1970 with this?" a reporter called out from the back row.

"We're being thorough."

"There is speculation that this is actually the third bombing at Crystal Waters this summer, the second being a lamppost outside the walls. What have you been doing since the house explosion in June?"

# Twenty-four

The Bohemian called at seven fifteen, his voice quivering like he was a hundred years old. "Four have died. Turn on your T.V."

"Till hauled me out there. I just got back." I held the cell phone next to my ear as I went down the stairs to the first floor. I'd left my television on the table saw.

"What the hell's happening?"

"Hold on." I switched on the little T.V., fiddling one-handed with the wire antenna until the snow went away. Agent Till was on Channel 7, standing at a plywood lectern in front of the green cinder-block wall at the Maple Hills police station. Black microphones with local T.V. logos were clustered in front of him. The crawler at the bottom of the screen said it was a live broadcast. "I'll call you back," I said, and clicked off. I turned up the volume.

Till was nodding at a perky young thing in a thin sweater. "Of course, we have to assume this explosion is related to the one in June. We're not ruling anything out."

The live shot on the screen switched to the composite renderings of Michael Jaynes. "What you are seeing now is computer-aged pictures of a man we are seeking for questioning," Till's voice said

The room went silent. Behind Till, Chief Morris took another step back. Till gripped the sides of the lectern.

"We're asking residents of Crystal Waters to vacate their homes temporarily—"

Pandemonium broke out as all the reporters began screaming questions at once.

"Are there more bombs?" someone shouted above the din.

"We're going to conduct a house-to-house search for evidence," Till yelled, holding up his hand for quiet.

He waited until the shouting stopped. "We have no reason to believe there are any more bombs. As a precaution, the road outside Crystal Waters is being closed to all public traffic, effective immediately. We need to keep spectators away while we conduct our investigation."

"Are you cutting the electric to Crystal Waters?" a reporter at the front of the throng asked.

To the side and back from the lectern, Chief Morris shut his eyes.

"We might have to shut off the current to check the security of the electrical lines. Again, we're just being thorough."

A female voice: "You mean the bombs might be hardwired into—"

"What about Anton Chernek?" the Channel 5 field man said loudly from the front row, cutting her off. I turned up the volume on the T.V. The Channel 5 man had good sources, maybe good enough to have learned that I was a suspect as well.

"What about Anton Chernek?" Till repeated, looking almost gratefully at the Channel 5 reporter. The other reporters hadn't picked up on the trampled question about hardwiring, the one question that, if answered, would have caused all the television stations to abandon local programming in favor of a vigil outside Crystal Waters, their cameras aimed for the big blow.

"You also have Chernek," the Channel 5 reporter prompted.

Till stared at the reporter, feigning confusion. "We don't 'have' Anton Chernek. We're A.T.F. Mr. Chernek was arrested on an unrelated financial matter by the F.B.I., and he's free on bond. Thank you," Till said abruptly, as he stepped away from the lectern. Chief Morris scrambled after him.

The sweet young thing in the thin sweater filled my four-inch screen. "That's the situation from Maple Hills," she said, signing off, as the screen went to a live helicopter shot of Crystal Waters. From up high, the fire trucks, police cars, and ambulances parked crazily along Chanticleer Circle looked like toys discarded by a monster child.

I stared at the helicopter shot of the charred ruins of the house that had exploded just hours before, the newly landscaped Farraday lot around the bend toward the guardhouse, and, across the wall, the lamppost next to where the school bus shelter had once stood. All were in the same northwest quadrant of Gateville. I kept looking at the screen, still seeing the helicopter shot, long after the picture had cut away to a commercial.

I went outside. This morning's Crown Victoria was black. The two young men inside were pretending to read yesterday's newspaper.

I tapped on the windshield pillar. The agent in the passenger's seat put down the newspaper and looked up at me, acting surprised.

"Tell Till I'm going to see Anton Chernek." I walked away.

Five minutes later, as I finished changing clothes, my cell phone rang.

"Why do you need Chernek?"

"Nice job on T.V., Till. You lied about everything."

"I kept you out of it, Elstrom. Now answer me, or I'll have you brought downtown. Why do you need Chernek?"

"He's got old blueprints of Crystal Waters. I want to look at them."

"For what?"

"For divine inspiration, Till. And for proximity. Have you noticed that all the bomb sites have been clustered together in one section of Crystal Waters?"

"I'll send an agent to get the prints."

"No. Let me talk to Chernek; he's not going to work with you. Besides, you know damned well it isn't him. Or me."

He paused. "Knock yourself out," he said.

I called the Bohemian.

Till must have told the agents tailing me to give me some space. I was already out of the Jeep and going into the Bohemian's building when they pulled into the parking lot.

Griselda Buffy sat at the desk in the empty reception area.

"He's expecting me," I said.

She gestured toward the door to the general office. "*Entrez,*" she said in what might have been flawless French.

The office was a crypt. No one was in the cubicles. I walked to the back.

The Bohemian's door was open. I tapped on the jamb, and he looked up.

"Vlodek," he said, trying to roll the first syllable on his tongue like always. But there was no enthusiasm in it now. He sat small behind his desk, a paled man going through the motions. On a table in the corner, a small color television flickered, its sound turned off. He motioned to a chair.

"A man, his wife, two daughters barely starting school." His voice was dry, raspy. His eyes searched my face. "How can they think I did this?"

"They don't. Remember, they're watching me, too."

"Agent Till mentioned Michael Jaynes on T.V. Are they getting close?"

"I doubt it. Till said that to give the illusion he had a lead."

"Was there a note like the other times?"

"Two days before. Two million. But the bomber didn't wait for the reply."

The Bohemian put his elbows on his desk and leaned forward. "What is to be done?"

"I'm here to look at your blueprints again."

He sank back in his chair. "Surely you don't think I'm involved in the explosions."

"No."

"You don't think I would kill a man, a woman, and two little girls." His eyes looked like they were pleading.

"No."

"Why not?"

"You give people chances, not take them away. Like you did when you hired me."

He gave me a tired smile. "I'd like to take credit, but it wasn't me. Your friend Stanley said you would be ideal and could use the work. I liked the spirit of his suggestion and recommended it to the Board." He pushed himself up. "Let's get the blueprints."

We went to a storage room. He unlocked a cabinet and took out the big paper roll. As he did, he dislodged a tan folder that fell to the floor. He leaned the roll against the cabinet, bent down to pick up the folder, and handed it to me. "I found this among the other papers. The sales brochure. Very selective, very private. We only printed three hundred and didn't use half of them. As you know, the sites sold out immediately." He picked up the roll of blueprints and locked the cabinet, and we walked down the hall. "Might as well use the big conference room. Keep the dust off the table."

He switched on the lights in the large room we'd used only a few weeks earlier, when Till, Chief Morris, Stanley, the Bohemian, and I had met to strategize. Just a handful of weeks. Now a whole family was dead because the people in that room couldn't put anything together.

The Bohemian set the drawings down on the table. "I will leave you to it, Vlodek," he said, and went out.

I sat midway down one side of the table and started to unroll the blueprints, but then set them aside and picked up the manila folder the Bohemian had handed me. The sales brochure inside was printed on the kind of heavy tan parchment stock they use for menus at high-end restaurants. CRYSTAL WATERS, the cover proclaimed in two-inch dark brown script. Stacked below, one word per line, it read: BEAUTY. TRANQUILITY. SECURITY.

The first five of the six inside pages presented lavish half-tone drawings of the various stone and brick houses that were going to be constructed. Each residence was shown surrounded by mature trees and featured a view of the fountain in the middle of the pond. Superimposed on the renderings were short, pithy blurbs in tall script: "Secure in our world," "Safe, because our children trust us," and, across one idyllic scene of a family picnicking under an oak tree, "Chanticleer Circle, the safest street in America." The bottom of every page was bordered, side to side, with a drawing of the brick wall that would enclose the development.

With serene drawings and soothing words, the marketing people had rendered the perfect world well. The only thing they'd missed was a sketch of the Stepford Wives, sauntering along in gingham, clutching bouquets of daisies.

The sixth page was the only one that gave details. As I started reading, I recognized the verbiage; they were the same words that had been used by the corn soufflé lady in the *Maple Hills Assembler* before Crystal Waters had been built.

I reread the closing paragraph several times. "From the impenetrable walls that enclose the community, to the fireproof construction, the security of the guardhouse, and the safety in the underground shelters, Crystal Waters will be the safest community in America."

*Underground shelters.*

I unrolled the drawings, flipping quickly over the grading elevations, landscaping details, drainage specifications. I was looking for specifications for concrete, any kind of concrete. The road specifications were there, along with the foundations for the guardhouse, the fountain in the pond, even the base of the wall. But there was no information about underground shelters.

Without the torn-off index sheet, I couldn't know for sure, but it was likely that at least some of the missing blueprint pages had to do with the underground shelters.

I rerolled the prints and took them to the Bohemian's office. He was reading a computer printout on his desk, eating a small bowl of cottage cheese. "About the only thing my stomach can tolerate these days," he said, gesturing with his spoon.

I leaned the roll of blueprints against the side of his desk. "Any chance the missing blueprints I told you about before had to do with bomb shelters?"

He set down the cottage cheese. "As I said, I keep the prints; I don't use them."

"It was you, though, wasn't it, who drew light *X*'s on the Farraday house and on the old bus shelter?"

He nodded. "I was wondering about their closeness to each other."

"And the house that just went up, that was close to the other explosion sites."

"Yes."

I set the brochure in front of him and opened it to the last page. "The last paragraph says there are underground shelters in Crystal Waters."

He looked down at the brochure and read.

"They were never built," he said, looking up when he was done.

"Why not?"

He pointed to the roll of blueprints I'd leaned against his desk. "Set those up here and I'll show you."

I put the roll on his desk, site plan on top. With a pencil, he drew five evenly spaced square hubs along Chanticleer Circle, centered within the edges of the street. "There were to be five bomb shelters, built under the road for additional protection," he said.

Next, he connected each house to a shelter with double lines, in clusters of five or six houses for each shelter. "These were to be the tunnels, running from each basement to the shared shelter." The tunnels fanned out from each shelter to a rough circle of individual houses. "I think some of the tunnels might have spurred off of one another, depending on the layouts of the houses, but this was the general idea." He studied the clusters he'd drawn. They looked like five rimless wagon wheels running along Chanticleer Circle.

"That was the plan, anyway." He picked up his cup of cottage cheese. "Narrow escape tunnels leading from the houses to central shared shelters under Chanticleer Circle, capable of withstanding a massive blast."

"You say they were never built."

"The first buyers weren't comfortable with the idea of shared underground vaults. One who objected was your former father-in-law, Wendell Phelps."

"Better to die than sweat together in fear?"

A tiny smile flitted across his face. "Perhaps, but by the time Crystal Waters was built, the big fear wasn't nuclear war. It was the riots, the fires, the uprisings of the students and the poor, storming the citadels of the rich. Bomb shelters couldn't protect against that. In fact, the shelters planned for Crystal Waters could be a threat. As Wendell, among others, pointed out, those tunnels were a way into the homes. Someone could break into one home, go through its tunnel to a shelter, and from there break into other homes. Wendell was right. The developers reconsidered and filled them in."

"You just said they weren't built. How could they be filled in?"

He tossed the cottage cheese cup in his wastebasket, picked up a pencil, and tapped the eraser on one of the hubs he had drawn along Chanticleer Circle. "The shelter vaults under Chanticleer Circle had to be built before the road was laid. I guess it would have been the tunnels that had to be filled in."

"So the shelters are still there, under the road?"

He shrugged. "I would presume so."

"And the tunnels going to them?"

"As I said, Vlodek, the idea was scrapped."

"And the tunnels were filled in? Filled in, or never built?"

"Filled in—" He stopped when he saw the look on my face.

"For sure?"

He started to shake his head, then froze as the impact of what I was asking hit him.

"Where were the entrances to the tunnels?"

"Small openings, maybe three feet square, through the basement walls."

"How about air shafts? Other ways in?"

"I don't know. Shit, I don't know."

I looked down at the rimless wagon wheel he'd drawn in the northwest quadrant of the development. I grabbed a fountain pen from a tray on his desk, unscrewed the cap, and started darkening the blueprint lines with black ink. From the hub under the road, one spoke went to the site of the Farraday house. A second led to the house that had just exploded. I darkened the lines of a third tunnel and looked at him.

His mouth worked for a minute before the words came out. "Amanda's house," he said. He looked up from what I had drawn. "Did you ever see an entrance in the basement?"

"There was none. But I only lived there a few months. I never had reason to examine the basement wall."

"I don't think the entrances to the tunnels were ever cut in."

"You don't think, or you don't know?"

He started to say something, but I already had my cell phone out, punching in Till's number. I got his machine. I clicked off, called Stanley, got his voice mail, too. All of Gateville could be blown to the moon with the flip of one switch, and nobody had time to answer the damned phone. I told Stanley's machine to tell Till to comb the grounds looking for air shafts leading down to tunnels and to begin in the northwest quadrant, where the two exploded houses had been. I said to check every basement for ways into the tunnels, starting with Amanda's house.

I said that was where the bombs were.

# Twenty-five

I was leading my two-car parade home on the Eisenhower, the Crown Victoria tight behind, when Stanley called. "It's a mess here, Mr. Elstrom," he yelled into the phone, trying to be heard above what sounded like large truck engines. "The Members won't leave without their furniture and clothes. Everybody has hired moving trucks, and now Chanticleer Circle looks like rush hour downtown. Gridlock. Agent Till is bringing in tow trucks to clear the street so he can get his own equipment in, but I don't know how long that will take."

I took the next exit off the expressway, swung into the corner of a gas station, and cut the engine so I could hear. The Crown Victoria screeched to a stop behind me.

"Stanley," I shouted into the phone, "do you know anything about underground tunnels and bomb shelters at Crystal Waters?"

The sound of diesel motors at his end was deafening. I didn't think he heard me. "I said, do you know anything—"

"Tunnels?" he shouted back. "I never heard that, except from your message. There are no tunnels here."

"I think you're wrong. Get Till to comb every lawn, every foundation, every basement, looking for ways into those tunnels. I think the D.X.12 is hidden there."

The sound of truck engines got louder.

"Stanley?" I yelled into the mouthpiece.

"Got it, Mr. Elstrom. Tunnels. I'll tell Agent Till."

"Start with Amanda's house."

"You don't think Miss Phelps—"

"Of course not," I shouted. I took a breath, trying to slow down so I could be precise. "It's because her house is so close to the two that have been blown up and because it's been unoccupied. Tell Till to start there."

"I'll tell him, Mr. Elstrom. Wait at home until you hear from us." He clicked off.

I drove to the turret. Before getting out of the Jeep, I picked up the cell phone, toying with the idea of calling Amanda. I could use the pretext that I was making sure she'd gotten her artwork out of Gateville, but it would be pointless. She knew about the bombs and knew about the link between them and me. It was why she hadn't been taking any of my calls.

I put the phone in my pocket. I couldn't repair anything over the phone.

I got out of the Jeep. I didn't recognize the two young agents back in the Crown Victoria, trying to appear to be looking everywhere but at me, but they looked the same as the others: dark suits, white shirts, close haircuts. Till must have had dozens of them. I gave them a nod, which they ignored, and walked up to the turret, scanning the ground around the base for small packages, containers, anything big enough to hold an explosive. It was my habit now, since the shed had gone up. I did the circle, unlocked the heavy door, and went in.

It was only eleven thirty in the morning but I had a hundred pounds of fatigue clamped to the base of my neck. From too many nights on the roof, I supposed, watching the sky over Gateville. But things were ending. Till was up to his knees in Gateville now. He was taking things apart; he'd find the tunnels. Then he would find the D.X.12, or at least the wiring, and no one else would die.

I went upstairs to the third floor and lay on the cot and checked out.

A cold gust of wind blew in from the river, arcing the metal slats of the window blinds into a crazed kind of St. Vitus' dance. It was dark, the only light in the room a gauzy, narrow beam from the moon outside the slit window. I pulled the blanket over my ears to shut out the clatter and tried to will myself back to sleep, but images of what must be going on at Gateville, of diesel searchlights and teams of men in bomb suits, probing the grounds, going into tunnels to rip things out, popped me all the way awake. I squinted at the clock. It was twelve thirty in the morning. I'd slept for thirteen hours.

I put on my jeans, Nikes, and the red sweatshirt, stenciled with I LOVE ARKANSAS in green below a Tweety Bird, that I'd gotten at the Discount Den during Bill Clinton's impeachment hearings. I like to be stylish, even in the middle of the night. I went downstairs to make coffee.

I filled my travel mug, grabbed a two-pack of Twinkies, and went outside. A Crown Victoria, black in the white light of the moon, was in the usual spot, a hundred yards down. I recognized Agent Other behind the wheel, Agent Blonder riding shotgun. I smiled at them, held up my Twinkies in salute, and rejected the idea of asking them for an update about Gateville. They wouldn't tell me; zipper-lips was the first commandment of being a junior G-man. No matter, things were under control.

I walked down to the bench by the river. Behind me, the Crown Victoria started up and eased quietly forward to keep me in sight. I sat on the bench, and the car's engine stopped.

I sipped coffee and took small bites of a Twinkie, making it last.

For the first time since Stanley Novak had come to see me in June, the greasy tingle of impending disaster was gone from my gut. I felt good, rested. Things were going to get better.

Trucks rumbled along the tollway. Somewhere closer a railroad signal clanged, and Rolling Stones music filtered out of one of the joints along Thompson Avenue. Mick was complaining about getting no satisfaction. Right, Mick. And from a car parked in the dark fringes of the city hall lot, a woman laughed, not in joy but in need. Too bad she couldn't hook up with Mick, I thought; they could do each other some good.

Normal sounds; Rivertown sounds.

I slid the second Twinkie out of the package. It was cool for the end of August, and I was glad for the sweatshirt. I looked up. The sky was that startling black that comes when there is a full moon and the summer air has suddenly gone crisp. The lights along the river stood out bright in the night, temporarily freed from the humid haze that shrouds them in summer. It was a good night, a clear night.

I watched the river reflect lazy silver ripples in the moonlight, ate slowly at the Twinkie. By now, Till's men were in the tunnels. I imagined dozens of them hand-digging, pulling out wires and packets of D.X.12. With luck, they'd also be pulling out evidence that would lead them to the bastard that had set off the bombs. And that would finish it forever. There would be epic battles with insurance companies, and people like Bob Ballsard were going to lose a lot more than his inventory of boat shoes, and Amanda might lose her house. But she'd still have the art. And no one else would die.

I checked my watch. One thirty. I finished the last of the creamy white nutrient they inject for health reasons into Twinkies and went back up to the turret. I waved at Blonder and Other. They didn't smile.

I climbed the stairs to the third floor, thinking Till might take my call. He'd still be at Gateville, far enough along to have made some real progress. He'd have to thank me for the tip on where to start digging; he might even drop his stony facade to congratulate me on the brilliant sleuthing that had yielded the presence of those long-abandoned tunnels. It was probably just oversight that he hadn't contacted Blonder and Other to call off the surveillance on me.

The cell phone wasn't on the wood table by my cot. I checked the floor and poked under the mound of clothes on the chair. Not there, either. I thought back. The last call I'd had was from Stanley, in the Jeep, when I'd told him where to hunt for the bombs. I went downstairs and outside. Blonder and Other watched me from the Crown Victoria. Blonder picked up his phone.

I looked through the plastic passenger window of the Jeep. The cell phone lay face up on the seat. I opened the door, turned on the phone, and sat on the passenger seat. The message indicator started flashing. I punched in the code.

"Hi, Dek." Amanda's voice was guarded. "I don't know if I should be calling you. I have no one else to call. I don't want to put you at risk, but I have to know what's going on. Two weeks ago, Stanley Novak called me, saying there have been bomb threats at Crystal Waters. He also said that your storage shed blew up and that you are being falsely considered a suspect. He told me there was no danger of any bombs actually going off and that you would be cleared shortly. Then he said that you would be better off if I avoided contact with you. I asked him how long that would take. He said less than a month. I didn't understand, but I said fine, I would wait one month for him to give me the go-ahead to call you. Now somebody from my father's office just called and said there's been an explosion at Crystal Waters. He said it's all over the news, that the police are going to search my house, and that I should get my paintings out of there. What is going on, Dek? I'm over Ohio now. I'll call you when I get to O'Hare."

I held the phone tight while I listened to the second message. "Where are you, Dek? I'm in a cab on the tollway. I'll be at Crystal Waters by ten thirty. Call me on this cell phone."

Something sick danced in my head.

She hadn't known about the bombs. Stanley had called her a couple of weeks before but had said nothing about the Farraday house or the lamppost. He hadn't told her to get her paintings removed.

Maybe that was understandable, if I had the time to think.

But the time of her last message wasn't, at least not why she hadn't called again.

She'd said she'd be at Gateville at ten thirty. That meant she would have been stopped around then, at a police roadblock or at the gate, and told that her house was off-limits. She would have become furious. She would have stayed right there, demanding to be let in to get the Monet, the Renoir, and the other works safely out of her house. She wouldn't have walked away. Her artworks were her soul. She wouldn't have left them.

*"If there were ever a fire, I would get the Monet out of the house before I'd call the fire department,"* she'd said the first time I'd come to Gateville. Never had I doubted that.

She would have grabbed her cell phone in a fury, to call her father to use his pull to get her inside Gateville. She would have called Ballsard, and every other Board member she could locate, to bully to get her in.

And, in her rage, she would have called me again, demanding to know what was going on.

She hadn't. There was no third message. No call demanding information. No call saying she'd gotten in, had grabbed her oils, was safe, and would call me tomorrow.

I called her cell phone, listened to four long, slow rings, got the voice mail message.

It was wrong. She should have picked up.

I waited a minute, redialed. Again I got the voice mail. I leaned over to look in the rearview mirror. Back in the Crown Victoria, Blonder and Other were watching me.

My mind flitted across options. The smart move was to get out of the Jeep, walk back, and get Blonder and Other to call Gateville and ask at the guardhouse if Amanda had arrived. But that would take time, assuming they would even do it.

The dumb move was to charge out to Gateville myself. Dumb. But fast.

I slid onto the driver's seat, fumbling in my pants pocket for the ignition key. Before my fingers could close on it, headlamps flashed from the Crown Victoria as it shot forward to stop diagonally across my left front fender. Blonder and Other jumped out with their guns drawn. I pulled my hand out of my pocket. It hadn't even touched the key.

Blonder was just outside the driver's door. "Step out of the car, Mr. Elstrom," he yelled through the plastic window.

I put my hands on the steering wheel so they could see I wasn't holding a weapon.

"Out of the car," Blonder shouted again. He raised the gun in his right hand, steadied by his left. Something moved out of the corner of my right eye. Agent Other stood in front of the Jeep, his gun also raised to firing position.

I got out, slow, hands high. And stupid. "Call Till. I know where the bombs are."

"Palms on the hood," Blonder yelled.

Agent Other came around, holstering his gun. He pushed me against the hood of the Jeep. I managed to push out my palms in time to break my fall as I hit. Other kicked my legs apart and patted me down, then pulled my arms behind me, sending my chin onto the metal. Two snicks and I was handcuffed, trussed, wings back, like a Christmas turkey. Other pulled me up. "Back to our car."

They marched me to the Crown Victoria. Agent Other opened

the rear door, put his palm on the top of my head, and gave me a quick nudge. I fell sideways onto the cold vinyl of the backseat like meat.

I pushed with my feet, managed to struggle upright, found a tinny voice. "What the hell are you guys doing?"

But I knew. I'd made the moves of someone trying to flee, and, when cornered, I'd made it worse by announcing that I knew where the bombs were, sounding every bit like the person who had planted them. They were rookies, but they knew to get me bundled up and neutralized in a heartbeat.

Other got in behind the wheel. Blonder took the front passenger's seat and pulled out his phone.

My shoulders felt like they were slowly being torn from their sockets. I shifted on the seat until I could lean against the door and ease the pressure off my arms.

"My wife's trapped inside—"

"Be quiet," Other said from the front seat.

Blonder had reached whomever he called. "Yes, sir, I think he was attempting to escape." He listened, then said, "He said to tell you he knows where the bombs are." He'd called Till. There was another pause. "We'll be right there."

Blonder clicked off and nodded to Other. Other started the car and nailed the accelerator, throwing me back against the seat like a bottom-heavy punching dummy.

He sped west on Thompson, toward Gateville.

As on the night of the last house bombing, the road was blocked just past the crest of the hill by a Maple Hills squad car and white sawhorse barricades. Unlike the last time, there were no flames shooting into the sky at the base of the hill. From a distance, Gateville was a cluster of trailer searchlights, surrounded by a half-mile-wide ring of dark landscape. Till had cut the power to the area all around Gateville.

Two blue-uniformed young police officers, holding yellow-nosed flashlights, stood in front of the barricade. Agent Other slowed to a stop and held his I.D. out the window. One of the officers approached the car.

I rocked forward as best I could. "Can you tell me if a brunette in her midthirties tried to get through here in the last couple of hours?"

The officer bent down to peer through the back-door window, saw the way my arms were pinned behind me, and looked at Agent Other. Other shook his head. The Maple Hills officer nodded and handed back Other's I.D., ignoring me. Other put the car in gear and started down the hill.

Blonder was back on the phone. "Yes, sir. Still cuffed." He listened for a minute, nodded at nobody, and thumbed off the cell phone.

Agent Other had to pull off the road well before the entrance. Ahead of us, fire engines, ambulances, several squad cars, at least three tow trucks, and, at the very end, a lone yellow cab were lined along both sides of the blocked-off highway. Forty or fifty people milled around on the pavement, talking. A couple of them smoked. Most were in uniform: firemen in opened yellow slickers, police in dark blue, paramedics in white or light blue. Those wearing civilian clothes I guessed to be forensic technicians waiting for orders, or reporters with enough connections to get past the police barricade. I scanned them all slowly. Amanda wasn't there.

I twisted on the seat to look at the compound to my left. Behind the brick wall at the east end, the sky and the tops of the houses were white, almost colorless, from the glare of the portable searchlights.

I pressed my face against the glass. The lights were all at the east end. I turned my head to check the northwest quadrant, where I'd told Stanley to tell Till to begin the search.

The sky above Amanda's house was black.

They were searching at the wrong end.

I pushed myself forward and tried to sound calm. "Till is looking in the wrong place."

Blonder spoke without looking at me. "Agent Till will come out when he can."

"The bombs are at the west end, in the tunnels." I spoke to the back of Blonder's neck, slowly, making each word distinct.

This time both of them turned around.

I wanted to scream at their young, unmarked faces. "I left a message for Stanley Novak to search for tunnels in the west end. The bombs are there."

Blonder's eyes were unblinking. "How would you know that?"

"Get Stanley Novak."

Blonder and Other looked at each other. Other shrugged. Blonder got out of the car and hurried across the highway to two Crystal Waters security guards standing a few feet from the entrance. He said something to them, and the two guards turned to look at our car. Blonder said something more, and then all three walked quickly across the highway to the Crown Victoria. One of the guards bent down to look at me through the side window. I recognized him from last Halloween. He'd been the guard that had pulled off my Wendell Phelps mask.

He moved to the open driver's window. "Mr. Elstrom," he said.

"Get me Stanley Novak."

"The agent here tells me you know something about tunnels?"

"I left a message for Stanley."

"What tunnels would those be, Mr. Elstrom?" the guard asked.

"Has my ex-wife been here?"

He made no secret of studying my red I LOVE ARKANSAS sweatshirt. "Are you here because of a marital issue?"

"Has Amanda Phelps been here?"

"No one's been allowed in since five this morning."

The other guard bent down. "Actually, that's not true," he said to the first guard. "Miss Phelps phoned the guardhouse from the barricade a couple of hours ago, demanding to be let through. Said she had to remove some paintings. She insisted we call Stanley. We did, and he OK'd her coming through. He said he'd meet her at the guardhouse."

"Where are they now?"

The guard shrugged.

"Let me out. I need to talk to Stanley."

Blonder bent down to the window. "In a minute. You told Stanley Novak to search the west end first?"

"I left a message on his cell phone early yesterday morning, telling him about the abandoned tunnels at the west end. Then I talked to him. He was going to tell Till. Let me out."

Blonder straightened up, and he and the two guards stepped away from the car. Blonder got on his phone and spoke for a minute. I heard the word "tunnel" three times. Blonder came back to the car. He opened the rear door.

"Agent Till wants you to wait for him in the guardhouse."

I slid out of the car and wobbled to stand up. "How about the handcuffs?"

Other looked at Blonder, who nodded. Other took out his key and removed the cuffs.

My arm throbbed as I raised my hand to point at the end of the row of cars and trucks parked along the road. "Is that my wife's cab?" I asked the Gateville guards.

"Don't know," the first one said.

"Amanda may be inside." I started for the cab.

Blonder held out an arm to stop me.

"She can tell us where Stanley is," I said, thinking no such thing, hoping she'd gotten rebuffed at the gate and was fuming in the cab, with a dead cell phone.

Blonder dropped his arm. With him at my left, Other on my

right, and the two security guards following, we moved quickly down the line of vehicles.

The cabbie was slumped back behind the wheel, asleep. I looked past him. The backseat was empty.

I reached in and shook his shoulder. "Did you drive a woman here tonight?"

"Hey." His eyes popped open, startled by my hand still on his shoulder. "Easy."

"Did you bring a woman here tonight?"

He straightened up on the seat, rubbing his eyes. He looked over at the meter. It was running. He smiled. "She told me to wait."

"Where is she?"

"In there." He pointed at the entrance to Gateville.

We hurried down to the guardhouse.

"Where's Stanley?" the first security guard asked the man at the console. The console was dark. The only light came from a portable electric lantern.

"Around someplace. Haven't seen him in a while."

"You hear anything about any tunnels in Crystal Waters?" the first guard asked.

The console guard shook his head. "There are no tunnels here."

"Did Amanda Phelps get in here tonight?" I asked the console guard.

The console man shook his head. "Strangest thing. She's almost always gone. Then tonight, of all nights, she shows up, demanding to get some stuff out of her house. Stanley kept telling her, 'No way,' over and over, but she wore him down. You know Stanley: anything for the Members. He finally folded and took her up himself."

"When was that?" I asked.

The console guard checked the log sheet on the masonite clipboard. "One hour and forty-eight minutes ago. Funny, I didn't see them come back." He reached for the console microphone. "Stanley, come in, over." He waited a minute and repeated it. "Stanley, come in, over." He pushed the talk button again. "Cassidy, you there, over?"

"Cassidy to base, over," a voice crackled back.

"Where's Stanley, over?"

"Haven't seen him, over."

The console guard checked the other guards. No one had seen Stanley.

I looked out the window, toward the dark, west end of Chanticleer Circle. "I'm going up to Amanda's house."

"You'll do no such thing." Blonder gestured to a chair. "Park it right there until I come back with Agent Till." Other took out his handcuffs and jangled them in his hands. Blonder put his hand on my shoulder, hard enough for me to realize he could push me down one-handed.

"You'll be back right away?"

"He wants to talk to you about those tunnels," Blonder said.

I sat down. After a glance at Other, Blonder paused at the door and spoke to the console guard. "Mr. Elstrom is a material witness. He can't leave." He went out the door and started running toward the lights at the east end of Chanticleer Circle.

Ahead of him, a small army of men with hand shovels worked slowly in the bright lights, poking and digging around the foundations and across the lawns. Their silhouettes were black against the glare of the lights. They looked like ghost soldiers, burying their dead.

"How long have they been working down at that end?" I asked the console guard.

"Since first thing this morning."

"They haven't been up by the Phelps house?"

The console guard shook his head. "They won't get up there for a couple of days."

"Try radioing Stanley again—"

The sky to the west lit up a fraction of a second before the guardhouse windows blew in. A roof of a house hung suspended for an instant, then it began spewing out a thousand glowing embers, just like the Farraday house on the videotape. The guardhouse shuddered, rocking on its foundation. Next to me, Agent Other swiped at the back of his neck. It was a lazy move, confused, as if he were swatting a mosquito at a summer picnic. Then blood spurted from between his fingers. I turned for help from the guard. He was on the floor beneath the console, not moving.

I turned back to Other. He had his hands locked behind his neck, stanching the flow of blood. "I'm just cut. Get out of here."

I ran out into the smoke and the fire in the sky. The smell of chemical explosives, thick and sweet, hung everywhere. Behind me, a hundred men were yelling, their shouts lost in a muddle of noise, as, outside the wall, the fire trucks and the ambulances rumbled to life.

I ran up Chanticleer toward the hail of embers that was falling into the flames at the northwest bend of Chanticleer. Amanda's house was around that bend, obscured by two dark houses on my left.

If her house was still there.

I tripped, on a curb or a yard stone, fell to my elbows. I got up. Pain ran down my leg; wet and raw. I'd been cut. I ran on, screaming into the night, pleading with every deity I knew.

Let her be alive.

# Twenty-six

Amanda's house loomed out of the smoke, dark against the back-drop of leaping fire. Its massive double front doors gaped open, sprung out on their hinges like huge hands, framing the black mouth of the entry. In the pulsating orange light from the inferno next door, the house looked like it was screaming.

Stanley's station wagon was parked in the driveway, colorless, strewn with charred pieces of wood and roof tile and ash. I pulled open the front passenger door. It was empty. I ran up the brick walk to the entry.

"Amanda? Stanley?" I yelled. There was no light inside; none of the windows faced the flames. I shouted their names again, holding my breath to hear above the pounding in my chest and the rumbling of the motors at the other end of Gateville.

Only cold air came back at me from the darkness inside.

I stepped into the foyer. Grit crunched under my shoes like I was walking on pulverized glass. I turned to shut the ruined doors to the noise outside so I could hear in the house, but they'd been knocked loose on their hinges and wouldn't pull back. I moved further into the foyer.

Something creaked above my head, and suddenly a curtain of coarse grit, some of it the size of hailstones, started raining from the ceiling. I threw up my hands to shield my face and slammed back against the wall, eyes shut tight. Dust filled the foyer. Then, just as suddenly as it started, the shower of grit stopped. Coughing, I peered through my fingers. Barely visible in the faint light from outside, a massive crack, two inches wide, had split the ceiling, running from above the entry doors into the blackness of the center hall. It had been plaster that had fallen, bits and chunks of it. The blast next door had shaken Amanda's house loose on its foundation.

The jimjams started in my head, taunting: *Why was the station wagon still in the driveway?*

I tried to force them away. The station wagon meant nothing. They could have left on foot, carried the art the few hundred yards to the guardhouse. Simpler, and quicker because they wouldn't have stopped to load the car.

The jimjams tittered: *Why haven't they been seen?*

I squinted across the foyer, to the darkness where the center hall was. Thirty feet into that hall, then into the living room, to the wall above the fireplace, and I'd know the Monet was gone. Then I could run.

I started moving along the foyer wall.

POP. POP. Loud, like gunshots, from upstairs. I stopped, pressed back against the foyer wall.

POP. POP. Closer now, right above my head, but not gunshots. Worse. They were nails, ripping out of the walls upstairs. The house was coming down.

Behind me, the orange glow beckoned through the open, ruined front doors. Perversely, it was now a beacon to safety. I turned away from it.

POP, this time followed by the long rip of wood splitting.

I turned and pressed my chest against the wall, hoping it was safer there, away from the center of the falling ceiling. Following my outstretched fingertips like a blind man, I pushed into the dark along the foyer wall. Fist-sized chunks of plaster nudged at my feet. I kicked at them, unseeing, sending them skittering noisily across the ceramic tile. The rubble on the floor was getting thicker the farther I got from the support of the outside walls.

I got to the entrance to the hall. Ten shuffle-steps, then twenty; my hand found the edge of the arch to the living room.

Something heavy crashed above, a ceiling joist or a roof rafter. I pressed under the arch, holding my breath, certain whatever had broken loose was going to come through the hall ceiling. A minute passed, then another. The house settled and went still.

I moved around the arch, following the wall into the living room, struggling to remember the location of every chair, table, and sofa.

My fingers nudged cold, curved metal. It was the first of a pair of wall sconces, directly across the room from the Monet. I moved faster along the wall, sure now of where I was in the room. I touched the other sconce, then next to it, the lined brocade fabric of the living room draperies. I felt past the window and found the frame of a small print. It wasn't valuable; she could have left it. The wall ended. I turned right. Five more paces and my hand struck something, knocking it to a soft thud on the thick carpet. A pewter candleholder, late seventeenth century. Valuable, but not something she'd grab in a crisis. I moved on.

My foot kicked a table leg, setting something wobbling. I stabbed my hand at the noise in the dark, found the lampshade, stopped the wobbling. It was the Chinese red lamp on the wine table. Below the small Renoir oil.

My fingers moved up the wall, tentative, afraid, and too quickly found the little bumps on the beaded frame. The jimjams danced on the skin of my scalp. *Shut up*, I heard myself shout, maybe aloud, maybe only in my mind. She could have left the Renoir, if there'd been no time. It was not the grand prize.

I was almost there.

*If there were ever a fire, I would get the Monet out of the house before I'd call the fire department.*

Five steps and I bumped the glossy, carved wood of the fireplace mantel, the fireplace she would never use because of the risk of smoke. Palms curled, I worked my fingers upward, willing them to find nothing but the smoothness of bare plaster.

I touched wood.

I felt along the gilded surface, needing to distrust my touch, to be wrong, but there was no doubting the double curve or the intricacy of the outer edge. My fingers came to the lower right corner, followed the odd angle. The hexagonal angle.

The Monet was still on the wall.

The jimjams roared.

She and Stanley had come into the house. The car on the drive and the yawning entry doors had told me that.

But they'd never left.

A staccato burst of *pops* from upstairs echoed through the house like machine-gun fire. Then the rips came, four or five of them, each one long and loud and groaning, like the bones of the house were being ripped out by some giant, unseen hand. Something crashed and shattered on the foyer floor.

I tried to take deep breaths, tried to think. Amanda and Stanley had come to the house. They'd unlocked the doors. There'd be time, they would have thought, time to get it all; the Monet first, of course, but the Renoir, too, then the Remington bronze, the other oils.

She hadn't even gotten to the Monet. She'd been stopped the minute they had entered the house—and been kept from leaving.

The house groaned.

I put my ear hard against the wall, heard the distant sirens, the idling diesel engines, sounds transmitted from outside. Mixed in with them, I thought I heard the almost imperceptible sounds of wood and steel shifting. But maybe that was the sound of my own fear.

I could hear no voices.

There was no time now to hug the wall. The house was coming down. I started into the center of the living room, arms outstretched like a fool playing at blind man's bluff, kicking at the dark first with one foot, then the other. A dozen steps and I found the arch. Far to the right, down the hall, a faint orange haze came from the foyer. I turned to the left, toward the kitchen. Amanda kept a flashlight there, in a drawer next to the sink.

I followed the hall as quickly as I dared, finger touching the wallpaper in front of me. A right turn and I saw more orange light, stronger, flickering from the doorway to the kitchen.

The kitchen windows faced the burning house next door. The blinds were drawn, but enough light crept between the slats to make out the outlines of the counters. I walked across the room. More grit, more chunks of plaster. Every ceiling in the house was falling. I felt along the granite countertop, covered like the floor with fallen plaster, following its edge to the cold steel of the stainless refrigerator, then to the sink. I reached down and found the drawer handle on the lacquered birch front. I pulled it open. The round black rechargeable flashlight was in front.

I switched it on and aimed it low, sweeping across the debris on the kitchen floor—and stopped.

Blue pant legs powdered talcum white by plaster dust. Silver tape at the ankles, below the knees, and around the chest, binding her upright to the bentwood kitchen chair. Arms taped together behind the chair back. Funny bracelet with a single charm, a gold question mark, dangling loosely on an unmoving wrist. I'd given her that bracelet.

And, grotesquely, a brown paper shopping bag, a hole ripped for a mouth, jammed on her head. A wet splotch of something red seeped through the paper above the left ear, where it pressed against her skin. She didn't move.

Two steps and I ripped the bag up and off. Aimed the flashlight at the far wall, enough for me to see, but not enough to blind her. Bent down to look in the eyes I saw every night when I couldn't sleep. Sparkling eyes, laughing eyes. But not now. Now they were lifeless, unseeing, the blacks of the pupils crowding out almost all of the brown. My heart chattered. They were dead eyes.

Something was jammed in her mouth.

I dropped to my knees, holding the flashlight under my chin so she could see my face as I worked the fragment of towel out of her mouth. She was as rigid as stone. Then her eyelids fluttered, closed, jerked open to look again, and comprehended. Her breathing came faster then, and she started making rapid sideways motions with her eyes, wildly trying to see around the room. "Don't talk," I whispered.

I got up, stepped quickly to the knife block on the counter, and took the first one my fingers closed on. I cut away the tape from her legs, waist, chest, and arms.

"Don't talk until we're outside." I reached for her arms.

She stopped me, pulling my head down with cold hands. "Stanley," she whispered in a cracked, dry voice. "Stanley."

"We have to get out of here." I put my arms around her and pulled her up. Caught again the scent of her perfume, felt the familiar weight of her. For one crazy moment, I didn't want to move.

"Can you walk?" I said into her ear.

She nodded.

I held her for the first slow steps, then moved in front of her so she could walk with her hands on my shoulders. The flashlight beam was dimming as we followed it out of the kitchen and down the hall. She dropped her hands away when we got to the living room arch.

"No," I whispered behind me, but she had already turned. I hurried to catch up to her, aiming the weakening beam in front of us as we crossed the living room to the Monet. "Just that," I said. She nodded.

She'd never installed security hangers, saying once that she couldn't bear the thought of a thief damaging the Monet trying to get it off the wall. I handed her the flashlight, reached up, and took it down.

The flashlight was dying as I followed her out of the living room. *Pop. Pop. POP.*

I grabbed her arm and pulled her under the arch.

*"What is that?"*

"Nails from the roof."

The upstairs went silent. We hurried out from the arch, through the hall and the foyer, and out into the orange light. She looked down Chanticleer and stopped.

A hundred yards east, a small knot of men, some holding flashlights aimed at the ground, had stopped behind two idling fire trucks. She stared at the cluster of men standing in the flashing red lights, then looked at the flames leaping from the shell of the gutted house next door. She turned to me, a question forming on her lips.

"Not now," I said. "Come on." I reached for her arm.

She stepped back, touching her head where the blood had dried. The words came in a rush. "I made Stanley take me up here when I found out about the bombs. He didn't want to. He said it wasn't safe." Her eyes locked on mine. "I made him, Dek. I made him bring me up here."

"Did Stanley hit you?"

"Stanley?" Her eyes flickered from me to the knot of men down the road and back to me. "Why would you think—"

"He's got to be in this, Amanda." Saying aloud for the first time what had been working at me since I realized Till didn't know about the tunnels. "Did Stanley hit you?"

*"I don't know who hit me."*

Again I reached for her with my free hand. "No," she screamed, taking two full steps back. "Can't you understand? I made Stanley take me here. We were finding our way in the dark, to the kitchen to get my flashlight, when something hit me. Stanley must have been hit, too. It couldn't have been Stanley."

"We've got to find Till." This time I got her arm. I started pulling her with my free hand, toward the street, toward the men and the fire trucks stopped a hundred yards down Chanticleer.

The new blast flared high into the air, showering sparks into the night. At first I thought it was from the house next door, but then my eyes registered the dark space between the two fires. It was another house, the one beyond the burning pile next door. Something clattered behind us. I turned to see one of Amanda's front doors break away from its top hinge and fall to the ground.

"I made him, Dek," Amanda shouted. "I made Stanley take me up here."

I looked at her face, saw fear and panic, but saw the future, too. I saw the guilt that would haunt her for the rest of her life if Stanley died inside her house.

I grabbed the flashlight she was holding and shoved the Monet at her.

"Find Till," I shouted, pointing at the cluster of men behind the fire engines. "Tell him the bomber is in a tunnel that leads from your basement. Tell him everything is going to go up. Tell him Stanley is in the house."

"But where will you—"

"Do it," I yelled.

She hesitated, nodding her head, but still frozen. I grabbed her shoulders and shook them hard. Then she ran, the Monet swinging under one arm, stumbling in a contorted, hobbled jog down Chanticleer toward the group of men huddled behind the two fire engines.

I ran back into the house.

# Twenty-seven

Grotesque black shadows danced in pantomime on the walls of the foyer, dark reflections of the trees and the smoke and the flames in the new light of the second explosion. There was no noise. No sirens, no firemen yelling, no big engines racing up Chanticleer. They weren't coming. They'd been held back, away from the explosions at the west end.

More debris had fallen in the foyer. The plaster dust was thicker now, making the foyer look like a barnacle-encrusted stateroom caught in the glare of an underwater shipwreck photograph. Jagged cracks ran up the walls. Soon, the walls would start falling.

I crossed the foyer in the strange new light, to the base of the stairs going up. The staircase canted downward, loose from the wall. A main support had given way. I looked up. The crack in the ceiling had grown to be a foot wide. Beyond it, a trace of orange peeked from the second-floor landing. New firelight, showing through the collapsing roof.

My shoes ground at the debris as I hurried into the central hall. The house was dead quiet now. Chillingly, the pops and groans of just a few minutes before had stopped, as if the house were holding its breath for one last shudder, one final exhalation, before it let go and collapsed.

I moved down the hall, past the living room arch. Outside the dining room, my foot struck something that wasn't plaster. I looked down, then bent to pick it up. It was an old Army flashlight, olive plastic, with its head set at a right angle to the body. The lens and the bulb were gone. My finger touched something damp. I turned the Army flashlight around and held it to the light coming from the foyer. It was blood, mixed with plaster and several short strands of dark hair. I threw it down. It had been used to strike Amanda.

I switched on the rechargeable flashlight and went into the dining room. The beam flickered and then died as I swept it around the empty room. I shut the light off, rapped it hard against my leg, and turned it on again. No beam. I dropped it on the floor. Without a charge, it was worthless.

Down the hall, to the library. Like the dining room's, its windows were on the other side of the house from the fires. I made the circle around the walls, then crossed the carpet on a diagonal to make sure Stanley wasn't trussed up in the middle. The room was empty.

I hurried down the central hall, toward the little corridor that led to the family room. And stopped at the turn. A pale sliver of green light ran up the wall ahead. The basement door was ajar. The greenish light was coming from down below.

I wanted to run then, run like a man on fire. It was Till's job I was doing, hunting to save a man trapped in a collapsing house. I turned, started for the foyer. And saw Amanda, in the dark, in my mind, as she'd been outside her house, tormented by guilt, and pleading. I could give the basement a quick look from the top of the stairs, and then run to get Till. He could send his men into the basement of that collapsing house to find Stanley. I turned back.

But I wasn't going anywhere near that green sliver of light without a knife.

There was a door to the kitchen off that short hall. I eased past the basement door, went into the kitchen. It was brighter now, from the second fire; the light coming in through the slats was strong enough to bathe everything in soft, ghostly illumination. I went to the knife block, found the big-handled carving knife. I'd never been in a knife fight, and I doubted I could cut a man, but it might give me enough courage to make it a step or two down the basement stairs. I went out to the short hall.

Ten feet from the basement door, I got down on my knees, crawled as silently as I could through the grit to the sliver of green light. I reached with the blade of the knife to ease open the basement door. A cold draft of air came up, dry, as if from a crypt. Dropping to my belly, I pushed forward and looked down. The base of the stairs was dark, barely visible in the soft green gloom. For a second, I let myself hope that the green light was coming in from outside, but then I remembered that the houses in Gateville didn't have basement windows.

Someone was down there.

Head first, still on my belly, I pulled myself down one step, but I could see nothing. I was too high up. I pulled myself down another step. Still the walls blocked my view. I pushed back, got to my feet. I'd have to go down. At the third step, the staircase was open at the sides; no walls, just handrails. I could see there. But I'd be vulnerable. If somebody were waiting, a grab from either side would send me tumbling down onto the concrete.

Something crashed upstairs, shaking the whole house. A roof rafter or a ceiling joist had broken away. Down or out, I had to do it now.

I gripped the carving knife tight in my right hand, eased onto the first step, then stopped, partially hunched to slash at a first touch at my ankle. But nothing moved. I took a second step, then a third. Each time I stopped, tensed to cut at a hand coming out of the strange green glow. But only the faraway shiftings of the joists and rafters, vague and restless, stirred the house. I took the rest of the steps down, and moved behind the stairs.

The green light came from an opening cut into the center of the south basement wall. The cutout was roughly chiseled and about two feet square. Rock-sized, irregular chunks of cement lay on the floor underneath, where they'd fallen when the hole was cut.

It was the entrance to the tunnel to the bomb shelter.

I looked around the basement and saw the familiar outlines of the wicker lawn furniture that her father had left behind, the few boxes of Christmas ornaments, the couple of extra suitcases, and, toward the cutout, the black upright coffin shapes of the two furnaces. Nothing moved; the basement seemed empty.

I looked back at the cutout wall, and caught my breath at what I'd missed. A man was hunched in the corner of the south wall, huddled down, twenty feet from the cutout.

The green light dimmed, then surged brighter, then dimmed again.

And then it went out.

I stayed stock-still behind the stairs, tensed for any rustling in the corner. I clutched the carving knife, but I was wrapped in black gauze; in the darkness, I couldn't have defended myself against a blind man. I felt for the stair rail, then let my hand fall away. He'd expect that, expect me to run back up the stairs. I'd never make it to the top before he'd stab me, or shoot me, from behind. He wouldn't even have to aim. In the narrow stairwell, I'd be a rat in a tiny tunnel. All he'd have to do is slash or shoot at the sound of the fear coming ragged out of my lungs.

I waited, breathing shallowly, for the slightest change in the air around me. After a minute, I could stand it no longer. I was like a goat tethered to attract a lion, all fear and sweat and tingling instinct. I came out from under the stairs and moved in a crouch toward the furnaces along the west wall. He might not expect that, and in that tight space between the furnaces and the wall, I'd have a chance to cut him. It would be like a knife fight in a closet, its outcome determined more by chance than skill. But it was a chance.

I touched the cold metal of the ductwork and slipped behind the furnaces. My skin prickling, my lungs starving for oxygen, I steadied myself against the duct, locked my eyes on the spot in the darkness where the man had been, and breathed in.

The green light glowed back on, slightly brighter than before. The light was being run off a battery; someone had just changed it. I looked in the corner. The man was still there. Incredibly, he hadn't moved.

At best, it was Stanley Novak, bound and gagged, but alive. At worst, it was Stanley, dead. No, at worst it was someone with a knife, ready to slit my throat. I supposed the good news was the house might come down on both of us before he could do that.

I came out from behind the furnace, low, knife tight in my right hand, eyes on the corner. Ten feet, eight feet, the shape didn't move. At three feet, I stopped, reached to touch it with the knife-point. The shape puckered. I bent down and touched cloth. It was the empty sleeve of a heavy jacket. I pushed at it. It fell to one side. It was just an empty jacket, tossed upright in the corner.

I crouched down and felt familiar flapped pockets with Velcro closures and a zipper set into the collar where a thin hood was stored. I knew those kinds of pockets; I knew that kind of zipper. I'd bought a jacket just like it from a surplus store when I was a kid. They came in only one color: Army olive drab.

I got down on my knees, grabbed the jacket, and crawled toward the green glow spilling out of the cutout. I needed to see; I needed to know. I stopped two feet to the right of the opening and turned the jacket so I could make out the nametape that every one of those jackets had sewn above the right pocket. I held it close to the light. JAYNES, it read.

All my theories, all my smug posturing about Jaynes being long gone, had been crap. He'd come back. He was on the other side of the cutout, in the tunnel, twisting wires, connecting the circuits that would soon blow the rest of Gateville to the moon.

But he had to know that Gateville was crawling now with cops and Feds. He couldn't get away.

The jimjams tittered, a sneering chorus: He wasn't doing it for money, not anymore. He was acting out a different last act of the play he'd written in 1970. And this finale had him exiting in a blaze of twisted, deranged glory, taking the cops, the firemen, and everybody else outside with him. I saw Amanda among them, clutching her Monet.

Something huge thundered upstairs, banging the ducts, ringing the pipes. For a second I let myself hope that the sudden loud noise might be pounding boots, Till's men, storming down the hall with flashlights and guns. I turned toward the center of the basement, to the stairs I could not see, praying for the first flash of a handheld light. But nothing lit the staircase, and the noise upstairs stopped. Till's men wouldn't come, not into a house laced with explosives.

I got to my knees and peered over the top of the roughly cut ledge. There couldn't be much time left now.

The tunnel was made of poured concrete, five feet high, four feet wide. Just big enough for a family to run through, single file, bent over. The only light came from the lone green bulb hanging by the tunnel opening, strung with two skinny wires that ran along the ceiling from deep inside the tunnel. Twenty feet in, the tunnel dissolved into darkness.

The bulb flickered and brightened again, and I saw the wires to the bulb, one black, one white, jangle slowly below the tunnel ceiling. He was doing something with the wires, deep inside the tunnel, connecting them to something else.

I looked down. Stacked low against the concrete wall were several spools of wire, a dozen black-box timers, and a dozen square batteries, each the size of a baking-soda box. Farthest in lay an object wrapped in silver carpet tape. It was another battery, this one attached to a timer, and to something else: a small cube wrapped in plastic. It was a timer bomb.

I didn't let myself think.

I crawled over the jagged, chiseled ledge of the cutout and dropped down, hands first, onto the floor of the tunnel. The cement was chalky from being entombed for so many years. I moved to the pile against the wall.

Each of the spools looked like it held hundreds of feet of fine thin wire, yellow, red, black, and white. I heard again the puzzled voice of the old electrician I'd hired to check out the lamppost. "These wires don't belong here," he'd said. "Too skinny for residential or commercial use." Maybe, old friend. But they were all that was needed to carry a spark from a battery through a timer a few hundred feet to one of those little plastic-wrapped cubes of D.X.12.

Just a few spools of that wire and some timers, batteries, and cubes of D.X.12 would be enough to blow all of Gateville to hell.

I saw it all in a second. Jaynes would have told his crew the extra, thin wire was for battery lights, or alarms, or any of a number of low-voltage items. They wouldn't have questioned him; he was their supervisor, and there were lots of things that were hush-hush about the construction of Gateville. They wouldn't have been around later anyway, when he came back to attach the thin wires to the little cubes that he then covered with a few shovelfuls of dirt. The other ends of the wires, the trigger ends, he would have already had his men run into the labyrinth of the bomb shelter tunnels. He'd have left those alone, for later, when it was time to attach the battery-operated timers with the round dials.

Next step was to test his plan. He sent the first note, demanding the ten thousand dollars. Then, after a few days, he hung around after his shift at Gateville, twisted a timer onto the pair of wires that led to the little cube he'd buried behind the guardhouse, set the dial, and was probably having the pot roast special at some diner when the back wall of the guard house blew off. He'd probably mailed the second letter after dessert, telling them where to leave the ten thousand. So simple, he must have thought. Plans that work are always simple.

I squinted into the tunnel. Somewhere in there, dozens, maybe hundreds, of thin wires came together, needing only a battery and a timer and the final twist of a dial to make them lethal. Jaynes was in there, too, probably so crazy by now he didn't give a damn about anything except twisting the last of his wires together. Maybe he had a gun and was hoping someone like me would come looking, so he could put a bullet into my brain and have a last giggle before he twisted the dial.

Maybe I didn't have to get that close. Maybe I just had to get to the wires.

I clutched the carving knife tighter in my right hand and started crouch-walking into the dark of the tunnel. As an afterthought, I reached down and picked up the duct-taped timer bomb with my left hand.

Frickin' Rambo.

The dry air stank of something acrid, something old, trapped long ago. It smelled like death. I wanted to run forward, find the wires, but he might hear me. I moved forward slowly.

Every few paces, I stopped to look back, to make sure I could still see the green light. When it came time to run, I was going to need that light.

But after twenty-five or thirty paces, the green bulb had disappeared in the darkness behind me.

A faint speck of light appeared in the darkness ahead. I moved closer. It was the same green as the bulb by the tunnel entrance, but this was softer, more diffused. When I got within fifty feet, I dropped down and started crawling on my knees and elbows, the knife still in my right hand, timer bomb in my left.

At twenty feet, I stopped. The light was coming from the left side of the tunnel ahead. I shut my eyes tight, opened them after a minute, and made out a wall straight ahead. My tunnel was dead-ending into a cross tunnel from another house.

And then I saw it, lying on the floor of the cross tunnel, to the right, directly across from the green light. I crawled forward, ten feet, five feet, and then stopped. It was a boot, a dusty, dirt-clumped boot, poking out from denim jeans. It didn't move.

I set down the knife and the timer bomb and crawled forward. "Stanley," I whispered. "Stanley."

I shook the boot. It was rigid, immobile. I slid forward on my left side, all the way into the green light at the intersection of the cross tunnel.

White halogen light hit me from behind. In the sudden glare, the shrunken, bearded face with wild dark hair stared at me from empty eye sockets, screaming noiselessly from an open, dead mouth. His tobacco-colored flesh had pulled taut against his skull, mummified from the dry air in the tunnel. A foot below his chin, three black bullet holes had pierced his chest. Below his wounds, the yellowed T-shirt was stained with a long-dried torrent of crusted blood.

"I stopped him," the calm voice said.

I rolled over to face the blinding light coming from his end of the cross tunnel. I couldn't see him in the glare.

But I knew the voice.

# Twenty-eight

"He was no good, Mr. Elstrom." He angled the super-white beam of the handheld spotlight off my face, down onto the cement floor ten feet in front of me, but still I could not see him.

Suddenly I was tired, bone-heavy from being too stubborn to accept what my mind had been tiptoeing around since—hell, since the beginning. I pushed myself up to sit against the wall of the tunnel, two feet from Michael Jaynes's dead foot.

"I knew him from working security those nights." Stanley spoke conversationally, his voice almost lazy behind the light. "Michael always stayed late, checking the work, I thought, and we'd get to talking when I came by on my rounds. He was your basic liberal lefty, but he seemed like a dedicated Joe on the job, working overtime after his boys had left, making sure things were being done right. We got along."

Clipping noises came from Stanley's end of the cross tunnel, and above my head, something stirred. I looked up. Red wires, black wires, and white and green wires were vibrating an inch below the cross-tunnel ceiling. He was snipping at those wires with a wire cutter, attaching them in some lethal combination.

"That April night in 1970," he went on, "after I'd dropped off the ten thousand behind the restaurant, I came back to make my rounds. I got to the Phelps house, though it wasn't yet called that, and went down to check the basement. I checked all the basements those nights, for kids at first, but then extra careful after the two letters. Anyway, somebody had pulled away the concrete forms from the tunnel entrance. It was odd, because they were scheduled to seal up those entrances the next day. I looked inside the tunnel, saw a faint light from far in. I supposed it was a worker making sure everything was ready, but I figured I ought to check to be safe. I crawled inside. That's when I saw Michael, sitting right where he is now, working with some wires."

" 'What are you doing?' I asked, thinking it was no big deal. But Michael smiled the sickest smile you'd ever hate to see, and I noticed his eyes were all sparkly. 'Fixing things,' he said. 'What things?' I asked. 'They made a mess with their greed, Stanley: Vietnam, ghettos in the cities, rural poor. Everything is being bled to make rich people richer. Ordinary folks can't do much. They march, they sing their songs, and the angriest of them riot and burn. None of that stops the greed, of course, but it does make rich people nervous enough to build places like this, thinking they can protect themselves from what they created.' "

Stanley clipped faster behind the bright light. "It sounded like crap to me, Mr. Elstrom. I told Michael he was making up phony baloney just so he could get ten thousand dollars. Michael laughed at that. 'The ten thousand is still in the Dumpster, Stanley. I'm just going to show those rich bastards they can't hide in a place like Crystal Waters. They're going to pay, more and more, but this place is still going to disappear, one house at a time. And when the last house is gone, they'll realize that no amount of money can protect them behind their fancy walls, and they'll act better.' "

The wires above my head danced.

I snuck a look down the main tunnel to Amanda's basement.

The knife I'd dropped next to the timer bomb was only a couple feet from my shoe.

"So you shot him, Stanley? Just like that, you killed him?"

"Small cluster right to the heart, as you can see." He sighed. "He couldn't let me get away. I knew too much, and I would stop his grand plan for world peace. So yes, I shot him, and the letters and explosives I found down here afterward would have justified it."

"But you didn't report it." I'd have no chance if I just took off. The tunnel to Amanda's basement was too straight. He'd come to the tunnel intersection, find my back with his spotlight, and pump a few rounds into me before I was fifty feet down.

"Report it, Mr. Elstrom? Why stir up a ruckus? If this place were known to be full of D.X.12, none of the Members would have moved in. They wouldn't have gotten their money back, either, because the developers would have gone bankrupt. The town of Maple Hills would have lost, too—a sorely needed source of new income. Everybody would have lost."

"And you would not have become security chief," I said, while I thought about what I could do.

The snipping stopped. "I was not thinking of myself, Mr. Elstrom." There was an edge to his voice. It was good. He was getting mad, maybe enough to distract him, from the wires, and from my legs. I'd started pulling my feet up under me.

"Of course not, Stanley." I laid it on thick enough so he couldn't miss the derision in my voice. "Just like I'm sure you left that ten thousand in the Dumpster to get picked up as garbage."

"I went back and retrieved the money, sure, but it's still in my garage, untouched after all these years."

The clipping began again.

"Sounds like what you call phony baloney, Stanley," I said to the glare. My feet were up under me, my knees high.

"I told you. Michael Jaynes was going to keep blowing things up."

"Forget Jaynes. You're the one who reactivated his plan. For money, Stanley. You've been planning your big score for years, thinking over every detail, right down to sending money to Nadine Reynolds, so that when you started bombing, people would think Michael Jaynes was still alive."

"I was helping her," he snapped from behind the light. "Michael used to tell me his girlfriend was just barely getting by. I got her name and address from his wallet, sent her what I could, every now and then."

"That's right, Stanley, just like when you called out to Clarinda every once in a while and left Michael's name. You've been jerking Nadine Reynolds around for years, letting her go on believing Michael was going to show up someday. You're a prince of a guy, Stanley."

"What would you have had me do? Send her a little note, telling her he was dead? You don't know, Mr. Elstrom, but it's better to live with false hope than to live with no hope at all."

"I know one thing, Stanley. I don't believe you when you say this isn't about money."

"I didn't say that, Mr. Elstrom. This most certainly is about money." He paused and then said, "You heard about my son?"

"Nothing other than Anton Chernek said he died." Slowly, I moved my hands down to the concrete floor.

"We lost him one year, seven months, seventeen days ago. He needed an operation, but the insurance said it was an experimental procedure, and they wouldn't cover it. I went to Mr. Ballsard, asked if I could get the money from my Crystal Waters life insurance. He said it was term insurance, no borrowing value. So I asked, can I borrow the money from the homeowners association? Know what Mr. Ballsard said?"

"He's a shit, Stanley." My palms were flat on the floor now, my legs as tensed as I could get them. I started easing forward.

"He said the association wasn't a bank. All those years of watching out for the Members, of driving their kids home from the police station after they'd been picked up drunk or goofy with dope. All those years of guarding their fancy homes when they were off on their cruises, skiing vacations, and shopping trips to London. After all that time, all he can tell me is they're not a bank?"

"So you decided to start killing people?" I'd have to grab the knife left-handed and then charge. And hope I could cut him before he could get to his gun. Or to the wires.

Above my head, the air moved.

"Nobody was supposed to die," he yelled.

I pushed off the wall.

The spotlight swung on me; the gun flashed loudly from behind the glare. Something whispered past my ear.

I dropped to my knees. I hadn't even gotten close to the knife.

"I'd hate to shoot you, Mr. Elstrom."

I backed up and immediately bumped the tunnel wall. I'd gotten three feet. I sat against the wall again, my ears ringing from the sound of the gunshot.

The wires began to dance again above my head.

"I like you, Mr. Elstrom. You're not from here," Stanley said in that same maddening conversational voice.

He shifted the spotlight beam toward the floor at his end of the cross tunnel, and for the first time I saw him in profile. He was close enough to have killed me with that shot; he was only twenty feet from me, sitting under a nest of wires dangling down from the ceiling. He squinted at a blueprint on the floor.

"Yes, sir. I always liked you."

"That's crap, Stanley. You used me to keep the Board from calling in the Feds."

"No, sir, that was their own greed. Mr. Ballsard didn't want the federal agencies in here because word of that would get out and destroy the house values."

"You played me for an idiot, sent me off to look for a dead man."

He reached up to twist some wires above his head. "You didn't want the money, Mr. Elstrom? Even though you kept saying you weren't qualified for the investigation, you didn't need that money?"

"Not bad enough to follow the wrong lead while you killed a family."

He dropped his hands from the ceiling and turned his head abruptly toward me. *"They weren't supposed to be home."*

"Sure, you liked me, Stanley," I said, trying to find a button, any button. "When everybody was giving up on the idea of finding Jaynes, you liked me enough to give them a new candidate: me. You passed a quiet word to Till about my background, no doubt suggesting I was prone to irrational behavior. That got him to put a tail on me. And when I told you I was coming to get Amanda's paintings, you realized I might discover the hole you'd opened up to the tunnel. Then you liked me enough to set off a cube of D.X.12 in my shed, to tighten the link between me and the bombings."

"There was no D.X.12 in your shed, Mr. Elstrom, just a slow-burning fuse and an old can of paint stripper. Your own turpentine did the rest. Agent Till thinks somebody walking along the river tossed a cigarette into your shed."

His hands worked in the nest of wires. There couldn't be any time left.

"You'll die, Stanley. And you'll take a hundred firemen, cops, and medical techs with you."

And Amanda. She was out there, too. But I couldn't give voice to that.

"I don't know how much that matters, Mr. Elstrom. My boy is dead. My wife is dying because she can't bear that, and I'm dead, too. All because of Crystal Waters. Michael Jaynes was right. This place must be destroyed."

Just around the corner, next to the knife that I'd never get close enough to use, lay the timer bomb.

I started getting up then, slowly. He raised his spotlight to shine right in my eyes.

I looked away from the light. "I liked you, too, Stanley. I liked you when the lamppost blew up, when I couldn't get past the idea that the bomb had been triggered from inside Gateville. I liked you when, miracle of miracles, you came up with the name of Michael Jaynes, and I didn't think to question the sudden appearance of such a good lead. I liked you when that family got blown up, when you kept waving that Member vacation roster around, insisting they weren't supposed to be home. I liked you, Stanley, too much to take a hard look at you."

I was on my knees. "Even tonight, I liked you, when I was badgering Amanda to tell me it was you who had hit her. She wouldn't believe that, and I didn't want to believe it, either. Because I liked you. You weren't Crystal Waters. You were a working guy, a guy carrying a load, like me."

I was all the way up now, hunched an inch from the ceiling. "But most of all, Stanley, I liked you because you didn't put a clown hat on me last Halloween. You took me away from Crystal Waters, paid for a room at the health center because I was too drunk and too broke, and you left me with enough dignity to get through the night. I liked you for that, Stanley, and it made me blind."

He lowered the spotlight. His right hand, his gunhand, was raised, steady and motionless, but his head was moving, up and down, like he was laughing. Or crying.

"But I don't like you enough to sit here and watch you kill a hundred people." I turned and stepped into Amanda's tunnel, out of his sight, and stopped—to pick up the bomb. I gave the dial the slightest of twists, turned back around, and straight-armed it around the corner, toward the spotlight. Then I ran, crouched, down the tunnel toward Amanda's basement.

I remember what came next, but the remembering takes longer

than the time it must have taken. I remember the sound of my lungs wheezing in the dry, cold air, and the incredible pressure of my heart thudding in my chest as I pounded down the tunnel, hunched over like a broken man. I remember the speck of green growing in the blackness ahead of me as I got closer, and praying that it wouldn't dissolve into a flash of orange. I remember hitting the concrete wall of Amanda's basement, hard, the pain stunning me for an instant before I thought to reach up. I remember the way the ragged, chiseled cement cut into my gut as I started to pull my-self over the ledge.

I remember the first instant of the tornado coming, bright and white and hot, without sound.

After that, I remember nothing at all.

# Twenty-nine

Amanda moved at the foot of the bed. Her head was wrapped in a white towel and she was wearing my red I LOVE ARKANSAS sweatshirt. It hung down to her knees, but I let the thought linger that she was wearing nothing underneath it. She smelled of shampoo and bath soap, but that was wrong. There was no hot water in the turret. No tub, either.

I recognized the rough stone walls of the third floor but the bed was wrong, too. It was a bed, not my cot, and it was too big, the size of the bed we'd shared when we were married. I looked back at Amanda. The sleeves of my sweatshirt were gone. Cut off above the elbows.

I opened my eyes all the way. "What did you do to my sweatshirt? I paid five dollars for that because it had long sleeves."

"You shredded the sleeves being blown into my basement." She moved close to the side of the bed and bent down to peer into my eyes. I'd been right; she was wearing nothing but the sweatshirt.

"I demand you remove that sweatshirt and give it to me, so that I might fully inspect the damage."

"Not now, sailor. You've got wounds."

"None that can't be immediately healed."

"I'm going to call the doctor and tell him you're regaining your strength, and then I'm going to make tea."

"I'm strong now."

She looked down. "I can see. I'm still going to call the doctor, then we're going to have tea."

"And cookies?"

She pulled the sheet up to my neck. "Sweets come later."

Amanda helped me out of bed on the fifth day. I had a broken arm, a dislocated shoulder, burns on both my legs, and a million cuts, give or take a dozen, from the thousand bits of pulverized concrete that had blown through the tunnel. I'd been lucky; I'd been most of the way through the cutout when the blast came, and Amanda's foundation wall had protected me after I'd fallen into the basement. My head had stayed attached, too, in its like-new, mostly unused condition. I certainly hadn't put any strain on it during the Gateville investigation.

Amanda held my good arm as I levered myself upright. "Was someone pounding on the front door a short time ago?" I asked, grabbing for the headboard. The round room was spinning like an amusement park centrifuge, at that moment when the floor drops away.

She made a face. "It was that horrible man again from city hall. Odd fellow, with sprayed hair and very bad, oily skin. He comes twice a day."

"What does he want?"

"The first few times, he asked what I was doing here. He said this place was zoned for only one occupant, as if that could be true." She looked up at me.

"What did you tell him?"

"That I'm a temporary nurse."

"You could be permanent."

"You don't need a permanent nurse."

"That isn't what—"

She went on, ignoring me. "Then today, he asked me if I'd lost a lot of weight." The beginnings of a smile played on her lips. "This wouldn't have anything to do with the laundry basket of ladies' unmentionables I found under your table saw, would it?"

"I'd like to look out the window now," I said.

She helped me hobble to the slit window. Down by the river, a man with a tan paper lunch bag sat on the bench, tapping a hard-boiled egg against the metal armrest. He had gray, wiry hair, wore a brown suit, and appeared to be talking to a duck floating in the water.

"Is that Agent Till?"

"Another strange man." She told me he'd come by every few hours during the first two days when I'd been frolicking in dreamland, demanding to speak with me. Amanda's doctor, a tiny, peppy gynecologist—named Woody, honestly—had kept him out. She said that yesterday, day four, Till took a new tack: He brought his lunch and ate by the river. "I think he's going to do this every day until you talk to him," Amanda said.

"How did you know to keep him out?" I looked at her, amazed.

"You said, 'Don't let me talk,' when they carried you out of my house, so I told Woody. Woody kept them out."

I nodded. I didn't remember. It was best.

Two days later, at a little past noon, Amanda and Woody helped me down the metal stairs and out the door. I insisted on shuffling to the river by myself, though they followed close enough to pick me up on the first bounce.

I sat on the bench.

Till didn't take his eyes off the duck as he slid his tan paper bag toward me. "Have half a sandwich," he said.

"What kind is it?"

"Tuna salad. My wife says I need more omega oil, whatever that is, so she makes tuna salad three days a week."

"Is the sandwich any good?"

"It's horrible. She uses fake mayonnaise." He threw a scrap of his sandwich in the water. The duck circled around it, picked it up in its beak, spit it out, and flew away. "I could have demanded an interrogation, you know," Till said. "Your little pipsqueak doctor can't keep out the federal government. I've been cooperative, letting you recover."

"I don't remember much."

He had to be careful, with Amanda and Woody hovering ten feet away.

"Think it'll come back? Things you might not remember now?"

He turned his head to look at me for the first time.

"Ask Woody."

"I did. He's a gynecologist, but he did say that after a concussion, full memory can return."

"One can only hope, Till."

"Mind telling me what you do remember, starting with after you heard the second explosion?"

"Amanda and I had just come out of the house. I sent her off to get you."

"Then you went back in?"

"To find Stanley Novak."

"That was noble."

"I figured he was taped up like Amanda had been. I was going to free him and then we'd run like hell."

"Risking your own life to save Stanley Novak."

I'd considered the next part. "He helped people." It had been true enough.

Till bobbed his head up and down in exaggerated agreement. "Ah, yes. Left the lovely Ms. Phelps taped to a chair in a house that was about to explode."

"He was otherwise occupied."

"Going into the tunnels to get Michael Jaynes."

"Stanley Novak was a good man."

Till muttered something.

"What?"

"I said, 'Bullshit,' Elstrom." Till shifted on the bench so that his head was a foot from mine. He smelled like tuna and fake mayonnaise. "Small fragments of an unidentified male along with the noble Stanley Novak blew out of a sealed-up air vent above one of the tunnels. But you didn't go into any tunnels, did you, Elstrom?"

"Just got as far as the cutout in Amanda's basement."

"So you couldn't have seen what Stanley Novak was doing in that tunnel, then?"

"How about chasing down Michael Jaynes?"

"Why do you think it was Michael Jaynes who was down in there?"

"He left his fatigue jacket in Amanda's basement. Jaynes was our prime suspect, Till, or did you forget that somewhere along the way?"

Till's eyes were steady on the side of my face. "Funny thing about the remains of the person that was not Stanley Novak," Till said. "He was dead."

"So you said."

"No. Longtime dead. Years and years dead." He stared at the side of my face. "You wouldn't know anything about that, would you?"

I shrugged as best I could with one arm immobilized in a cast.

Amanda came up to the front of the bench. Woody hung back ten feet, but his eyes were on Amanda, waiting for a cue.

Till shook his head and looked up at Amanda. "And you, Ms. Phelps, the way you got the ambulance driver to take him here, instead of to the hospital. I'd like to know why you did that."

Amanda smiled. "I thought he'd be safer here."

"I was outside your house when they pulled him out, Ms. Phelps. He was cut up pretty bad."

"The E.M.T.'s said he could be treated at home."

"I talked to them. Both techs said you told them terrorists were after Elstrom and that he could get killed in the hospital. You also told them you would have guards here to protect him."

Amanda smiled. She had a lovely smile.

"Where are the guards?" Till asked.

Amanda smiled.

Till turned back to me. "I like having lunch here. It's calm, and peaceful. I might come here every day."

"It'll get cold soon."

"I love the brisk days of autumn."

"I didn't mean that soon. I meant in January and February." I gave him a steely look I'd practiced once in front of a mirror. "Maybe forever," I said.

Till picked up his paper bag and stood up. "Sure you don't want some? I left plenty."

I shook my head.

He held it out to Amanda.

She smiled.

Till walked the five steps to the trash barrel. "I should leave this on the bench. Keep the flies away," he said.

"One thing I forgot to ask, Till. Did you ever get the lab results on what blew up my shed?"

He paused, his lunch bag poised over the barrel, and he grinned. "Solvents. Paint thinners, turpentine, gasoline."

"No D.X.12?"

He dropped the bag in the barrel. "Rest up, Elstrom. I might be back." He started up toward his car.

"One can only hope," I said after him.

Amanda helped me stand. She waved Woody off, and we walked slowly up toward the turret.

"Did I really say, 'Don't let me talk'?"

"You told me you didn't want to talk under sedation. I called

Leo as they were rolling you up to the ambulance. He said if you were thinking clearly and could convalesce at home, it would be better for you. He said with the money that's going to be lost at Crystal Waters, and the lawsuits that are sure to be filed against the Board, the Board will be going to the ends of the earth to get out from under any negligence claims. Leo thought they'd start by trying to blame you for an ineffective investigation. Leo said you'd be in court for the rest of your life." She paused. "You know what I think, Dek?"

"I'm afraid to ask."

"I don't think you were thinking of your own skin, or what was left of it."

We got to the door of the turret. "Poor Stanley," I said.

"That's what I believed, and it almost got you killed." She held the door open for me. "But you're the only one who will ever believe that now."

The next week, the Bohemian came down to the bench by the river carrying a slim box wrapped in silver paper. "Vlodek." He rolled the name. "You look horrible. Much worse than you sound on the phone."

With effort, I slid down a bit on the bench so we could both watch the river. He sat down.

"How are you?" I asked.

"Right as rain," he said. He looked it. His skin was back to its usual prosperous bronze. "Miss Terrado, my accuser, got arrested for shoplifting the day before yesterday. 'Heiress Caught Stealing,' the paper said. After detailing her growing eccentricities, the reporter, a nice boy, the nephew of a friend, devoted some space to Miss Terrado's preposterous accusation against me, noting that the F.B.I. anticipated the matter would be dropped."

He started to hand me the slim, wrapped box, saw the cast, and said, "A token, Vlodek. Allow me." He slit the paper with his huge thumb, removed the top of the box, and held it out for me to see. It was the largest fountain pen I'd ever seen. "A 1928 Parker Duofold, in Blue Lapis. I restored it myself." He set the pen down. "You can use it to endorse this." He pulled a Crystal Waters Homeowners Association check from his suit-coat pocket and held it up.

"Two thousand?"

"The association is virtually bankrupt, and with the lawsuits—"

I imagined he had to shake Ballsard pretty hard to come up with the two thousand. "It's fine," I said.

He smiled, relieved. "Your suggestion that I visit the Novak house was most productive. I met with Mrs. Novak's sister, who is now her guardian, and presented her with a letter from Bob Ballsard, assuring her that the Board will begin paying Stanley's pension immediately and will also expedite her claim against his life insurance policy. Mrs. Novak will want for nothing in her current home, poor woman."

"I'll bet Ballsard was most enthused about writing that letter."

"As you predicted, but he was persuaded when I told him I had every hope of recovering all the extortion money. Besides, as you also pointed out, Stanley dying a hero might minimize claims against the Board for negligence."

"You looked around Stanley's garage?"

"Mrs. Novak's sister was quite cooperative once she realized I was acting in their best interests. She gave me the key and told me to take anything that belonged to Crystal Waters. It was in the attic of the garage: five hundred and ten thousand, untouched." He patted my good shoulder. "As you requested, I told the Board only that I recovered the funds through a confidential source."

"That ten thousand—"

"—did not have a bill newer than 1970." He beamed. "And the five hundred thousand was still in the attaché case. I don't think he ever opened it." He watched me.

"Attaché—" I started to stutter. "Son of a bitch."

He patted my good shoulder again. "Perhaps surveillance is not your forte."

"Thank you, Anton."

"You're a moral man, Vlodek. I like that." He stood up. "I told the Board you would be discreet."

He took a step toward the street but then turned. "I meant to bring you a bottle of ink for your new pen, but there are so many colors. I didn't know which you'd like."

I waved my good hand. "Anything will be fine."

The Bohemian glanced over at Amanda, planting bulbs for the spring by the base of the turret. She was wearing my cutoff red sweatshirt. "I think red, perhaps," he said. "Red is such a vibrant color."

I followed his eyes. "Red is perfect."

Leo drove me in the pink Porsche with the top down. "It's silver rose, not pink," he said again.

"Pink enough, Leo."

"Endora likes it."

"And for that it must be treasured."

He did some fancy downshifting, just to show me he could, and pulled up to the entrance to Gateville. A Maple Hills squad car was parked by the guardhouse, its uniformed officer talking to a guard. The guard came over to the Porsche.

"Brumsky and Elstrom," Leo said, handing up our driver's licenses. "Anton Chernek arranged it with Mr. Ballsard."

I loosened the chin cord and pulled off the tan big-brimmed Tilley hat Amanda had bought me to keep the sun off my stitches. The guard checked our faces against the license photos, and handed them back with photocopied waiver forms that absolved the Board of responsibility for anything that occurred during our visit, like us getting blown up by an undiscovered cube of D.X.12. We signed the forms and handed them back.

"Jeez, put the hat back on, Dek," Leo said as we started up. "You look like Frankenstein, post op."

I pulled on the Tilley as Leo turned left and started clockwise around Chanticleer Circle.

At first blink, the houses at the east end of Gateville looked the same: big and blessed in the sun. But then the uncut grass, untrimmed shrubs, and scattering of fast-food wrappers, dropped by the curious and blown over the wall, popped out like black teeth on a beauty queen. Nobody was at home in Gateville anymore.

We circled slowly around the east end and started up the back stretch. Around the bend ahead, the mounds of blackened bricks and charred wood looked like World War II photographs of Dresden, the day after the Allies had flown over and obliterated it.

"Jeez," Leo said, stopping the car. He shut off the engine.

For a time we sat in his open convertible and looked at the rubble at the west end.

"What finally made him set the plan in motion?" Leo asked, when the silence got too loud.

"Our divorce."

"Atta boy, Dek. Suck up the guilt for this, too."

"It's true enough, Leo. Obviously, the Board's rejection of his request for a loan, and then his son's death and his wife's deterioration, were the reasons. But they festered, and might not have gone any place, except that Amanda and I divorced, and she went to Europe for what was to be at least six months. God knows he'd had the motive; now he had the means and opportunity. He'd never forgotten the letters, blueprints, and D.X.12 that were in the tunnels with Michael Jaynes. Now he had the keys; he was supposed to check on the house. He cut into the tunnel and began blowing things up."

"And hired you to misdirect the investigation that was sure to come, by feeding you clues about Michael Jaynes."

"He controlled the investigation every step of the way. Using the old notes was genius, because it forced everyone's attention back to 1970, to someone who had worked building Gateville. When that looked to be a dead end, he fed me Jaynes's name to keep me going."

Leo turned from looking at the ruined houses. "And when that lagged, he set you up to take the fall."

I shook my head. "He didn't set me up."

"What about the money missing from the Dumpster? Stanley had to know you would stake it out, even if you didn't tell anybody beforehand."

"Sure, but he couldn't know I'd admit to being there. Nor could he anticipate I'd be so lame as to fall asleep and admit that, too. My announcing that I'd been there but didn't see the money disappear made me look worse than stupid; it made me look like I was lying *and* stupid. That's what got Till interested in me in the first place. He thought I was covering up the fact that I'd grabbed the money myself. I dug my own grave on that one."

"I don't get it."

"It made me look like I was lying—"

"That's not what I meant. What happened to the money?"

I gave him my happiest grin. I knew what was puzzling him, but I wanted to savor the sensation of knowing something he hadn't worked out.

"The money never went to Ann Sather's," I said.

"Jeez—" he said, and then the confusion left his face. He smiled.

I blurted ahead, though he already knew what I was going to say. "Even if I'd brought binoculars, I wouldn't have caught it. Stanley came to the drop with a white bag full of food scraps he'd picked out of Ann Sather's Dumpster a few days before and had kept refrigerated at home. Only he'd put the white bag inside a black bag. Assuming that I would be watching, he made a show of leaning into the Dumpster, like he was jamming the black bag all the way in so he could close the lid. What he was really doing with all that fumbling was ripping the black outer bag off and balling it up in his fist. It was just thin plastic. Then he drove away with his wadded-up black plastic bag, leaving behind a white bag full of nothing but authentic Ann Sather kitchen garbage. He figured when I saw no one come for the black bag, I'd rummage in the Dumpster. I wouldn't find the money, but worse, I would realize that if I told anyone that the money had disappeared right under my eyes, they wouldn't believe me. They'd think I took it. I must have really shocked him when I told everybody I'd been watching the Dumpster but had fallen asleep. That was a bonus for him; it made me look even more guilty."

"That wasn't setting you up?"

"No, because he never expected me to admit I was there."

"What about blowing up your shed? That wasn't a setup?"

"It was time to get me out of the picture, because I was making too much noise about doubting the bomber was Michael Jaynes. He needed more time to string out the bombings, to make the Members suffer slowly, like he and his wife had, watching their son die. But he didn't use D.X.12 on my shed, Leo, which would have tied me to the Gateville bombs much more closely."

"Jeez," Leo said.

"That's it exactly," I said. "Jeez." I looked down the street at the ruined houses.

"So he was never looking for money?"

I shook my empty head in my Tilley hat. "It was too late for money. His son was dead, his wife was headed for an institution. No, he wanted to punish the Board, and the Members, by destroying all of Gateville."

"Wanted it bad enough to kill."

"No. I saw his face when he learned that that family had come home from Door County and was in the house he'd blown up." I pointed at the pile of rubble that had once been the dead family's home. " 'Bastards,' Stanley said that night. I thought he was referring to more than one bomber, but it was actually a slip. Stanley was referring to the Board, blaming them for the family's death just like he did for the death of his son."

We sat for a while then, in the sun, without speaking, like we were waiting in a graveyard for a grounds crew to come to cover new graves.

"Drive on, Jeeves," I said finally.

Leo put the Porsche into gear and eased up Chanticleer toward the turn.

"What's going to happen here?" Leo asked.

"This last batch of destroyed houses will be scraped away. Their owners, including Amanda, are the lucky ones. They'll get insurance money to buy someplace else. I don't know about the others, because technically their houses have not been damaged. The Board will plant grass and trees, like they did earlier, to try to perfume the development, but it won't work. The story is out. No one wants to live in a minefield."

"What about the report in the paper that said the whole development would be rewired? Won't that end it?"

"That's just whistling past the graveyard. The D.X.12 is still here. They've found a lot of it, maybe even all of it. But even if they bulldoze all the houses, they'll never know if they missed one tiny cube. That's what makes this place a ghost town for a long time to come."

Leo started the Porsche and crept along in first gear. "So Stanley Novak got what he wanted?"

"More like what he needed."

Leo nodded at the justice of that, and we continued around Chanticleer Circle until we got to what was left of Amanda's house. Two men in white hard hats stood in front of the pile, next to a dump truck loaded with debris. Only the front wall of Amanda's house remained.

Leo put the Porsche in neutral. "She sure had a lot of guts, bullying those E.M.T.'s to go in to get you, even as the roof was coming down."

"Never underestimate the force of Amanda's determination."

"Is she going to be staying a while in Rivertown?" Leo kept looking straight ahead, but I could see him smile. When he got that big slimeball grin on his face, I could swear his lips touched the lobes of both his ears.

"She bought a condo downtown. She'll be moving out in a month."

"No grand reconciliation?" The disappointment in his voice was genuine.

"She's leaving the hot water heater, the portable shower, and the big bed. She'll be back to visit."

"Still . . ."

"She says we're too young to get married."

"You're both looking at middle age."

"She's right, Leo."

The men climbed into the cab of the dump truck.

"Big greed," Leo said. "It's always big greed." He turned to look at me, his eyebrows riding high on his forehead.

I looked at my watch. "Fire it up, Leo. Amanda wants me back by three."

He slipped the shifter into first gear. "What's the rush?"

"Amanda said we're having sweets."